Perfecting the Proposal

ALSO BY CATHRYN BROWN

Wedding Town Romances

Runaway to Romance

Married by Monday

Finding her Forever

Bridesmaid or Bride?

Waiting for a Wedding

Perfecting the Proposal

Alaska Dream Romances

Falling for Alaska

Loving Alaska

Merrying in Alaska

Crazy About Alaska

Alaska Matchmakers Romances

Accidentally Matched

Finally Matched

Hopefully Matched

Merrily Matched

Surprisingly Matched

Perfecting the Proposal

CATHRYN BROWN

Sienna Bay Press

PO Box 158582

Nashville, Tennessee 37215

www.cathrynbrown.com

Cover designed by Najla Qamber Designs

(www.najlaqamberdesigns.com)

Perfecting the Proposal/Cathryn Brown. - 1st ed.

ISBN: 978-1-945527-64-7

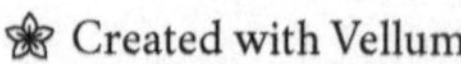 Created with Vellum

In *Waiting for a Wedding,* I created the character Amy Marchant, new owner of the *Two Hearts Times* newspaper and Nick's cousin. I thought she would be a minor character in that book and maybe have a line or two in a future book.

But when it came time to write *Perfecting the Proposal,* I knew she had to be the main character. When this book begins, Amy's newspaper is struggling a bit.

Scott is in town to visit his friend Greg. Instead of the simple vacation he's expecting, he's pulled into a surprising plan to help Amy, and a whole lot more.

I hope you enjoy their story as they become friends and fall in love.

*A*my Marchant added the final touches to her newspaper article, another one about weddings. But that subject wasn't a surprise in wedding-crazed Two Hearts, Tennessee.

This time, she'd interviewed Bella Walker, the owner of Bella's Brides, the wedding dress store. In the final version of the week's newspaper—*her* newspaper—that same page would include a farm report, a photo of last Saturday's celebrity wedding, and the mayor's weekly update.

The *Two Hearts Times* covered everything that mattered to this town and the surrounding countryside. With one more article tomorrow, she'd put this edition to bed and print it. Then she'd add some of the articles to her new website.

Amy pushed back from the tiny kitchen table in the equally tiny kitchen she used as a desk and office during her off hours. She had little privacy in the small house her younger brother Dexter rented and that she had shared with him since she'd come back home to Two Hearts a few months ago. A door divided it from the living room, where her brother watched a game, an activity he and the rest of her family loved. But to her, men and women who threw balls and swatted at pucks did so for no good reason.

Growing up, she'd rarely get to choose what she wanted to watch when a game was on. Both her parents and her four siblings—two brothers and two sisters—loved sports.

It was a welcome break when her phone rang with a call from her new friend Cassie.

Cassie started talking the second after Amy said, "Hello."

"Is there any way—*any way at all*—that you can help me tomorrow?" The panicked note in Cassie's usually calm voice surprised her. Before Amy could reply, Cassie continued. "My best wedding assistant helped with her sister's wedding last weekend and is now stuck in Miami because of flight issues. Two of my usual assistants won't be there, either."

"I'd love to, but I have to finish up the newspaper tomorrow."

A sound between a low scream and a groan made Amy cringe. Then the phone went silent. Cassie must be mentally sifting through everyone else she knew for possible aid.

If Amy finished the paper tonight, she'd be able to take tomorrow off. The bride article was the last piece. A couple of months ago, she'd been flipping through old newspapers in the archive that had been sold along with the business and had come upon a story about a 1937 wedding with a photo of the bride. Amy had scanned the photo and written an article to accompany it.

That had been the biggest hit with readers since she'd restarted the paper. A town that loved weddings as much as Two Hearts, Tennessee, loved everything wedding-related, so it shouldn't have surprised her. She'd done one of those articles every week since then. With more than sixty-five years of newspapers, she wouldn't run out of material anytime soon.

A late trip back to her office and a couple of hours of work would be all it'd take. "I'll rearrange my schedule so I can help you."

"Thank you! I was so desperate that, for a moment, I even considered calling my mother."

Amy laughed. She'd heard stories about Cassie's domineering mother.

"I'll text you the details. Your job will be assisting the bride. Oh, and please wear black." With that, Cassie ended the call.

Amy stared at her phone. She should have known she'd be pulled into the wedding industry when she moved back home to Two Hearts. She glanced over her shoulder at the door to the living room. To get her purse with her car keys, she'd have to pass through there to a table beside the front door. Her overprotective brother would no doubt then deliver a lecture about walking and working alone at night. He'd probably insist on taking her himself.

It was 7:30 p.m. and barely dark. She'd be perfectly safe in this town. Other than occasional celebrity weddings, nothing unusual happened in Two Hearts.

She scrounged around in the kitchen drawer that held everything from scissors to twine, finally finding the key to her building she kept there for Dexter. He usually worked from home but occasionally needed an office to do an in-person interview, so she let him use her place of business when she wasn't there.

With her laptop tucked under her arm, Amy started toward the back door. A three-block walk would do her good after sitting so long. It was a warm late May evening, so she didn't even need a jacket. After flipping on the outside light beside the door to light the way when she came home, she stepped out the back door and looked down.

Bunny ears immediately caught her eye—pink ones, followed by an embroidered pink nose and black eyes. Her mother's sense of humor had been in full force when she'd bought these slippers last Christmas.

Her shoes were neatly placed beside the front door. These

slippers would have to do. Besides, it was dark out, so even if she did come upon a late evening dog walker, they wouldn't notice her footwear.

She hoped.

As the newspaper publisher, she tried not to draw attention to herself. She wanted to appear professional and to have all eyes on her newspaper. Hopefully, she wouldn't run into anyone.

~

The last week hadn't gone as Scott had expected.

First, his sister had called him in the middle of the night, frantic because a tree had fallen on their house during the storm that had still been howling outside his window. He'd hurried over to see how he could help and found his brother-in-law trying to remove belongings from their home before they got soggy from the rain that had, thankfully, slowed to a trickle.

As dawn broke, he'd borrowed a friend's truck and had helped them haul everything to a storage facility. Then he'd invited everyone to stay at his house.

"Scott. Hello?" His friend Greg Brantley waved his hand in front of Scott's face. "I asked what made you take me up on my suggestion that you visit Two Hearts."

"You made this town sound like a great place. I decided I needed a vacation from Chicago's big city chaos."

Greg's unwavering gaze as he gave his next comment told Scott that his friend made a great sheriff. "Sure. The offer I've made every month or two for the last couple of years. And today—without any notice—you suddenly show up."

Scott rubbed his hand over his face. He'd wanted to keep his confusion to himself, but he'd been Greg's friend long enough that he knew he would get the answer out of him soon, anyway.

"Melinda and her kids were driving me crazy."

Confusion swept over his friend's face. "Your sister's children? How are they doing that when they live twenty or thirty minutes from your house?"

"They're *in* my house. A tree landed on their place, and they needed somewhere to go."

Greg nodded slowly. "I see. So you have your sister, her husband, and four kids under six—"

"Under five. A set of twins in the middle managed to make it even more chaotic. And they have two sheepdogs. My three-bedroom house was perfect for me alone and maybe an occasional out-of-town guest, but . . ."

Greg chuckled. "So you ran?"

"I wanted to be far enough away to escape the chaos. I told them it was perfect timing because I'd planned a getaway. And you keep telling me I need to visit, after all."

"Had you planned a getaway?"

Scott rubbed his hand over his face. "Every day. The commute is a beast. That day, I talked to the Captain about time off."

"He agreed to let you take some?" Greg's incredulous tone made Scott smile. Scott's boss was infamous in the department for refusing to grant time off.

"I had the leave accrued. But I'm on call if he needs me. If he does, I guess I'll be working from your mother's living room." He'd put his duffel bag and laptop on the coffee table in front of the comfortable, light green checked couch he now sat on. Scott had to admit it wouldn't be a hardship to stay here, but he was alone right now and not sharing the space with its owner.

"That's what you get when you arrive on a busy wedding weekend."

"It's a small town. Why would I have thought the one motel would be full? And what's the deal with weddings?"

"We're becoming known as *the* wedding town. Even

celebrities want to get married in Two Hearts." Greg stretched out in his chair.

Scott gestured toward the room around them. "Are you sure your mother won't mind my staying here?"

Greg laughed. "Are you kidding? My mother knows you, and she loves company."

"But she's out of town. I just barged in here."

"I asked her before I offered. She and her new husband—that's still a little odd for me to say—are on an island off of Florida for a couple of days. He's a wedding photographer. He keeps declaring he's retiring, but I think he enjoys weddings in exotic locations far too much to completely let go. Mom is happy to tag along."

Scott felt tension easing out of his shoulders as he leaned back into the sofa cushion. "The slower pace of a small town is just what I need. No rush hour." He sat upright. "There *is* a slower pace, right?"

Greg laughed again. "Definitely. I don't miss Chicago's busyness. But it does become more hectic around weddings. The sheriff's office provides security. The worst we ever get, though, is a guest who's had too much champagne." Greg cleared his throat. "There's a wedding tomorrow."

Why was he being told what he already knew? That had been made clear the second he'd tried to book a room at the motel. Then it hit him. Greg needed more people for security.

When Scott didn't say anything, his friend added, "I know you moved from beat cop to computer techie, but we can always use the help."

Greg's phone rang. Before he could do more than identify himself to the caller, he asked that person to hold while he answered a second call.

"Yes, Edna. I understand. I'll check it out. Thank you for reporting it." Then he switched back to the first and listened to the situation. "Square or round? Okay, I'll be there as soon as I can."

Greg put his phone back in his shirt pocket. "I spoke too soon about the calm. A farmer's trailer loaded with hay had a tire blowout, and half a load of hay bales slid out onto the highway. The farmer's trying to gather the bales and fix the tire without a car hitting him in the dark. I'm the only one on duty tonight, and the caller is in danger, so I'll have to go on that call first."

Scott got to his feet. There was no point in sitting here if Greg needed him. "And the other one?"

"That may be nothing. One of our nosier residents noticed a light on in the newspaper office."

Scott frowned. "Does the owner work at night?"

"Not usually. That's the main reason I should drive by."

Scott reached for his jacket. "Do I need the car, or can I walk there?"

Greg raised an eyebrow. "Are you sure? You're here to relax."

"I'm here to have a break from my normal life. This qualifies. Text me the address, and I'll check it out. I'll stop and get a bite to eat for us on the way back."

Greg laughed as they walked toward the door. "Dinah's Place and the grocery store are closed. You're in a small town that rolls up the sidewalks before dark. But don't worry. My mother left meals in the freezer, and she makes enough for a crowd."

Scott decided to take his car. He checked the address he'd been sent and started on his way. Considering everything Greg had told him about Two Hearts in the years he'd known him—first as memories of his hometown when he was in Chicago and then updates after he'd moved back—Scott was fairly certain he'd find a man his father's age or older working late to get tomorrow's edition out.

This should be easy.

CHAPTER TWO

Amy hefted down one of the giant books that bound six months of newspapers together. She'd been delighted to find this treasure of Two Hearts history stacked on shelves in the back. The books had been under decades of dust that she'd had to clean off, but they were still in good shape.

When she set the book on the counter over cabinets that ran around the perimeter of the small room, a poof of dust billowed up. Coughing, Amy stepped back and waved her hand in front of her face. Maybe she hadn't cleaned as well as she'd thought.

She flipped through the first newspaper in the bunch and searched for an article with a wedding and a photo she thought would scan well and be usable. However, January 1935's issues didn't produce anything suitable, so she kept flipping.

About the same time she turned to February's section, a sound from outside caught her attention. It hadn't sounded like a car but rather a human.

Amy turned toward the front of her office. A thud sent her heart rate through the roof. The sound and person were *inside* her newspaper office. A second later, the floor in the old building creaked.

Had she locked the front door when she'd come in? She was so used to leaving it open during the day that she probably hadn't.

Another creak.

She tiptoed to the light switch and flipped it off, hoping to stay hidden. Amy gulped. She might need a weapon—something to arm herself against this unwelcome intruder.

She felt around on the counter for a pair of scissors or a letter opener but found nothing helpful, at least nothing big enough that she could grab and stab or swing. Suddenly, her hand touched upon a fish, the largemouth bass the previous owner—Phil—had thought enough of to taxidermy and preserve.

Phil had installed it on the wall with a brass plaque under it that gave the weight and the date it had been caught in the lake at the edge of town. Amy had thought less of the fish than he had, so she'd taken it down and put it in the back. Right now, she liked it a little more.

She grabbed the fish by the tail and hefted it above her head, ready to strike, when a shadowy figure came around the corner. "Don't move, or you'll be sorry!" she yelled with far more force than her jelly-like insides summoned.

The figure yelped and lifted his arm to block the attack as the bass made contact.

"Wait! I'm not here to hurt you. Greg sent me."

His words interrupted a second swing of the fish.

"Who are you?" she demanded. "And you'd better speak quickly." She scooted along the wall to the light switch and flipped it on.

A man with dark, wavy hair held up a hand to block the light. When he dropped it, she saw clear blue eyes behind wire-framed glasses. His broad shoulders filled out his flannel shirt to perfection. She knew she'd never seen him before.

"Greg had to take another call, so I said I'd come over here to check the report of unusual activity." He glared at her and rubbed his arm. She *had* hit him with a fair amount of force.

Amy held her weapon firmly and stared at him. "I know all the deputies. You aren't one of them."

Slowly smacking the fish against her hand as a warning, she watched him, waiting for his reply. She did her best to appear fearless, even though her knees were ready to buckle.

"I'm one of Greg's friends from the Chicago Police Department."

Amy dropped the fish on the counter and stepped away. She'd just hit a cop? What was the fine for assault with a fish?

He spoke before she could apologize. "I assume you're the business owner. I'm going to need to have you prove it, though."

How did she prove that? Her driver's license didn't say *Owner of the Two Hearts Times*. She could call someone and have them come in to verify her identity, but then the unfortunate situation with the fish would probably come up. She'd like to avoid that. Forever, if possible. Then she remembered her website. "I've got you covered on that! Follow me."

She spun around to her laptop, flipped it open, and brought up the newspaper website with her photo. "Here I am."

Scott leaned over to look. "I'm pleased to meet you . . . Amelia." He straightened.

"People call me Amy. I just put Amelia, which is my real name, on there because it sounds more . . . businesslike." She realized she was babbling, so she extended her hand to shake his.

"Scott Miller."

When they touched, a warm zing traveled through her.

He held on for a moment longer than she thought he should have before he released her hand and smiled down at her. Down, because he must be at least six foot two to her five foot four.

"Scott, you said?"

He nodded, a curl falling onto his forehead. "I'd better get going."

"Wait!" The darkness outside appeared more ominous now. Maybe she should have at least locked the door. "Why did you come to my newspaper office in the first place?"

"Someone spotted a light on inside your building and reported it."

Annoyance at the intrusion into her personal life warred with happiness that somebody was looking out for her. She decided to let happiness win.

She still had to write the article, so she'd better get going, or her brother would realize she was missing and send out the cavalry. "I'll be out of here in about an hour."

"I'll leave you to your work. Remember to lock up after me." Scott stared at her for a moment longer, acting as if he wanted to say something.

She followed him to the door. As it closed, he glanced back, his blue eyes twinkling, as he added, "Nice slippers."

Amy flipped the bolt as soon as the door had shut behind him. Bunny slippers and assault by bass. Her evening couldn't get more embarrassing.

Scott seemed like a nice guy and certainly wasn't hard to look at. Something about the laughter in his eyes when he teased her made her wish she could get to know him better. But he wasn't staying, and she definitely was. Nice or not, Scott Miller was off-limits.

She hoped to get through his visit to Two Hearts without running into him again. With almost every moment of her life going into this newspaper, she had little time for socializing, anyway. She'd thought owning a paper would generate enough income to cover her expenses, but Amy was coming to realize that a small-town newspaper didn't bring in much money. That was a concern for another day. Right now, she had the next edition to get out.

CHAPTER THREE

*A*my wondered for the hundredth time if she should have agreed to help with this wedding. The one positive to her day was that no one had mentioned yesterday's bass assault. The story must not have made the rounds yet.

The limousine pulled to the curb in front of the small Two Hearts church and not a moment too soon. As always, the building looked inviting with its fresh white paint and church spire. It had never been more welcoming to Amy than at this particular moment.

"I don't know if I can go through with this." The frantic bride beside her was moments away from a full-on panic attack.

This had been the longest two hours of Amy's life. "It's a charming church, Maxine. You're just going to walk up the aisle and say I do. Easy." Amy had said words like that so many times today that she'd lost count. If this was what it was like assisting with weddings, she'd stay as far away from them as she possibly could.

The bride sucked in air, something between a gasp and a sob.

At that moment, the limousine door opened. "Can I help you

ladies out?" The male voice sounded familiar, but she couldn't quite place it. He must be someone from the security detail who helped with the weddings.

He reached down a hand, which the bride stared at for a moment before taking it. When she had stepped out of the vehicle, Amy released the breath she'd been holding. There had been a very real possibility that Maxine would have asked her to return them both to the motel and help her pack up to go home.

Once the man had the bride stable on her feet, he helped Amy out, and she came face to face with none other than last night's intruder.

"Mr. Miller. How nice to see you." She forced a smile. Her humiliation from last night hadn't faded, but the last thing they needed was more angst within a fifty-mile radius of this wedding.

"Scott works fine."

Amy stared into his eyes. They really were the most amazing shade of blue. A whimper brought her back into the moment. "Scott, maybe you could walk on Maxine's right side, and I'll take her left. Let's help Maxine into the church and to the bridal room."

His surprised expression said that hadn't been on his agenda, but his years in public service must have told him to go with the flow. When they were moving up the front steps, the bride slipped on a step and landed on the front hem of her skirt. A tearing sound and Maxine's strangled cry had Amy's heart racing.

Please, please, please tell me her dress is not torn. Amy stepped around to look at the fabric and saw that everything from the hem up was intact, but when she stood, she noticed one of the narrow bejeweled straps over Maxine's shoulders dangling free. If she could get the bride inside without her learning about the problem, she'd quietly call Bella to have her fix it.

Amy gathered up the dress and held it to one side while the bride continued up the stairs and inside the building. When they'd almost reached the door, Maxine put her hand on her chest and over the loose spaghetti strap.

"Oh, no, no, no, no, no! Maybe it's a sign! Maybe I shouldn't marry him!"

Amy did her best to stifle her groan. She went inside the room and thankfully found Maxine's maid-of-honor and two bridesmaids waiting. Their eyes widened when they took in the scene. One of them leaped to her feet. "Maxine, don't cry. It's going to be okay."

Maxine sniffed. They'd be in even bigger trouble if they needed makeup repair minutes before the ceremony started.

Amy tried for a cheerful tone. "Scott, follow me out here, and we'll see what we can do about getting some help for Maxine."

Scott backed away toward the door. Once in the vestibule, he said, "I hope you have a plan. I can't handle this wedding stuff."

That got the first laugh out of her today. "I want to stay far away from them after this. I've been running a weekly historical wedding article in the paper for a while. I don't know if I can handle even that now after this debacle."

He chuckled.

Amy texted Cassie and Bella. Bella responded first with, "On my way."

"I've been surprised that no one has commented on our meeting last night. No fish or bunny jokes."

His brow wrinkled in confusion. Then he smiled. "That's because I only said I'd asked you to prove who you were and left. No details."

Amy released a sigh. "Thank you. I need good news right now." Amy's phone chirped an incoming message. "Cassie says she'll be here soon." A quick check of the time told her they had twenty-two minutes until the bride was supposed to walk down the aisle to the groom.

When Amy looked up, she discovered Scott had disappeared. She didn't blame him for running. Besides, that fit in with her plan of not being around him.

Paige arrived with her camera and gear. "The bride said she didn't want photos before the ceremony. Do you think I should go inside to see if she's changed her mind?"

Amy cracked the door to see what was happening inside. The maid-of-honor was comforting the bride while the other two women stared in horror. Amy wasn't sure if it was because of the damage to the dress or the bride curled up in a ball on a chair in the corner.

After closing the door, she said, "The only decision she may have changed is whether or not she's marrying her groom."

Paige gasped. "You're joking, right?"

Amy shook her head.

"Then I'll do exactly as the couple requested." She moved a few feet away.

Bella ran through the church's front door with a tote bag in her hand. She slid to a stop in front of Amy. "Is it just the strap?"

Amy nodded. Then, after a second, she shrugged. "But I'm not a clothing expert. That's the only damage I saw. At first, I thought she'd torn the front of the dress when she stepped on it, but—"

Bella gasped. "I hope you're right because I can't fix major damage in—" she checked her watch, "twelve minutes."

"The hem looks fine to me."

When Bella reached for the doorknob, Amy put her hand on her arm to stop her. "And the bride is a basket case."

"Well, that's understandable with this happening at the last minute."

"No. The bride *already* was a basket case. This put her meltdown on steroids."

Bella gave a single nod before disappearing through the door. Amy wasn't sure if she should follow, but there wasn't anything she could do. She had offered all the comfort she could, and Maxine had her friends with her now.

A few minutes later, she heard a squeal of joy and cracked the door open to peer inside. The bride was smiling, and a bridesmaid was trying to touch up her makeup. After taking a deep breath first and releasing it slowly, Amy stepped back into the room to offer any help she could.

Bella gave her a nod as she checked her work again. "The dress is as good as new. And I checked the other strap." In Amy's opinion, Bella's perky, happy tone sounded forced, but no one else appeared to notice.

The bride reached out to hug her. "Thank you, Bella. The dress is beautiful again." Her voice was now filled with happiness. "I'm ready to walk down the aisle to Oliver. I'm glad this was the only big catastrophe this morning. I'd have hated to have my joy interrupted."

Could this be the same bride? Was this what it was like to work in the wedding industry? One moment the bride is freaking out, and the next moment she's happy. How did Cassie do it? She'd made a career out of this.

Cassie appeared just as the music rose. "I saw your message but knew you'd manage. The groom had a crisis, and I've been with him."

"Wasn't sure he wanted to tie the knot?"

Cassie nodded.

Amy hoped the couple had a long, happy marriage. She wondered, though.

Cassie opened the door to the bride's room. With a smile, she asked, "Ready? Your groom is waiting for you."

Paige moved over with her camera as the attendants stepped out and began their walk down the aisle first. She snapped photos as Maxine passed, a shockingly ethereal expression on her face. She appeared as though she truly did want to get married. But would she say yes?

Amy watched the ceremony from the back of the church, wondering if she should have Maxine's things ready to grab when she made her escape. When the bride said, "I do," and kissed her groom, Amy relaxed. Until that moment, she'd thought the wedding had little chance of ending well.

After today, she would do her best to stay far away from everything associated with weddings. While the bride and groom stood at the top of the front steps for photos, Amy waited inside.

Cassie stepped beside her. "You ready for the second half of the day?"

Amy sighed. "Does my answer have to be yes?"

After a laugh, Cassie leaned closer and, in a low voice, said, "Maxine was a trial from day one, but I knew you'd be able to handle her."

That made her feel better.

A little.

"I want to beat the couple to the reception." Cassie checked her watch. "Can I give you a ride?"

Amy watched the bride. She'd been stable on her feet, but Amy didn't trust her to go down the stairs upright without assistance. "I'll stay here to make sure everything's okay."

"Thank you."

A moment later, pink and white rose petals showered the bride and groom as they walked down the steps to the limo that would now transport the couple to their reception at Levi and Cherry's flower farm north of town. Amy had straightened the bride's dress before she'd started her descent to avoid any more incidents. Then she'd watched carefully to make sure the bride didn't get tangled.

When the newlyweds drove away, a weight lifted off her, but exhaustion slipped in, reminding her of the late night she'd had in order to free up time to be here. If only her wedding duties for the day were over.

Amy heard vehicles starting up and down the street. She'd walked the short distance to the motel this morning, so she'd need to walk home to get her vehicle.

The sheriff's car stopped at the curb, and Greg rolled down his window. "Need a ride?"

"I won't be able to get home if I take you up on that."

He shook his head. "Don't worry about it. I'm sure someone will be available. If you're there at the end, Cassie or I can help."

She'd foolishly chosen shoes that weren't ideal for the day she'd had, so Amy elected to take the easy route and avoid another walk. As she neared Greg's car, she realized someone else was inside.

Scott.

So much for avoiding him.

She could come up with an excuse for not getting in the car, or she could be a mature woman and climb in. After a moment's debate—long enough that Greg asked, "Is there a problem?"— she went with *maturity*. But it had been touch and go there for a moment.

Forcing a smile, she opened the door to the back seat and climbed inside. Greg greeted her, then started driving. Firmly in cop mode, Scott gave a single nod. Did the man ever smile?

Greg took a call a few minutes into their drive and stayed on it until they pulled onto the long driveway to the farm, thankfully eliminating the need for conversation.

Amy opened the door and had one foot on the ground as Greg put the car in park. "Thank you for the lift." She gave a single wave before starting her search for Cassie.

The reception was already in full swing under the big white tent set up in a cleared area. The backdrop of tulip fields almost took her breath away. Most guests had been seated, with the stragglers arriving and immediately being taken care of by

Cassie and her team. Amy headed in that direction. The bride glowed with happiness.

Cassie looked up when Amy neared. "I'm glad you're here." When she continued with the words, "If you don't mind," Amy tensed, panicking at what she might say next. After her earlier time with the bride, she wasn't in a hurry for more. "Could you help Paige with anything she needs? She may need help to get the shots right and people in the correct places. The couple was more focused on photos of the wedding and the reception than what happened before."

"Good thing," Amy muttered.

Cassie grinned. "It never gets old. Brides—and their mothers —keep me on my toes."

Amy nudged her shoulder toward the newlyweds. "She made me wonder if there would be a wedding today."

"Crying, hysterical, smiling, laughing . . . I've seen it all," Cassie whispered, "And you can't tell which marriages will last."

"Really? I'd think it's obvious."

"Oh no. There's no pattern. Maxine and Oliver could be married for six months or sixty years. I've had happy brides who don't last six months in the marriage. Of course, that could be the groom's fault." She shrugged. "You can never tell what will happen."

Amy couldn't picture that. But thankfully, she'd never be immersed in the wedding industry, so she wouldn't have the experience to tell one way or another.

She glanced around the tent and then pointed to her left. "Paige is over there." She rested a hand on Amy's arm when she turned to go there. "And thank you again."

"I'm happy to help." And she was. Mostly. The rest of the evening should go well.

Paige greeted her. "Ready to make some photographic magic?"

Amy grinned. "Just tell me how I can help you."

The next couple of hours passed quickly. Paige took pictures of the first dance, speeches, and the couple cutting and neatly feeding each other cake. Amy made notes of every shot for Paige's reference, fluffed the bride's dress, and assisted with lighting a couple of times.

As a journalist, she knew a thing or two about images. They were important in telling a story, especially in her articles. Paige's level of professionalism took the perfect photo to a higher art form.

When the party seemed to be slowing down, Paige said, "Let's get some fresh air."

"Gladly! You don't get breaks, do you?"

Outside, Paige set her camera on the table they'd used earlier to hold the seating assignment cards, rolled her shoulders, and stretched. "Weddings can be long, but this is truly my dream job."

"I feel the same about writing."

Paige gave her a pointed look. "Then why are you running a newspaper?"

The question took her aback. Why was she? "I wanted stability. I wanted a steady income I could rely on."

"I thought you had a job you quit to move here."

Amy sighed. "I did, but I was only there because of Logan." As soon as she said his name, she wanted to take it back. She'd been too embarrassed to mention him earlier.

Paige raised an eyebrow. "That's a name I haven't heard you talk about before."

"I guess that's what exhaustion can do. I won't mention him again."

Paige opened her mouth to speak, then closed it, but her expression said, *Tell me more.*

She hadn't spoken about her ex-almost-fiancé, but Paige had become a friend. "Okay. Here's the story. Logan told me he needed more time before making a commitment, so I followed him to North Dakota when he got a job there. I thought the man was going to propose a dozen times. Maybe more than that."

"Nothing?"

"Not to me. When I pushed for a commitment, we broke up. Six weeks later, he was engaged to someone he worked with."

Paige winced. "Ouch. That must have hurt."

"It did. So I did the smart thing and bought a defunct small-town newspaper." Even she knew that sounded ridiculous. "I don't plan to be proposed to any time soon. Nor do I want to be."

Paige picked up her camera. When they turned to go inside, Amy saw a couple beside the field of tulips. She and Paige weren't the only people seeking fresh air.

When the man knelt in front of the woman, Amy nudged Paige. "There."

"What?" When Paige looked, she held up her camera and started snapping photos.

He pulled what must have been a ring out of his pocket. They couldn't hear what he said, but the woman threw her arms around him when he stood. He spun her in a circle before leaning down and kissing her gently on the lips. The wedding she'd just seen had been beautiful, but this was unpracticed. The couple walked hand in hand toward them.

Paige stepped in front of them. "I hope you don't find this intrusive, but I'm the wedding photographer. I won't give any of these photos to the newlyweds, but I took photos of you when I noticed your moment."

"Thank you! We'll treasure those forever." The newly engaged woman reached out and impulsively hugged each of the women. Then she looked up at the man with a sweet expression. "I'll be so happy to have the photos."

As they started to walk away, an impulsive idea sprang to Amy's mind. "Excuse me." She stopped them. "I own the town's newspaper. Would you mind if I put one of the photos in the

Two Hearts Times? It's a wonderful moment." Amy waited for their response, hoping her request wasn't intrusive, knowing she had no right to ask what she had.

The woman smiled. "I'm fine with it. Carter?"

He nodded. "Sure."

Paige returned to the tent while Amy talked to the couple. Amy collected their names and contact information and then calculated whether she could squeeze the photo in this week's edition. It would be nice to have something that had just happened instead of week-old news.

Inside, Cassie greeted her. "How was your first wedding?"

How did she answer that? Slow torture? She cleared her throat.

Before she could reply, Cassie patted her on the back. "I know what you went through with Maxine. Bella told me the story. I'm sorry that happened." She motioned her forward. "Walk with me while I do my routine check on the room."

"It's fine, but I don't want to see another wedding soon. Or have anything to do with weddings."

Especially proposals.

They checked the drinks, finding everything fine. "Weddings are my life. But you probably have little to do with weddings with your newspaper." Cassie asked, "What's the most popular story you've done since you started the paper?"

Amy laughed and thought about it for a moment. "That's easy. When Nick proposed to Simone. Paige was in her backyard and saw the whole thing. She took photos with her phone, and the couple let me run one in the newspaper. I received a ton of great comments about that story."

Cassie nodded. "Maybe you should do a column in your newspaper with wedding-related things like tips and current trends."

Amy waved her hands in front of her face. "Today kind of put me off of everything wedding for a while."

Cassie laughed. "You've moved to the wrong town if you want to avoid weddings."

Amy was sure that was true. The town had been dying before becoming a wedding destination had brought it back to life. It had embraced everything bridal.

CHAPTER FOUR

*A*my tried to focus on the front of the church. The minister had chosen today of all days to talk about raising children, something that held zero interest for her. Unfortunately, she'd desperately needed something to grab ahold of her attention and not let go, and today's message had failed to deliver. In fact, she was having trouble staying awake.

She narrowed her eyes and willed herself to focus—rapidly blinked her eyes, then opened them wide to try to keep them open. Moments later, her head dropped forward. Embarrassed, she jerked it upright and glanced around, hoping no one had noticed.

Cassie, seated to her right, glanced over at her. She leaned closer and, in a low voice, asked, "Are you okay?"

"Tired." Staying up late to add the proposal photo to the newspaper may not have been a great idea. The wedding had already exhausted her.

Cassie nodded and sat upright again.

A moment later, Simone, to her left, nudged her with her elbow.

Amy turned to her with a puzzled expression.

Simone whispered, "You started to snore."

Humiliation swept over her. She had fallen asleep in church and *started to snore*. That had to be a new low for her life. How could she look anyone in the eye again? If someone came to the newspaper office to place an ad, they'd snicker about today. She'd need to move and go somewhere she wouldn't be known as the *snoring church sleeper*.

"Only for a second. I don't think anybody else heard it," Simone assured her.

Amy glanced around. No one seemed to be watching her, so maybe Simone had been honest with her. They were almost cousins since Simone was engaged to Amy's cousin Nick Barton. Amy quickly mouthed a *thank-you*.

Her friend smiled and gave her a little thumbs up.

Amy dismissed plans to get a rental truck to move this afternoon. Actually, all it would have taken was stuffing one suitcase in the trunk of her car, considering she was still living with Dexter, and her few other possessions were in her parents' garage in Missouri.

When everyone stood to sing, Amy felt like rejoicing. She'd made it to the end of the service with what she hoped was only a minor embarrassment. She hustled out of the pew as soon as she could and hurried outside. When she stepped outside, she was immersed in the summer heat. But taking several deep breaths, she felt as if she'd be able to function for the rest of the day. Or at least until she could get home and crawl into her bed for a nap.

Cassie and Greg came out of the building, followed by Simone, Nick, Bella, and Micah. When they all clustered together, Amy noticed Scott off to the side.

"Amy?"

"Huh?" Turning toward Simone, she realized she'd been staring at Scott.

Simone raised an eyebrow but, thankfully, didn't mention it.

"We're heading over to Bella's for lunch. You're welcome to join us."

Amy's mouth watered. "Lasagna?" She'd once had Bella's lasagna and would make her way there even if she had to crawl.

Bella chuckled. "Lucky for you, the baby loves lasagna." Bella put her hand on her pregnant belly.

"I owe you a future night of babysitting if you feed me some of that."

Everyone laughed.

Cassie spoke up. "That isn't a bad trade-off, but it wouldn't work for me. I haven't been around babies, so I may not be a good babysitter."

"This is where being a middle child in a big family comes in handy. My oldest sister already has two kids, and I've babysat many times."

"In that case," Bella said, "I will not only feed you lasagna, but you can have leftovers to take home."

"Sold!" Being around these people who had quickly become friends washed away some of her exhaustion and her fear of the unknown when it came to her business.

Greg motioned Scott over and invited him to join them. "I think everyone has met my friend Scott."

Murmurs of agreement went around the room except for Bella and Simone. After Greg introduced them to his friend, Amy learned a bit more about him. "I've known Scott for, what, six or seven years?"

Scott nodded. "We were in the same academy class. Greg went on to love the job. After a year on the street, I moved to the IT department. Computers are more my thing."

That still didn't tell her why he was here other than maybe visiting a friend.

The group turned and headed toward Bella and Micah's house. Two of her friends had been absent from church, even though both had been at the wedding last night. "I didn't notice CJ and Paige this morning. Are they okay?"

Cassie nodded. "They headed out of town early this morning for a concert in Nashville with a couple of CJ's sisters. They got tickets and invited Paige and CJ to come along. They'll be home later today."

When she entered Bella and Micah's house, the scent of garlic and herbs drifted around her.

"Everyone, get comfortable. I put the pan in before we left, so we're almost ready to eat."

The conversation became lively. Scott seemed to fit right in, but he also appeared more serious. Maybe the warmth of Two Hearts would help him lighten up.

Then she realized she was thinking again about this man who was simply passing through. Why had he become intriguing to her? She wasn't one for casual relationships. Besides, she hadn't gotten over her relationship with Logan.

When Bella brought out her big pan of lasagna and set it in the middle of the table, everyone took a seat. Conversation swirled around her as Bella put a serving on each plate, then, when everyone had been served, faded to quiet as they picked up their forks and started eating. Amy glanced over at Scott again.

And there she went again, focusing on Scott Miller. He seemed like a really nice guy, though. And he was undeniably handsome. *Distractions, Amy. You don't need distractions. Focus on your business and getting your life pulled together.*

Simone pulled her out of her musings. "I think I'm the only one who noticed Amy fell asleep in church." She chuckled.

Amy felt all eyes on her and heat on her face. "Thank you for sharing."

Everyone grinned.

"I stayed up late working on the newspaper," she explained. Thinking about it brought on a yawn that she covered her mouth to hide. She reached for the salad bowl to divert attention from herself.

Cassie frowned. "I'm sorry for pulling you into the wedding. I didn't realize that you'd have to work in the middle of the night to make up for lost time."

"This wasn't your fault." Amy explained about the proposal and the photo she wanted to get in the next edition. "The printer will start working on it today, so I had to make the changes to the file when I did." She shrugged. "I'll be fine. I've pulled all-nighters to meet publishing deadlines before. Tomorrow afternoon, I pick up the printed paper in Nashville."

Micah asked, "How's the newspaper going?"

Amy paused with a bite almost to her mouth and debated her answer. Sometimes, people asked questions expecting a simple *everything's fine*. When she glanced around the table, she realized these people knew her well enough that they would want an honest answer.

"I thought it would be easy to make enough to support myself. Running a small town newspaper takes a lot of work, which I don't mind, but it has proved challenging to bring in more than a small profit." She put her fork down as she waited for everyone's response in a room that had gone quiet.

Micah was the first to speak. "I didn't realize. I know Bella and Cassie have placed ads. I'll have one for the next edition."

Amy waved her hands in front of her. "I don't want to take your money if I can't bring results. The paper needs *more*. A special idea to bring positive attention. I built a website,"—she glanced toward Scott because she'd used it to prove her identity the other day—"and that gets some traffic from people checking out the town, probably for weddings. But I haven't figured out how to bring more attention to the site." She raised her hands in defeat.

And I'd love to get out of my brother's spare room.

Cassie nodded. "I can see where you'd want your own space."

Had Cassie read her mind? When everyone seemed to understand Cassie's reply, Amy knew she'd said the words out loud. She was even more tired than she'd realized.

"Agreed. Dexter is a great brother and a nice guy, but I want my own home."

Bella leaned back in her chair. "Hmm. How can we help?"

"I'm not sure."

Cassie stared at her plate for a moment. Then she looked at Amy and replied with a confidence that surprised her. "Don't worry. We'll figure this out. Together."

Amy wasn't sure what she was getting into, but she nodded. She hadn't found an answer on her own. Maybe her new friends could help.

Bella patted Amy's arm. "We'll think of something. Remember—anything is possible in Two Hearts."

CHAPTER FIVE

Cassie's historic yellow house looked just as inviting as it always did. Amy walked up the driveway and around to the back door. She'd received a mysterious text from her this morning asking her to drop by at 9:00 a.m.

Simone answered her knock. Feminine laughter in the background told her other women were there too.

Cassie called from across the room. "Come on in. I'm sure you were surprised to get my message."

Amy chuckled. Cassie's comment made this sound very spy-like. The text message simply said, *Meet at my house at 9 a.m. Tell no one.*

Cassie grinned. "I was hoping to make it intriguing."

"You succeeded."

Paige, Bella, and Simone were already seated at the kitchen table.

Cassie glanced around the room. "I'm sure you're all wondering why I brought you here together this morning." She laughed. "This sounds like the moment when the sleuth is about to reveal who committed the crime. I may have been reading too many mysteries."

"You're right. I could almost hear the dramatic music." Bella got up and went over to one of the cupboards. "I'm going to make a cup of tea. Would anyone else like one?"

Amy sat in the extra chair pushed up to the four-person table. "I do. Whatever you've got is fine with me."

A few minutes later, they had tea, coffee for those who preferred it, and pieces of pie Simone had picked up at Dinah's Place on the way over.

When they were all comfortable, Cassie said, "We need to brainstorm ideas to help Amy."

Amy gasped. "What do you mean? I'm okay."

Cassie shook her head. "You told me yesterday things haven't turned out exactly as you'd hoped. You're staying at your brother's house because you can't afford a place of your own. That isn't okay for someone running a business in Two Hearts. We want you to succeed."

Tears welled up in Amy's eyes. It felt good to have friends by her side.

Cassie continued. "But we don't want to intrude on something that feels too personal and private. Tell us if you'd rather we dropped the discussion." She picked up her fork. "We eat pie, and that's it."

"I'm happy that you care." Amy glanced longingly at the piece of chocolate pie. The stress of her problems had pushed her appetite away. "The newspaper itself is fine. I've gotten some advertising. Thank you to all of you for that." Her gaze went to each of the women in the room because they'd all advertised at one point or another. Cassie and Bella every week. "But I hadn't thought through the purchase of this paper before I jumped on the opportunity." She muttered under her breath, "Hasty decisions seem to be the story of my life."

More loudly, she added, "Newspapers should make money from advertisers, but the town is just coming back to life. There are only so many advertisers for me to work with. You can't support me out of pity. You need to have a good return on your investment. Earning money because an ad works is smart business."

"It's nice having a newspaper," Bella said. "It makes Two Hearts feel more like a community than before. I want you to succeed."

They all nodded in agreement.

Paige offered, "You know, I always think about photographs first. Could you add more local photos to your newspaper?"

Amy thought about it for a moment and then sighed. "I could make it more appealing to the people who live here, I suppose. But that still doesn't bring more income to the town, and that's truly what we need."

Cassie drummed her fingers on the tabletop. "Come on, ladies. You all run businesses in this town. There must be something we can do. Don't filter yourself. Just call out ideas."

Bella shrugged. "Wedding dress of the week?"

Simone said, "I could give away a small cake every month."

"I could increase my advertising budget with you." Cassie raised her hand in a stop motion to silence the others when Amy tried to speak.

"Two Hearts has been good to me." Amy sighed again. "I appreciate all of your suggestions, but I can't become a charity. This newspaper has to support itself."

Bella asked, "Do you have all the basics down? You mentioned a website. Do you also have a newsletter list people can subscribe to? Are you on social media? Those sorts of things? They help with my business."

"My website went live a couple of weeks ago. I've set up all my social media accounts. But I wasn't sure what people would want to see there."

Paige leaned forward excitedly. "That's a place where photographs do really well." When everyone laughed because of her championing everything to do with photos, Paige crossed her arms and said, "You know they do."

Amy brought up a social media site on her phone to check for feedback from viewers. "I added the proposal photograph you took to the paper with an article about the couple. I also put that picture on social media with a shortened version of the article."

Cassie said, "That was the last-minute addition that made you so tired at church on Sunday?"

Amy's face flamed with heat. "Simone had to elbow me in the side because *I was snoring*."

Simone chuckled. "It was only for a few seconds."

"I'm sorry I missed that." Cassie laughed.

Amy stared at her screen. Comment after comment said how much they loved the photo. She swallowed hard. "I can't believe this happened."

Paige reached out and touched her arm. "What's wrong?"

Amy shook her head in amazement. "I think the proposal photo has gone viral."

Paige grabbed the phone out of her hands. "Oh my goodness! She has thousands of views on this post." She passed the phone to Cassie.

Cassie exclaimed over it as she checked it out. "This is amazing! Maybe your financial situation will take care of itself, and we won't have to worry about increasing your income." She gave the phone to Bella.

Bella swiped down the list of comments. "This is awesome!"

"Maybe. Let me see if it's made any difference to the newspaper." Amy brought up her subscription numbers. "No new newspaper subscribers either from Two Hearts or elsewhere. I set it up so I could mail a copy of the paper anywhere." She went into her email. "Wait! I may have a possible new advertiser from Nashville." She frowned as she read through the message. "She's from a jewelry store and will advertise if I'm going to continue with similar photos."

Amy looked up at the group of women seated around the table. "This was a random moment. Paige and I happened to be there. I've used two proposal photos in the newspaper—the one Paige took from her backyard when Nick proposed to you, Simone, and this one. They drew interest, but you can't pull engagement photos out of thin air."

A noise at the back door had them all turn in that direction. It opened to Greg. When he saw all the women, he paused. "I was stopping by to visit Cassie on my lunch break, but it looks like I've interrupted something."

His fiancée waved him in. "Please join us."

He entered the room, followed by Scott, who looked startled at what he'd been drawn into.

Cassie had a thoughtful expression. "Greg, drag a couple of chairs in from the living room. We can squeeze you guys around the table. I'll fix a sandwich for each of you."

"That's okay. We'll just head over to the diner." Greg turned toward the door.

"Wait! We really do want your input. Let me explain." Even with the offer of a meal, he and Scott remained standing and near the door.

Cassie told him about the engagement photo and their lack of ideas for repeating that.

Greg shrugged. "You just need more photos. Does the proposal have to be real?" The room went silent.

He chuckled. "Uh oh. Did I make a mistake in suggesting something as wonderful as a proposal be acted out instead of real?"

Cassie slowly said, "You may have hit on something."

Amy watched the women nod their heads in agreement. Was it a good idea to put fake photos in a newspaper? "But—"

In his more formal law enforcement voice, Greg said, "You'll need to say they're mockups, not the real thing."

She still wasn't sure. "Could it work if they weren't real?"

Paige cocked her head to the side. "I *think* so. And I'd be happy to take the pictures. I think it would be kind of fun to broaden my wedding business into engagement photos. This would give me something to put in my portfolio."

Cassie clapped her hands with glee. "Then it's settled. Amy is going to have mock proposals in her newspaper."

Amy laughed. "I have the best imagination in the world, but I have to ask, how many times can Paige photograph a man on his knee offering a ring to the woman in front of him? Doesn't that get boring? And who is she going to photograph?"

Bella reached for another slice of pie, saying, "Eating for two," as she did so. She had a thoughtful expression as she broke into the crust with her fork. "We were all proposed to in different ways. There must be a million ways to offer the ring."

Amy had limited experience with proposals. Actually, zero beyond those she'd seen.

Greg said, "You ladies seem to have come up with a good plan, so we can leave now. But before we go, I want to mention that you need a man and a woman for these proposals, don't you?"

The bubble of bliss that had begun to surround Amy burst. She sighed. "You're right."

Bella nodded. "We need a man and a woman to be our actors. I think we can all agree that using the same couple every time is fine, can't we?" Bella glanced around the room.

"I agree," Cassie said. And then her gaze turned toward Amy. "But we have a single woman in our midst, so we don't need to search for one."

Amy gasped. "Me? Other than a couple of plays in high school, I haven't acted in anything."

Cassie laughed. "I think that makes you the most experienced actress in the room. But we need a single man to pose too. I don't think using one of the men in town who already has a girlfriend, fiancée, or wife would be appropriate."

Greg grinned. "I think I may have to respond to calls about loud arguments if that happens."

Cassie tapped her chin as she stared at their visitor. "How long did you say you were staying, Scott? I think it was a month, wasn't it?"

He nodded slowly, looking suspicious.

"Then it's settled."

Amy shrugged. "How is it settled? You've roped me into this, but we still don't have a—" Her gaze whipped toward Scott. "Oh no, Cassie! You don't mean to pull him into it too?"

Cassie rubbed her hands together with glee. "All he has to do is pose a few times and get his picture taken. That's about as easy as it gets. It won't interrupt his relaxation."

Scott now had a deer-in-the-headlights expression.

Greg laughed and patted his friend on the back. "Welcome to Two Hearts."

Cassie stood. "I believe this meeting has come to an end. Let's all get back to our businesses. Thank you for coming by. We can heartily recommend Dinah's chocolate pie today."

Cassie moved at a fast pace, kissing Greg on the cheek as she passed him, then hurrying toward her front door.

Amy stared at Scott for a moment before she followed along. The man would look great in photos—if he agreed to their plan.

Cassie herded the women toward the door—the one she didn't usually use and the one not blocked by Greg and Scott. When Amy got there, Cassie said in a low voice, "I needed the idea to settle in a bit with Scott. I think he was just about to say no. We're not going to give him a chance."

Amy stepped out the door with Cassie right behind her.

Apparently, even she needed to leave her own house. This situation was getting stranger and stranger. Then Amy remembered the wonderful comments and the number of people who'd shared her post.

Maybe this wild plan had a chance of working.

CHAPTER SIX

"Greg, what just happened?" Scott stood near the door, unsure what his next move should be.

Greg continued staring forward, then he turned toward Scott and sighed. "I think we've been expertly directed on our path."

Scott swallowed. Amy was definitely attractive, but he wasn't interested in a relationship or even the illusion of one. "I don't want to pretend to propose to someone."

"I don't think many men would want to. But I agree this could benefit Amy's business."

He didn't want to be a jerk, but he really didn't want to do this. Before he could answer, Greg continued. "And it won't be difficult. Not compared to your former job. You've faced down criminals."

Scott nodded. "And I stopped doing that to be the geek in the corner office." He had a couple of options. One, he could play along. Two, he could tell them he refused to do this.

"You could leave town. But I don't want you to do that."

Three options. The problem was that in the short time he'd been here, he'd come to enjoy the small town. It'd been a good break for him and had given him the chance to relax. "For right now, I'd like to stay."

Greg grinned and clapped him on the shoulder. "I was hoping you'd say that. And it really is a great little town. A good place to get away." He gestured toward the door. "We may as well leave. I know Cassie well, and she won't come home as long as we're here. She's probably sitting next door at Simone's house waiting for us to drive by."

As they walked down the driveway toward Greg's sheriff's vehicle, Scott thought over the last few days and started to laugh. "Is it always this crazy here in Two Hearts? I've only been here a few days, and in that time I've worked at a wedding and am now going to be an actor in a proposal. This town's love of weddings doesn't stop."

"This all started with Cassie. She rode into town on a motorcycle and wearing a wedding dress. I dismissed the first report that came in that said a woman in a wedding dress was walking down the sidewalk. When the calls kept coming, I went to check it out. Sure enough, a runaway bride had run out of gas in Two Hearts."

"She does sound like a character."

"That she is. She's also a fine wedding planner. She started a chain of events that is bringing our town back to life." Greg rested his elbows on the top of his vehicle and looked across at Scott. "There is one more thing that I need to tell you, though. And remember, you said you were staying."

With those words, Greg got back into the car. Scott hesitated before opening the door. He thought nothing would happen in a small town. But maybe he couldn't have made it through a whole month of nothing. To help out, he'd play his role with the proposals. Otherwise, everything seemed to be going pretty smoothly.

Inside the car, he glanced at his friend and waited for him to explain what he'd meant earlier.

Greg rolled down his window and waved as they passed what must be Simone's home—an older blue house beside Cassie's. He drove to the corner and turned right, back toward the highway, what was actually Main Street through the middle of town.

"I think you're happy at Mom's house, but I got a call from her this morning."

"She wants me out of her house, doesn't she? I knew I shouldn't stay there when the owner wasn't home."

"No. It isn't that. Mom loves having guests." Greg hesitated for just a second before continuing, but Scott noticed it. "It's just that she and James are coming home today. You're welcome to stay, though."

"This sounds both good from your words and bad from your hesitation. Give me the skinny on the situation."

"They're newlyweds." Greg drove up the highway a distance and turned left. They made their way toward the lake as the sheriff made his rounds through the town. "I remember when my sister got married. She acted the same way."

"I don't remember my siblings doing anything unusual, but then again, I wasn't with them all the time."

"They giggle. It's, well, disturbing. But I'm her son. Don't misunderstand me. I do want her to be happy. I'm glad she found joy and love again. But it's kind of like being around a high school couple, and I find it difficult. I walked in one day, called out to them, and my mom said, 'We're in the living room.' I went in there and found her sitting on his lap. Freaked me out."

Scott laughed. "As a cop, you've seen worse."

Greg reached up and rubbed one of his eyes as though to erase the image. "Not with my mother. I know she'll extend a warm welcome and ask you to stay. I just need you to know what you're walking into. And to add to the confusion, she kept the name Brantley instead of taking his name." He followed the curve around the lake, then turned back toward town. "The motel will be busy off and on for weddings so that really isn't viable. Besides, my mother would feel like she'd failed a visitor if you moved out of her home and into the motel. She's very big on promoting Two Hearts. And my place is just too small. We'd want to kill each other within twenty-four hours."

The situation here had changed. Did he care enough to want to leave? Probably not.

At the end of the day, they returned to Greg's family home. With a promise to get together for dinner, Scott went into the house, and Greg went to his apartment over the garage.

"Are you sure it's okay for me to join your mother and James for dinner?"

"My mother is in favor of anything that brings people together and especially anything that benefits her town."

Scott kept catching snippets of things about Mrs. Brantley. He still felt welcome but also had the feeling there was something no one was telling him, whether or not it was intentional. He rapped on the back door, and a voice called out to come in. When he did, he found a woman about his mother's age standing at the kitchen counter stirring something.

When she turned, he knew where Greg had gotten his features. "You must be my houseguest. I'm glad to have you here." An older man walked through the door, came over and kissed her on the side of her neck. "This is James. My husband." When she said those words, a light flush stained her cheeks, and she smiled.

~

Scott woke up to the scent of bacon and something sweet. Cinnamon. Last night had gone well. He'd had a delicious meal that included roast chicken, green beans with bacon, and mashed potatoes with gravy. All of that was followed by strawberry shortcake. Mrs. Brantley could really cook. He'd been warned by Greg and Cassie, but if this was the extent of his interaction with the lovebirds, he could certainly handle this. The tradeoff was worth it.

When he went downstairs, he found the two of them seated at the dining room table. Mrs. Brantley scrambled to her feet. "Let me get you some breakfast. Sit yourself down here across from James. I've got a coffee cake, eggs, and bacon for you."

Scott sat as he'd been told to and breathed in the wonderful scents. This was better than staying at a bed and breakfast. He had a room of his own. No one bothered him. And he was fed wonderful meals night and day. What could possibly go wrong?

She put the plate in front of him, and he reached for his fork.

"I have everything for the day planned out."

Scott forked eggs into his mouth, only half paying attention to Mrs. Brantley's words to her husband.

Then she added, "I think you'll enjoy it, Scott."

"Excuse me?" He paused, his fork midway to his plate for another bite.

"I was talking about the day I have planned for us. I want to make sure you get full immersion into Two Hearts. I can show you the schedule if you'd like."

Scott stared up at her. Maybe she was just a helpful tour guide. "I'd like to see that," he muttered, trying to be polite.

She slid a clipboard with a week-long grid over to him. One-hour time blocks were labeled on every day. Even lunches had been scheduled. Today's visit said "TBA wedding business," so she hadn't firmed up the appointment yet. Tomorrow's first stop was a wedding cake place. The next day took him to a wedding dress store, a feminine domain he and most men of his acquaintance hoped to avoid. Each of the visits to a business came after a drive somewhere and lunch.

Today's first stop was McDonald's Farm with a side note to show him where they'd held the Fall Festival last year. The farm sounded fine, but he didn't care about an event he hadn't attended. And though she was a very nice woman, what was he going to say to her during these hours spent together every day?

"This is very kind of you. But I think I'm just going to relax and maybe ride around with Greg some."

She shook her head vigorously. "We can't have that. You're a guest. It's my duty to take care of you while you're here."

And that's what led him to be on his way to Dinah's Place. They'd arrive late—more than a half hour off from the planned time—because the tour of the farm had run long. The morning had started fine, but the afternoon's unknown festivities loomed on the horizon.

CHAPTER SEVEN

Amy drove home from Nashville with every thought about the newspaper. Actually, thinking about the paper was too mild. She was obsessing. She played different scenarios for saving her business over and over again in her mind. Nothing solved her problems.

No, she needed to come up with a different approach. When the long drive home with the papers stacked in her trunk didn't produce any other ideas, she knew that she was back to where she'd been that morning.

She owned a small-town newspaper that would bring in enough money—she hoped—to support itself. The problem seemed to be that the *Two Hearts Times* wasn't going to support her. She was going to have to get a job working for someone else. That would involve a long commute, though. She'd have to sell the newspaper and move. But who would want a paper that could barely keep itself afloat?

Her haste in buying the business had gotten her into a sticky place. Her friends had come up with one idea to save the newspaper. Maybe they could come up with a second one.

The landscape morphed into a scattering of houses, then

farmers' fields. She passed the questionable motel that had a police car parked in front with the lights on and, not long after that, saw the sign welcoming her to Two Hearts.

When she saw the sign, reality kicked in. Her friends had come up with a great idea, and the odds of them producing a second one were slim. She'd have to figure out something else on her own. At this point, she wanted a cup of coffee and one of Dinah's fabulous pieces of pie. It might not solve her problem, but it was a good start.

Inside, Michelle greeted her, and Amy chose a table off to the side. Being led to her favorite table helped her feel like she belonged here. She sat here every time she came in alone or with a friend. Just one more thing to love about her small town.

Once seated, Michelle hurried over, her order book in hand and a glass of water in the other. "We had a busy lunch rush. There are fewer choices of pie." She gave Amy a steady look. "You are getting pie, right?"

Amy grinned. "Every chance I get."

"After lunch or instead of it?"

"I'll be sensible and have pie after whatever the special is."

"Fried chicken, mashed potatoes, and green beans. And I have cherry and key lime left."

"I'll take the key lime. I don't think I've tried that flavor, but Dinah does everything great, so I know I'll be happy. "

"Coming up. That and your usual cup of coffee."

As Amy waited, the door to Dinah's opened. Mrs. Brantley walked through the door with a determined expression and a clipboard tucked under her arm. That woman ruled the town as mayor with everything organized on her clipboard.

Scott followed behind her.

For a flicker of a moment, Amy considered asking them to join her. Then she remembered she didn't want to spend time with Scott.

She was surprised when he followed Mrs. Brantley to her

table in the middle of the room. They were close enough that Amy could hear some of their conversation with Michelle. Perhaps conversation was the wrong word. Mrs. Brantley spoke, and Scott listened and nodded.

"We got back from our trip in time to show Scott our town. He could have missed everything we had to offer, especially our new wedding businesses."

Scott looked directly at Amy. Instead of his usual calm expression, she saw panic.

After Michelle had taken their orders and left, Mrs. Brantley checked her phone. As she tucked it back in her purse, she said, "I have great news, Scott. I was able to schedule a time for you to observe at Bella's Brides today while she has an appointment with a bride. I want you to experience everything Two Hearts has to offer. That's much better than the simple tour of her business I had down for the day after tomorrow."

Amy hid a snicker behind her hand. Scott's fear had clearly morphed into horror.

Her meal arrived, and Amy picked up her fork to dive in. As she ate, she glanced over at the pair. They'd also gotten the special and pie, with Scott also choosing the key lime. That might be the first thing they had in common.

Before taking a bite, he stared directly at Amy and mouthed the word "help."

Amy sat back in her seat and watched them. When Mrs. Brantley got rolling on something, she definitely was a force to be reckoned with. She had set her sights on giving Scott the ultimate tour of Two Hearts, probably hoping he'd be so enamored with the place that he'd move here.

She ignored little facts like his long-term career in Chicago. He took a bite of pie as Amy watched them. Mrs. Brantley somehow managed to eat gracefully and lay out plans for the day at the same time.

When he said what looked like "please" with his hand beside

his mouth so his host couldn't see his mouth moving, Amy knew there was no way she could leave without helping. Besides, he'd done her a huge favor by not reporting the fish or mentioning her slippers. Then he'd agreed to stage the proposals with her. Well, he'd been roped into it, but he could have said *no* as they'd fled the room. No matter what, she owed him.

Amy polished off her pie and then, with a sigh, pushed back from the table and went over to pay. She could feel Scott's eyes on her the whole time because, at this moment in time, she was his one way out. Michelle and Dinah didn't know him.

Michelle took her money and said, "What do you have planned for the rest of the day?"

Amy gestured with her thumb toward the parking lot in front of the restaurant. "I picked up the newspapers today, and I'm going to distribute them." She glanced toward the door. "Do you think I could put some over there? I have these cute little stands now."

"Dinah!" Michelle called over her shoulder.

Dinah stepped out of the kitchen area, wiping her hands on her apron. "Everything okay?"

"Delicious as always." Amy repeated her request to the restaurant's owner.

"Of course, hon. I think that's a great idea. We've started to get more visitors, so we may be able to sell quite a few of them. That reminds me. I've been thinking about doing something with the newspaper. Do you think you'd be able to use a recipe from me once a month?"

Amy couldn't fight the grin that came to her face. "I know everyone would love that. Just get it to me whenever you have time, and I'll find space. By Wednesday or Thursday of each week would be helpful, though, if you wanted the recipe in the next issue."

Dinah waved her hand through the air. "Timing doesn't

matter much to me. Not unless I have something special for a holiday, and we don't have any of those coming up soon." She gave a nod. "I'll get to thinking more about it."

She turned toward the back. Amy gave one more moment's consideration to what she'd do next before she turned and went straight to the table she should avoid. The one with the man she'd hit with a fish.

"I couldn't help but overhear your plans for Scott. But I know you've been away, Mrs. Brantley. I'm sure things related to your mayoral duties have been piling up."

Mrs. Brantley said, "I have a few issues. But I'll get to them soon."

Scott's eyes had gone hopeful for a moment, but now he let out a sigh as he assumed his shot at getting out of this planned day was over.

"I may have a way for both to happen. I need to get the newspaper out, and I could use Scott's help to do that. At the same time, I can give him a tour of Main Street and some other parts of town."

Mrs. Brantley looked from Amy to Scott and smiled. Oh no! She thought Amy was interested in this man, and that was the last thing she needed right now.

Scott jumped to his feet. He must have decided to take the bull by the horns. "I'd be honored to help you distribute the newspaper. I enjoy a little workout in the fresh air." He turned toward his host. "If you don't mind, Mrs. Brantley. You've been so kind to me today."

Mrs. Brantley kept smiling the smile that concerned Amy. "It's a lovely idea. You two kids have fun."

And that brought Amy to the point where she was walking out the door of the diner with Scott directly behind her, all with a promise of spending the next few hours alone with him. The day had certainly not gone as anticipated. A quick glance towards Scott's face said he felt the same way.

~

As he left Dinah's Place, Scott felt as if he'd broken out of prison. His afternoon at Bella's Brides had been canceled. "Thank you."

Amy giggled. "She had your day planned down to the second." She stopped and turned to him. "I distribute the newspapers every week by myself. I don't really need your help."

He glanced back toward the restaurant. "I think I need to do what I said I would. She's such a nice lady . . ."

"Good point. Then climb on board. We'll drop off papers at the grocery store and hardware store. A short visit to Simone's bakery should take care of the wedding requirement. We'll get something to eat there. You can tell Mrs. Brantley about your visit later."

"She has that location scheduled for tomorrow. At least, I'll have one place knocked off her list." He sighed. "Everything there is probably pink."

Amy laughed, and he liked the sound. "You're right. Pink has become the town's color and pairs well with weddings. I understand the trend started when Bella painted the park's picnic tables pink."

When he pictured family photos taken during a picnic, he winced. At the grocery store, Scott jumped out to carry the papers. He had volunteered, so he would do this. Not that he thought for a second that Amy couldn't. She seemed to be singlehandedly running the newspaper.

Amy stood with her hands on her hips, looking as if she wanted to argue, then shook her head and led him inside. She'd given him notice, though, that she wasn't a delicate flower. She was used to doing her job on her own.

After a quick visit with Sam at the hardware store, where Scott learned about a new line of hammers that had just arrived and that Sam felt would revolutionize hammering, they pulled up to the bakery.

A sign over the pale pink door said *Delicious Weddings*. As they approached the door, he stopped. "I only see wedding cakes in the window." Wedding-only businesses weren't a guy's favorite place to be. "Are you sure we can buy a cupcake?"

"I know we can't."

"Then why—?"

"Because we'll get a sample or two. Simone gives me one every time I visit her shop."

Scott reluctantly opened the door and then stepped back to allow Amy to enter first.

"Besides, you were scheduled to come here tomorrow, and there's no way that Mrs. Brantley hadn't booked that with Simone."

In the back, Simone was intently focused on the cake in front of her. "Welcome to Delicious Weddings. I'll be with you in a sec. Please look around." Now that they were closer, Scott could see she was adding a yellow border to a cake with words across the top.

Amy called out, "It's just me, Simone. And I have a visitor with me."

Simone finished her work and turned toward them. Her gaze went to Amy, then to him, and she got the same smile Mrs. Brantley had. Before he could clarify their relationship—or lack of one—Amy did.

"I just rescued Scott from a day with Mrs. Brantley. She'd scheduled him for tours. Including Bella's place."

Simone nodded. "Right. She contacted me about tomorrow afternoon. I don't have anything special ready to show him."

"Don't worry about anything. I brought Scott here, so that's one stop off the list."

Simone cocked her head to the side. "If you'd like to try a new flavor, I could give you a taste." Before he could ask what flavor, she added, "You'd be my first taste tester. I usually make Nick do it because he's a chef and has no choice since he's engaged to me. But he's working at his Nashville restaurant today."

Amy quickly said, "I'm game."

"I am too." He didn't see a downside to trying any cake flavor.

A couple of minutes later, she handed each of them a dainty plate with a square of frosted cake and a fork. When he saw the color, he laughed. "We were just talking about the town's love of all things pink."

"I love pink, too, so it works for me." Simone bounced on her feet as she watched them. She was a bundle of energy.

They each took a bite. Simone leaned forward as she waited for their responses.

"Strawberry." And a tang he couldn't figure out.

"You're right about that. It's strawberry cream cheese frosting on my regular white cake." After a few seconds pause, she asked, "Well? Is the frosting a keeper?"

Amy didn't hesitate. "Unexpected and delicious."

"I agree." Scott peered into the glass case in front of him. "Is there more?"

Simone laughed. "Of course. But not in there." She boxed up a piece for each of them.

When they left the bakery, Scott realized that instead of time passing slowly as he would have expected with newspaper deliveries and a cake bakery, he'd enjoyed the last couple of hours. "Thank you for rescuing me."

Amy seemed to hesitate before saying, "Anytime. Can I drop you off somewhere?"

He knew she had more papers to deliver. He also knew she didn't need a stranger's help. "I can walk back. Thank you again."

As he started toward his temporary home, he realized he

would like to see Amy again. However, spending time with her when he knew he'd be leaving wouldn't be his best plan. But he'd agreed to be the man in her photos, so they'd be together again.

CHAPTER EIGHT

The next morning, Scott watched as Amy parked her car in front of the Brantley's house. She stepped out and called, "Aren't you coming?"

He held up his key ring. "I'd like to drive today."

She walked up the driveway toward him. When she reached him, she said in a low voice, "After yesterday, you want some control?"

He grinned. "I'm glad you understand."

As Amy went toward the passenger door, she said, "Look! It's a rabbit."

He glanced in the direction she pointed but didn't see the animal. "We *are* in the country. I'm sure there are lots of squirrels and rabbits."

"This one didn't look like the wild rabbits I've seen here."

"Was it wearing a vest and carrying a pocket watch?"

"Ha!" She smacked his arm. "I still think it looked different from normal." She continued toward the truck door. "I guess we'd better get going. Head north out of town."

He backed down the driveway and drove toward Main Street. "What's our destination?"

"The flower farm where the last wedding took place."

Flowers sounded fine, so they were on a good path. Better than the one he'd been on yesterday with Greg's mother. Even proposal photos were an improvement over full wedding immersion. They were soon in the country and passing by farms and farmhouses.

Amy kept shifting in her seat and fidgeting nervously. He was unnerved about the whole proposal thing, but he was surprised to find that she appeared to be, as well.

Distracting both of them would probably be good. "Why don't you list places where we can take photos? Even if we add more later, at least we'll have a starting point."

Amy reached for her phone. "Great idea." She started typing. "There's the two city parks, the one downtown and the one at the lake."

"Those sound good. Are there any other property owners you can think of who would welcome us?"

"The McDonalds let us have a festival on their property last fall, so I know they'd be willing."

"A farm?"

Amy nodded. "There are lots of animals."

They drove past rows and rows of pine trees. "A Christmas tree farm?"

"The man who owns this one is an old friend of Dinah's. Over Christmas, they started dating. I'm sure he would let us go there, but I don't know how to make Christmas work in May."

"Good point."

Amy pointed to their right. "The turn is just up ahead. It's always pretty out here. Well, in the middle of the winter the fields aren't particularly attractive, but Cassie puts up other decorations. This farm is often chosen by couples because of the option of using the barn or the large area with a tent. Cassie can make any setting beautiful."

More weddings. This town truly was wedding crazy. He'd

already heard enough from his wedding crazy former girlfriend Elaine to last years. Maybe longer.

When they approached a gravel driveway on the right, Amy pointed, and he pulled in. He saw a house off to the side, the fields of spring flowers she'd mentioned, and a red barn.

"Is that barn also used for animals, or is it only for weddings?"

Amy laughed. "It *was* a barn with animals. Cherry is very entrepreneurial, so they moved them out, cleaned it up, and now rent the building as a wedding venue." She pointed to the other side of the house where a brand new metal barn stood, but in the same color as the house to make it less obvious. "That's where their livestock lives now."

Scott pulled up to the side of the barn and stopped.

"I just realized I should have called first. This is incredibly rude of me. I got so caught up in the plan that I forgot." She grabbed her phone and quickly brought up Cherry's phone number. "I'm so sorry. We were already on your property when I realized I hadn't asked you first if we could come out here. We're looking for places to take wedding proposal photos to use in the newspaper."

Scott heard the reply through the speaker. "Of course! Do you need anything from me? I just put the baby down for a nap."

"No. I'm sure you want to enjoy your quiet time. That's what my older sister always says."

Laughter came through the phone. "Thank you. I think I'm going to relax. Now that she's mobile, there's hardly a moment when I'm not on the go. Anyway, you let me know if you change your mind about needing me for anything." The call ended.

Amy chuckled. "There's a fun story about the baby. When Cassie and Greg first met, he got a call from Cherry saying she was in labor and couldn't get a hold of her husband, Levi. So the two of them raced out here to the farm and helped until the paramedics arrived."

Amazing. Scott was sure there were stories like this in Chicago, but they seemed harder to find when you were in a big city. They stood out less because you often didn't know your neighbors.

They got out and walked over to the edge of the fields. His mother's love of gardening had given him an education about flowers. Peonies and other late spring and early summer flowers decorated the fields before them.

"What do you think?" she asked.

"It's beautiful. I wonder, though, if it would be so decorative that it'd compete with the two of us and the ring in the photo."

"Good point. I could blur the background to help with that, but I just put a photo taken here in the newspaper. Maybe we need other locations for the photos." She turned back toward the truck.

Scott put his hand on her arm to stop her. "What about the barn?"

Amy frowned. "Without the lights Cassie brings in for an actual event, we'd just have a dark hole."

When they went around to the front, Scott pointed to the traditional barn door. The large rectangle with a crisscross of wood had country charm. "This could work."

When Amy stood and stared at the side of the barn for a bit too long, he added, "But remember, I'm a computer geek and don't spend much time with actual humans. I could be wrong."

"I was trying to picture us standing there, and you . . ."

He swallowed hard. His trip to Two Hearts had been full of unexpected surprises. This one would have to go down as the largest of those.

"You had a good idea. I like this for the first . . . event." She clearly struggled to say the word *proposal*. "But let's go check out some other places too. Maybe the town park? There's a bandstand there that was refurbished last year."

He walked toward the driver's side of the truck. "Then let's head on back to town."

As they pulled out onto the highway, he said, "I'm glad we found a place for at least one of the proposals." As soon as the words came out of his mouth, he realized how ridiculous this situation truly was. He was driving around with a woman he'd met just days ago and trying to find a location where he could propose to her. Not a real one because that would scare him instead of baffle him. But the situation felt a little too real all the same.

She intrigued him, but her roots were firmly planted in Two Hearts, and his were in Chicago. He'd stay friendly but not cross a line beyond that.

To keep conversation going, he asked, "Should we go through some ideas for proposals? Or are they tied to the location, so we must wait until we've chosen a place?"

The calm feeling that had filled the vehicle flew out the window. Now, they were focused on proposals again, and Amy tensed up every time they talked about them. He wondered what she had in her past that made that happen. There must be something.

She swallowed before replying. "Well, we talked about the pattern of the guy kneeling and handing the girl a ring. There's always that."

"He looks nervous, and she appears surprised, as if she never saw this coming in a million years."

Amy chuckled. "Because they've probably been dating for a long time, and she should have been expecting it."

"Right? If you date someone for a while, the intention of the relationship should be serious. And nothing is more serious than a proposal."

"That's the truth," she muttered.

He sensed a story there, but he didn't dare ask. He was

surprised when Amy added, "I dated a guy for almost two years."

He waited for her to explain the proposal she must have turned down. Amy was cute and kind. Overall, she seemed like a great person. He couldn't imagine someone not wanting her.

Whoa! Where had that thought come from?

"He never proposed." She punctuated the sentence with so much venom on the word *never* that he didn't dare ask for more details. But she'd opened up the door on an interesting subject.

Time to lighten things up, or they would never get anywhere on this, at least never in a pleasant way. "Tell me what you think should be in the photos. What would make them something you think would get you the business you want?"

She scrunched up her face as she thought. "I just don't know. This whole proposal thing is so weird to be participating in. Do you know what I mean?" She turned to him with an earnest expression.

"I do. I really do. I've never proposed to anyone. I have zero experience. This is why I spent the night studying online. If I'm going to do this, I want to do it right."

At this, she smiled. "So we focus on the newspaper, and we're just acting?"

"Of course."

"A proposal seems so important, more than we should play around with. But maybe readers will enjoy the photos."

He knew just enough about social media to know readers would more than enjoy them. "They're going to have fun waiting to see the next proposal."

"And don't worry. You aren't actually going to have to propose to me today."

Elaine had tried to lure him into a proposal for weeks. Suddenly focused on that nightmare, Scott jerked the wheel. When the vehicle started to cross the line, he realized what he'd done and corrected it.

"What's going on?" Amy asked, holding onto the side of the truck.

How could he explain this? "Let's just say I've never proposed to anyone, but someone wanted me to propose."

He could feel her eyes on him, and the mood in the vehicle was decidedly icy. "So you dated someone for a long time, and you didn't propose?"

Ah. Now he understood. She thought he was like her ex. "We went out about five times."

Silence greeted him, and he figured she must be waiting for the rest of the story. But that was all there was to it.

"And?"

He shrugged. "She started planning the wedding."

Amy settled back down into her seat and seemed to calm down. That guy had really done a number on her.

After a stop at Fred's Christmas tree farm—where they decided it definitely was not going to work for their purposes— they went to the city park. To his eye, there wasn't anywhere special to propose here. He didn't think there was a man alive who'd want to propose in front of a pink picnic table. The bandstand without a band seemed incomplete. But maybe Amy would see something in it that he didn't.

"I don't know if this is going to work, either." He heard the frustration in her voice.

"What if we focus on the first photo and try not to think about the others? Maybe something will come to mind, or someone will suggest a place you haven't thought of."

She looked up at him with a beaming smile.

Scott took a step back. A smiling Amy startled him. She was always pretty, but that smile changed her. Made her more.

"Then we'll do as you suggest and talk to Paige about shooting a proposal in front of the barn."

He stared at her, and he felt as if her emotions were

mirroring his own. Pure panic as the whole thing became real. "When?"

Her obvious distress increased when she said, "Tomorrow? We probably should do this sooner rather than later."

As much as he hated to admit it, he agreed. "Then I guess you can pick me up tomorrow morning. I didn't bring a suit or anything like that. I feel like I should dress up for a proposal."

"I disagree. I think a proposal should happen while wearing whatever is comfortable and happy for you."

She just kept surprising him. He had a feeling no one he'd ever dated would agree with her sentiments. They would have wanted him in a tuxedo with champagne and roses and a violin playing in the background.

CHAPTER NINE

$\mathcal{B}$ack in his truck, she said, "I can walk back to the newspaper office from Mrs. Brantley's house, so just take me there. I know you must be having a good visit overall because she's a wonderful hostess."

He snorted. "She's a newlywed."

Amy glanced over at him. "And?"

"She and James are a couple my parents' age acting like twenty-year-old newlyweds."

She laughed. "Well, you're only here for a week or two, right?"

"A month."

He put his turn signal on to leave the highway. "That's a long time. Why?" She held up a hand in a stop motion. "Forget I asked. It's none of my business."

"No. You're okay. The short version is that my sister and her family are staying at my house while they have their house repaired."

Amy pictured the boisterous family gatherings she'd experienced growing up. Even if he'd come from a similar type of family, he was single, so that wouldn't be his daily life. "You're used to quiet at home, aren't you?"

"Yeah. Her kids are great. I love my niece and nephews. But it was a lot. Besides, the department kept telling me I needed to take some of my leave or I would lose it. Every time I talked to him, Greg asked me to visit. He said Two Hearts was a great place to come and get away from a hectic life. I thought, why not now?"

Amy wanted to ask if he agreed with Greg. Scott hadn't been here long, though. As they drove down the street, she saw an old woman standing at the end of a driveway and holding onto a walker. The woman waved to them frantically, teetering on her feet as she did.

"Something's wrong." He pulled to a stop at the curb.

Amy got out of the truck and walked over. She was surprised to find Scott at her side when she was within a few feet of the woman who she now recognized as Mrs. Robinson. She must be ninety-seven if she was a day.

"Have you seen my Nosey?"

Amy glanced over at Scott with her eyebrows raised. "Excuse me, ma'am?"

The older woman swiped at her cheek, and Amy realized she'd been crying. "Nosey! He got out sometime this morning. I must have left the door open a crack after the mailman brought a package."

Scott asked, "Your cat or dog escaped?"

Mrs. Robinson balanced wobbly on her walker. "Rabbit. A small brown rabbit."

"I saw him!" Amy exclaimed.

Mrs. Robinson's face lit up. "Oh my goodness!" When she pressed her hand to her chest, Amy wondered if the woman was about to have a heart attack. "Where? Around here?"

"Over at Emmaline Brantley's. I saw him in the front bushes. Scott and I will go over there right now and see if we can't find him. But first, let's get you inside the house and resting."

The older woman protested, but Amy was afraid she'd find her face down in the street if they didn't get her seated soon. When they reached the front porch, Mrs. Robinson said, "Just sit me down here on one of these rocking chairs, and I'll be fine. Please go find my Nosey!"

They both assured her they would and started back toward the truck. Scott said, "Maybe we should walk and keep checking our surroundings. The rabbit could have moved since you saw him." After a pause, he added, "And I'm sorry I didn't believe you when you said you saw a rabbit."

They walked through yards between Mrs. Robinson's house and Mrs. Brantley's, probably about a block in distance. When they finally arrived, Amy spotted a bit of light-brown fur exactly where she'd seen it earlier. He must have gotten scared and holed up here.

"You go on the other side, and I'll come on this side. The one thing I know about rabbits is that they can hop fast, probably quicker than we can move."

They snuck up on the rabbit from both sides. When they were close, Scott swooped down and picked up the bunny in his arms, holding him snugly to his chest so he couldn't escape. But instead of trying to run away, the rabbit leaned into Scott.

"I think he's happy to be rescued," Amy said in a soothing voice so she wouldn't startle the bunny.

A few minutes later, they were within viewing distance of Mrs. Robinson. She squealed with delight, sounding more like a teenager than the nearly centenarian she was. "Thank you, thank you, thank you! Why don't you take him into the house? I'll follow you in."

Amy opened the door for Scott, and he went through.

Mrs. Robinson called out, "Take Nosey to his bedroom. Down the hall, last door on the right."

Scott acknowledged her statement and kept going while Amy helped Mrs. Robinson into the house and into her recliner. Once the door was closed, the older woman leaned back in her chair and sighed. But then, new tears started streaming down her cheeks. "It would have been my fault if something had happened to Nosey."

Amy pulled a tissue out of the box on the table next to Mrs. Robinson and handed it to her.

She dabbed it on her cheeks as the tears slowed. "I'm sorry for getting so emotional. As you can tell, this rabbit is special to me."

Amy felt the weight of the world on her shoulders. She was many things, but an elder counselor was not one of them. "Nosey is safe. He had a big adventure today, but was scared when we found him. Maybe that will discourage him from running away again."

Mrs. Robinson patted Amy's hand. "You are wise for your age, dear."

Scott called from the hallway. "Should I bring the rabbit out here now, or does he stay in the bedroom?"

"Oh my goodness! Bring him on out. I just wanted to make sure he couldn't escape while I was getting back inside. I seem to be moving a bit slower in the last little while."

Amy's eyes went to Scott as he came around the corner with a rabbit hopping just ahead of him. The rabbit moved toward his owner and a pet bed beside her chair.

"If you wouldn't mind getting Nosey a treat out of the refrigerator before you go? I have some fresh parsley in there. He loves that."

Amy did as asked, and the bunny gobbled up his treat. Then they were on their way.

When they were outside, Amy said, "I think I'm just going to walk to the newspaper office from here."

"Thanks for keeping life interesting."

"Hey, this wasn't me. It's Two Hearts and a bunny named Nosey."

He looked at her for a moment before he turned toward his truck. "No. I think it's you."

She stood in the driveway and watched him disappear down the street. Had he just said he'd enjoyed the time with her? Considering they'd been looking for a place to stage the fake proposal he hadn't even wanted to be part of, she had to admit she was surprised. As she continued to her office, though, she realized how much she'd enjoyed the time spent with him too.

When her office came into view, and her car wasn't parked on the street in front of it, Amy stopped. Then, she remembered she'd driven to Mrs. Brantley's house to pick up Scott. She reversed her path and headed toward her car. With her job, she sat more than she should anyway, so extra exercise couldn't hurt. But she might deserve a slice of pie on the way back.

CHAPTER TEN

Amy woke up and blinked, staring at the bedroom ceiling. She heard movement beyond her bedroom wall and realized Dexter was up and moving around. The best part of his being an early riser was that coffee would be waiting for her by the time she got out of bed. The worst part was that she hadn't gotten to sleep late for the entire time she'd been sharing the little home with him.

As she always did, Amy thought through everything she would need to do for the day. She was scheduled to interview the mayor for an article about spring events. Cassie would be there, too, because she was taking a bigger hand in most of the events here. A wedding planner and an event planner seemed quite close in job descriptions.

A door closed, and then she heard water running as the shower came to life on the other side of the wall. This small house was adorable but a little too tight of quarters for her. After his shower, he'd start working. Being a blogger who writes about small towns meant he could work anytime he wanted.

Amy rolled over and pulled the pillow over her head, but the fluff didn't muffle the water. Besides, any minute now, he would break into his rendition of Hound Dog, which didn't compare well to the original.

As her eyelids started drooping, the song's first words exploded through the wall. She bolted upright and sat on the edge of the bed, rubbing her bleary eyes. What Dexter lacked in skill, he made up for with volume.

Last night, she must have spent an hour or two nodding off and immediately waking up again as she pictured being proposed to for the first time. By someone who didn't actually want to marry her.

In her last relationship, she'd expected and hoped for a proposal from Logan for months. Make that close to a year. All for nothing.

And now she'd actually receive one.

Be careful what you wish for, Amy.

She grabbed a robe, slipped her feet in her bunny slippers, and shuffled off to the kitchen to get some life-giving elixir. With a steaming mug of coffee in her hands, she leaned forward and breathed in the scent, already feeling more awake.

Forty minutes later, she had showered, dressed, and driven to the newspaper office. She went through her list of articles for this week, satisfied that everything was under control. Not much happened in most small towns. Two Hearts was no exception.

Her phone rang with a call from Scott.

"Do khaki pants and a navy blue button-down sound okay for a proposal?"

She grinned. Before she could reply, he added, "I may be obsessing just a little. I'm new to this."

"That makes two of us. Your outfit sounds fine, and I'll wear something to coordinate with you so we make a good couple in the picture."

There was such a lengthy pause with no response that she

was about to check her phone to see if he was still there when he said, "You'll pick me up in an hour?" Then he added, "I'm sure I'll get better after this first proposal."

If she had to be proposed to, Scott seemed like a good person to do it. He had a mixture of seriousness and comedy about him that should make today go more smoothly.

"I'm over at the newspaper office. Paige says she could meet us out there at about noon, so I'll get some work done here, and then I'll swing by to pick you up."

He whispered into the phone, "Just a second." Then she heard footsteps and a door opening and closing.

"Mrs. Brantley was in the other room, and I was afraid she would overhear us and give me things to fill my day."

Amy laughed.

The man was definitely perceptive. He'd figured out Emmaline Brantley's personality right away.

"I'm going to take a long walk and meet you at your office."

"You know, you could tell her you'll take Cookie for a long walk first. She loves her dog, but I don't think she has time to walk him as much as she'd like to. Then you won't seem to be sneaking out."

"Good idea."

She heard the door open again, then footsteps as he must have been returning to the house's main living area. He whispered, "Thank you," before hanging up.

To her surprise, just after eleven o'clock, Scott walked in the door. The room instantly felt smaller.

"Please tell me you have something I can do to help you." He ran his fingers through his hair in frustration. "That woman plans everything to the second. I've got to be able to explain my time."

Grinning, Amy pointed to the desk at her side. "First, sit down. Give me a second. I can probably come up with something for you to help me with."

"Bless you."

He sat down and leaned back in the chair. "Mrs. Brantley is one of the most amazing people I've ever met. She's kind and helpful, but I don't know how Greg and his sister survived growing up with her. Everything must have been incredibly organized—and by the minute."

"Being mayor is still new to her, so I think her being super organized helps. She probably wasn't that way before."

"You'd be wrong in that. Greg said she organized their Cub Scout troop better than anyone else. He also said they had a lot of fun. Maybe I should just let her take over and plan my stay."

She watched him for a second before replying. She wasn't sure she should say this but realized it would be fine.

"I think you're an introvert by nature, so being pushed out and on a regular timetable is hard."

He stared at her.

Amy gulped. Maybe she'd gone too far and said something too personal.

"You're right. Most people don't see that because I can act like an extrovert, but I'm really not. I prefer being on the computer."

"For me, it's a good book every time. I use the computer, of course. I have to for my work and life. But I love books."

He looked around the room. "You need to have bookcases somewhere."

She sighed. "When I get a place of my own, I'll bring my books out of storage." Her parents would be very glad to get everything that belonged to her out of their garage.

"So what would you like me to do?"

Amy frowned. Unless Scott wanted to be interviewed for an article—and Amy knew he didn't—she didn't need much. Then she looked at the computer in front of her, and an idea came to mind.

"You said you're in IT now?"

He shrugged. "I can do pretty much anything. I write code, do deep-dive internet searches, and use a bunch of programs. What do you need?"

She brought up the program she used to put together her newspaper. "Can you help me format the newspaper while you're here? I always do it, but that piece of publishing isn't my favorite. I would love to have a break."

He leaned over to see her screen. "Sure, I know that well." Scott reached into the backpack he had set beside him on the floor and pulled out a laptop.

Amy laughed. "Don't leave home without it?"

"I told you I was a computer geek."

"I don't have a budget for buying the program for you, though." She frowned.

"No worries. I already own it."

She stared at him with suspicion. Was he trying to humor her and pay for the program himself?

He held up both hands. "Don't worry! I do actually own it. I like to play around on the computer. I've even designed a few things for the police department with this."

She shared her work with him and explained what she needed, and he got right to work. As she edited an article, he worked on the rest of his part. "Oh no."

He jumped in his seat. "What happened?"

"I just realized I'm going to owe you for two things. You're already helping me with the proposals, and now you are helping me with my newspaper."

Scott leaned back in his seat and grinned. "But by doing this, I'm avoiding a tour of a wedding shop. I would do a lot more to avoid the tour."

When that man smiled, her heart did a double beat. Not good. The last thing she wanted was a romance, especially with someone who would leave soon. But even if he didn't, she was years away from being ready to have another man in her life.

CHAPTER ELEVEN

Amy and Scott stood in front of the barn as Paige pulled down the long drive toward them.

"I guess we're going to do this, huh?" Scott said. He followed that with a nervous laugh.

"You ready to pop the question?" were Paige's first words as she stepped out of the car. Dead silence greeted her. "I guess that's a no?"

Amy got the humor, but stress wouldn't let even a smile through. "The proposal's a yes. But a no."

"I can go, and we can pretend this never happened."

Amy blew out a big breath. "No."

"Let's do this."

Paige turned to Scott. "You still in?"

He nodded but didn't say anything.

"Okay, I've only done a couple of engagement photo sessions, so I have limited advice. Except try to be natural as much as possible. That's what I tell my wedding people as I'm about to take pictures."

Amy shook out her arms and tried to loosen up a little bit. Looking natural was about the last thing she felt at this moment. Scott stood ramrod straight beside her, so he was feeling the same thing. "Do you have one of those rubber duckies, stuffed bunnies, or something that helps kids relax in photo sessions?"

Paige grinned. "I usually just tell them to think of the person they're about to marry or just married if the photos are after the ceremony. But that isn't going to work for you two, is it?"

Amy's face flamed with heat. Thinking about Scott shouldn't do that to her. So far, he'd made her heart beat faster, and now, just standing near him made her feel warm all over. She didn't want or need that.

When the two of them didn't move, Paige laughed. "Okay. Let's get you two set up while the light is good. At this rate, we'll be trying to take the pictures at midnight." She went to work arranging them. As they had planned, Amy stood against the barn for the backdrop with Scott facing her.

Paige pulled a piece of plastic out of her pocket and set it on the ground in front of him. "I thought this might save your pants if you put your knee there. I'll set up the shots so no one can see the plastic in the photos. Also, where's the ring box?"

Amy tugged the red velvet box out of her pants pocket. The ring inside was a cheap one she'd worn for years. The box itself had come with cute rabbit earrings her mother gave her a couple of years ago for her birthday. She'd had to pull out the part the earrings fit on and set the ring inside. They'd be fine as long as the inside of the box didn't end up on camera.

"Let me get set up over here for just a second." Paige stood off to the side. "I'm going to move around you guys in a circular pattern. If you can manage to stay in position, I can get a bunch of photos, and we can use the best of the bunch."

Scott dropped to one knee. He held up the open box, and Amy feigned a surprised expression. At least, she hoped she looked surprised and not hysterical or panic-stricken.

Considering how she felt right now, her face probably showed something closer to terror.

Paige started snapping photos as promised. Amy focused on Scott as much as she could and ignored the photographer. He was easy on the eyes, that was for sure.

"Okay, you can relax." She came over to them and fussed with the neck on Amy's top. Then she turned to Scott and straightened the line of buttons running down his shirt. "Let's go in for the second batch."

Amy and Scott groaned at the same moment.

"Don't complain. I think we got good photos on the last batch, but I want more to choose from. So now, I'll move back a little and stay in one place. Scott, I want you to be in a standing position to start with."

"I like the standing position part, but *start with* makes me think I'm going down on my knee again, aren't I?"

Paige grinned. "Very perceptive of you. Put the ring box in your pocket, Scott. I want you to take it out slowly. Give the box sort of a nervous look if you could."

"No problem there," he muttered.

Paige's laugh at his comment made Amy smile for the first time since they'd arrived here. "I'd like you to drop to one knee in front of Amy. Then, pop the box open and hold it up for her to see. Amy, I want the expected reactions from you. Your eyes widen when you realize what's going on. There's excitement when he drops to one knee. And I want you to squeal. Yes, squeal," she added when Amy frowned. "And hug him after he pops the question."

Hug him? Her head whipped around to Paige. This wasn't going at all as she'd anticipated. *Deep breath, Amy.* She needed to go along with Paige's plan. This had to seem real. Besides, Amy could choose any photo she wanted for the newspaper and social media.

Paige positioned the two of them and stood off to the side so she had a clear line with her camera, and said, "It's showtime."

Scott did as directed. Amy's shock was real when he opened the lid, but not because of his actions. A cow's nose reached in to check out the jewelry box.

"Mabel! What are you doing here?" Amy put her hands on her hips.

The brown and white cow let out a long moo.

Scott burst out laughing and stood. "Mabel?"

"She's basically a pet cow, but she's supposed to be fenced in. I know she has a habit of getting out, though. I did a newspaper feature on Mabel a month ago. She's kind of a legend around here now."

Amy rubbed her hand down the cow's side. "She likes to nose in between people. That's probably why she came over to us. You were standing close to me."

Paige snapped a closeup of the cow. "She's also very photogenic. But now," she held her camera to her side, "this gives me a great idea for a photo. Amy, I still want you to hug Scott. Throw your arms out wide and wrap them around him. If Mabel comes in to break you two up as we think she will, I'll get a fabulous photo." She stepped back to where she'd been. "Ready whenever you are."

Amy and Scott stared at each other. He stood still, seeming to be waiting for her to act.

Amy had to remember this was all for her newspaper. She closed her eyes and focused on the emotions and the excitement she'd feel if this was a real proposal. Then she smiled and threw her arms around Scott, pulling him close.

As soon as she did, her world rocked. Scott wrapped his arms around her, pulling her close. This man knew how to hug. He rested his head against hers. But just when she started to forget all about Paige and her camera, a wet nose pushed between them.

Laughing, the two of them sprang apart.

Amy pushed away her emotions and absentmindedly patted the cow's head. "Exactly on cue, Mabel."

Scott chuckled. "Paige? Did you get that on camera?"

She glanced at him and then at Amy and smiled widely. "I did. *All of it.* I'll leave you two alone now." Paige went over to her car, turning back once as she was about to open the door. After a chuckle, she got in, and Amy could still see the smile on her face.

Amy watched her leave. "I don't know what that was about, do you?"

He shrugged. "I'm a guy. I'm not supposed to get these girly things. If you don't, I'm not going to."

Amy grabbed the collar with a cowbell around Mabel's neck and tugged her toward the house. The cow went along at her usual slow pace. "I'll knock softly on the door so the baby won't wake up. I want to make sure Cherry secures Mabel in her pen. Then it's time to head back to town."

She'd have all night to think about the hug to end all hugs.

"So what does the rest of your afternoon look like?" Scott asked as she pulled into a parking space in front of the newspaper.

"I'm going to come up with a list of possible articles for the newspaper for the next month. I try to work on that at least once a week. And anytime someone mentions a possibility, I note it."

"I never thought of the problem of constantly needing things to write about. You have to find a newspaper's worth of articles every week."

"This is easy compared to the daily newspaper I used to work at. Of course, it was in a medium-sized city, so there was a lot more to talk about too."

When they got to the newspaper office's door, Scott said, "I don't really have anything else to do. Maybe I'll just go back and give the dog another hourlong walk, or maybe Greg has something for me to do over at the police station."

Amy opened the door and waved him to come inside. "I have something for you to do if you're interested."

He perked up. "Another computer situation?"

She'd been about to ask him to move something off the top shelf for her since he was so much taller than her. But maybe she needed to come up with something else. The poor man seemed bored, and he didn't want to return to where he was staying. "I'll have you look at my website and let me know if you see anything that doesn't look right."

He smiled. "Consider it done." He gleefully went over to his laptop and sat down.

"In about an hour and a half, I'm supposed to head over to Bella's for a women's meeting. And before you ask, I have absolutely no idea what the meeting is about. I'm new enough to the town that I don't know if this is unusual or normal."

He made a few sounds as he looked at her website, some of apparent happiness and some not as enthused. Maybe she hadn't done as great of a job as she'd thought. "This isn't bad. I'll make a few tweaks."

"Thank you!"

"I need to thank you for giving me something to do to avoid going back to the Brantley house." Maybe some of his less-than-enthusiastic mutterings had been about his vacation abode.

"You know there's probably a room at the motel you could move into for at least the weekdays if that would help. Then you could avoid her schedule completely and spend your days doing whatever you want."

He swiveled his chair to face hers. "I've thought about that. I can't find a way to make that not seem rude to my host. She's kind. I wouldn't want to do anything to upset her."

"You do have a good point. Unless you had a place to go that made sense to her, it might seem that way." She checked her watch. "It's time for me to head over to Bella's. Do you want to stay here or leave together?"

He stood and stretched, the fabric on the front of his shirt stretching over muscles she wouldn't expect a computer nerd to have. She tore her eyes off of his chest and stood. "If you want to come with me, you could just sit off to the side. I do have a bonus waiting at the end. Every week, I do a little write-up about Simone's flavor of the week from her bakery."

He quirked one eyebrow. "Samples?"

Amy laughed as she grabbed her purse and went toward the door with Scott beside her. "Absolutely. She sometimes gives me a slice or two to take home."

"Sold." When they turned onto Main Street, Scott asked, "Isn't Bella's house over there?" He pointed to the left.

"The meeting isn't at her house. Bella's at her bridal shop."

Scott stopped in his tracks. "I didn't think about this properly. A man at a women's get-together." He turned around and started walking in the other direction before she could say a word.

"Are you okay, Scott?"

"I'll head over to the diner and get a cup of coffee and a piece of pie. I won't need the cake sample."

He waved with his hand and moved away at an ever-quickening pace. The man had a serious aversion to wedding dress stores.

CHAPTER TWELVE

aige came out of her photo studio up the street and headed toward Bella's. Amy waited for her to arrive before she headed inside.

"Do you know what this is about?" Paige asked when she was crossing the street.

Amy shrugged. "I have no idea. But Bella made it sound urgent, didn't she?"

"She certainly did. But I didn't have any clients this afternoon. I usually keep the middle of the week open for other work."

Amy wondered if that's why she'd called the meeting in the first place. She'd known everybody would be available. Inside, she found Bella and Simone.

"Ladies, take a seat, and let's get started." Bella glanced toward the door with a furtive glance.

When Cassie wasn't here and didn't seem to be expected, Amy wondered what was going on.

"And before you ask, Cassie hasn't been invited because we're going to talk about her."

A collective gasp sounded in the room. "And no, we're not

spreading gossip. I just want to talk about something Cassie recently said. The rest of you were there, too, but maybe it didn't stick in your mind like it did in mine."

Amy took a seat in one of the comfortable upholstered chairs the brides and family used when they came to shop for a wedding dress.

Bella sat down in the chair next to her and leaned forward. "I think we all know Cassie wants to get married."

The four of them nodded.

"We also know that her almost-wedding last year was a fiasco."

Amy had been told the story on more than one occasion. Cassie had discovered her groom in a room kissing a bridesmaid he'd passed off as a cousin. She'd run from the ceremony on a motorcycle and had ended up in Two Hearts. And that's when the town started turning around. She'd brought a wedding here and then another and another.

Bella continued. "Do you remember a couple of days ago when I asked her if she was ready to get married, and Cassie got a dreamy smile?"

Amy remembered this conversation. "Of course."

"Me, too," Paige added.

Simone interrupted. "I followed up by asking if she'd started planning it. The woman is a planning genius."

They all leaned back in their chairs. Cassie's reply had been strong. *I love Greg and want to plan the wedding. But every time I try, I think of the last time, and I just can't do it.*

Amy's journalist mind remembered every detail. They'd fled next door to Simone's house after pulling Scott into the proposal and sat around visiting for a while. "I replied with, 'Wouldn't it be fun if you could just show up on your wedding day and not have to plan anything?'" It had been an offhand remark without a moment of consideration afterward.

Cassie had responded with a grin and the words, "That's a great idea."

After laughing, they'd moved on to other conversation.

Bella leaped to her feet. "That's it! I knew I remembered it right." She rubbed the base of her spine and paced back and forth. "So I had this crazy idea. I can help my closest friend achieve her dream of marrying the man she loves."

Amy waited to see how Bella thought this could happen without the wedding planner planning it because she couldn't picture it.

"I have all Cassie's measurements. I'm sure nothing has changed. She looks the same as she did last year."

Silence reigned, as apparently Amy wasn't the only one who couldn't figure out what that meant for the wedding.

Bella stopped her pacing. "Don't you see? I can make her a wedding dress. I did it before. I know exactly what her measurements are. I checked, and I even have the original muslin I made that was pinned and fitted to her at the first fitting."

Simone said, "For those of you who haven't known Bella as long as I have, these custom wedding dresses are first done in plain, simple muslin fabric. That's fitted to the customer, so the expensive fabric isn't ruined if there are significant changes. So she has an exact pattern to work with."

That was smart, but Amy still couldn't see the plan. "But that just gets her a dress. How do we do everything else? And aren't weddings expensive?" Amy thought about her own bank account. It couldn't fund much beyond a meal at the diner, so paying for part of a wedding reception was out.

Simone smiled. "I think I see where you're going with this. Cassie has brought me so much business over the years that I would happily donate a wedding cake. And she has tasted enough of them when she's brought in her brides that I know the flavors she prefers. She's even mentioned her favorite cake decor numerous times."

Bella clapped her hands with glee. "That gives us a dress and a cake."

Paige sighed. "But it doesn't give us food or a place to hold the reception. A ceremony at the church would be lovely and free, so that's easy. Oh, and she needs flowers and invitations."

Bella frowned and sat down hard in the chair. "You're as much of a planner as she is."

The bell over Bella's door rang. "That should be Michelle. She had to finish her shift at the diner."

Instead of Michelle, Mrs. Brantley joined them. She stopped when she came upon the group. "I came by to ask Bella a question, but it looks as if I've interrupted something more serious."

Bella stared up at her for a moment, and Amy could tell she was processing what she was going to say. "I should have thought to invite you. But you have to know that what we're discussing is a secret and cannot be mentioned."

Mrs. Brantley grinned in a way that made her look like a teenager and sat in the empty chair to Amy's right. "Bring me up to date."

Bella filled her in on what they had so far.

Mrs. Brantley took out a notepad. "I think Cassie always uses the same tent company. Maybe they'd donate a tent along with the setup and take down. I could ask them."

Paige shrugged. "I have no idea who they are."

Bella said, "I do. We had that bridal event last year, and I have all the contacts from that."

Amy spoke up. "I'd like to help. Is there anything I can do?"

She felt all eyes on her.

Mrs. Brantley went down the list on her notepad. "You have the cake, the dress, and the photographer." She looked over at

Paige. "I'm sorry. I put you down for photos without even asking."

Paige smiled. "That's because you knew I'd do it."

"And if you need a second photographer on site, Paige, I'm sure my wonderful new husband James would help."

Paige beamed at the offer. "I love learning from him. He's been so kind about sharing his decades of wedding photography experience, so I'll happily take you up on the offer."

"That leaves us without flowers, tables, portable bathrooms, invitations, and probably other things I haven't thought of yet." Bella looked around at them with a defeated expression. "In my mind, this would work because we had so many things just among us. Now—" She shrugged.

Mrs. Brantley made a *tsk-tsk* sound. "Don't give up so easily. It's a good thing I dropped by. I think we can do it all. Cassie has worked with most of these vendors for a long time. She has an excellent reputation with them. I've been there when they've come out with their equipment, and they're always smiling and happy to see her. She's kind and pays on time every time."

"How does this help us?" Simone asked.

"I think we can get them to do her wedding for free."

They all sat back and stared at her.

Paige said, "But that's a lot of expenses for them. They have to bring everything out from the city."

The door chimed, and a woman called out, "It's Michelle. I was finally able to get away." She appeared around a rack of dresses. "Thank you for inviting me. What's going on?"

Bella filled her in.

As she took a seat, Michelle said, "Maybe it's easier than you guys think. I helped with that festival last fall."

Mrs. Brantley made a snorting sound that had them all sit up in their seats. "My dear, you ran that whole thing. You did an amazing job. And the town certainly benefited financially from your efforts."

Michelle blushed. "Well, I was going to say that it's about the same amount of work. Couldn't we hold the reception in Cherry and Levi's barn? Do you think that's the wrong place for Cassie? I know she's done a bunch of receptions there."

Bella spoke up first. "I love it. And you know what, we can talk to her florist because I know that Henri absolutely adores Cassie. I believe he would help with this."

Mrs. Brantley nodded. "Agreed. As to the tables, we could have a few of the guys drive into the city and pick them up. I bet we could talk her vendor into that."

Amy considered everything they'd said. "And I can do the invitations."

Mrs. Brantley patted her arm. "My dear, that would be far too expensive for you to take on."

"I have an idea. What if we only mail invitations to a select few? I'm pretty sure I can get the company that prints the newspaper to print up a few invitations for me for little to no cost. I have good graphic design skills because of my work. And if there's a program I don't know how to do, Scott can help me." As soon as his name left her mouth, she wanted to call it back.

Every one of the women stared at her and smiled knowingly.

Simone cleared her throat. "Are you spending time with Scott? I know the two of you were in the bakery the other day, but you said you had just taken over on the tour." Her eyes twinkled with delight as she asked the question.

"I've been helping him with—" she remembered Mrs. Brantley was right beside her "—having things to do while he's in town. He seems to get bored easily. But he's a genius with a computer." Trying to direct them back to the invitations, she said, "We could send digital invitations to everyone else. We would need to get email addresses, but we'd have to get mailing addresses if we were doing it the other way. It's probably the same amount of work."

Mrs. Brantley started to make sounds of an objection when

Bella chimed in. "I have received some of those for events, and they can be gorgeous. The person clicks on a button, and it opens up an envelope and shows a pretty invitation. Amy, I think this is wonderful." She looked back down at her list. "We have a venue, invitations, flowers, and the possibility of getting the tables we need. We still need the tablecloths and everything that goes with that. And food."

"I know I'm already doing the cake, but Nick and I can provide the food too. I know food for a group won't be cheap, but we'll consider it our gift to Cassie."

Paige said, "You're already giving her a wedding cake."

Simone chewed on her lip. "I'm just not sure of another way to do this piece of the wedding."

Michelle, who had been quiet after her initial comments, said, "Do they need a sit-down meal, or can it be more like appetizers? Maybe some people in town could help make food if it was just appetizers."

Mrs. Brantley frowned. "I'm trying to decide if Cassie would appreciate a potluck wedding reception. I know her mother wouldn't approve."

Bella grinned. "That would almost be enough reason for Cassie to want potluck. She loves her mother, but her mother can be contrary. And I know that Cassie is excited whenever someone drops off a meal. Nick's mom found out she loves her chicken salad, so she brings some every month or so."

"Let's revisit the food later. Other than that, I think we've covered everything big. We can do this wedding." Mrs. Brantley tapped her pen on her pad. "The big question is the date."

Amy said, "If we're using Cherry and Levi's farm, we need to make sure there's no other wedding happening that weekend. How can we do that?"

"I usually make the cakes. There's a wedding this weekend with a reception out there. And one the following weekend."

Simone frowned. "We probably want more time than that, anyway."

"I think the minimum lead time is three weeks. I have to make the dress, and we need to contact and book the vendors. Does everyone agree?" Bella asked.

Simone nodded. "I agree. That's really rushing it, but the longer we leave this hanging out there, the more likely someone will accidentally tell Cassie."

Mrs. Brantley made a note. "In that case, it looks like nothing is scheduled three weekends from now."

An incoming text sounded on Bella's, Simone's, and Paige's phones.

Paige swiped to see it. "This is hard to believe. Cassie just messaged that she booked a wedding that weekend—at Cherry and Levi's farm—and the couple will call me to book photography."

"Same here, but for a dress," said Bella.

"And a cake," Simone added.

An idea came to Amy. "This might be a problem with any Saturday we choose. Maybe it would be better to have it on a weekday right before a wedding. The vendors would already be bringing everything. They probably wouldn't mind leaving the tent and all the extras here for a couple more days."

Mrs. Brantley clapped her hands. "Perfect. Three weeks from now, on a Thursday?"

Bella tapped her phone. "That works for me."

The others agreed.

"They'll need time off for a honeymoon, but I guess that will have to wait until after the wedding on the following Saturday. That isn't ideal, but it will work. And what about everything else on Cassie's schedule?"

Bella drummed her fingers on the chair's arm. "A honeymoon means that Greg needs time off. The bigger thing is that we have to somehow prevent Cassie from scheduling anything during that next week. Appointments could probably be moved, but weddings can't. How do we do that?"

"That is a bit of a conundrum," Mrs. Brantley said. "I've noticed that she likes to accommodate brides and will squeeze them in with very little notice if there's an opening. As you mentioned, her vendors are happy to work with her as needed."

Amy thought about it. "Greg."

Everyone turned to look at her.

Mrs. Brantley smiled. "Of course, my dear. My son needs to be told he's getting married. I know he'll be thrilled. Besides, he's going to need a suit, and we don't have his measurements."

"Good point," Bella said. "I always think of what the bride is wearing, but I sometimes forget that the man has to show up looking good too. He can tell Cassie he has a surprise for her the weekend they need off for their honeymoon."

"A big event he's scheduled," Michelle offered. "Something that can't be moved. And it would be completely true because he'll probably have plane tickets for them."

Mrs. Brantley grinned. "This is wonderful and devious. I will be so happy to have Cassie as my daughter-in-law. I already feel she's that in my heart, but now it will be official."

As they stood to leave, Paige told Amy, "I just need a couple more minutes with the photos for the newspaper. By the time you get back to your office, I'll probably have them to you." She leaned closer and dropped her voice. "The ones with the two of you hugging and the cow butting in are absolutely adorable."

Amy stopped where she was, and Paige kept going. She'd almost, *almost*, been able to forget that awesome hug. She knew many of the other women in this group had moved to town because of the man they were in love with, but she had no intentions of falling. And Scott had a very full life and family in Illinois.

Amy thought about him too much as she walked back to her newspaper office. Once there, she sorted through the photos

Paige had sent, each one more disturbing than the next. They weren't of a crime scene.

They were just the promised proposal photos with Scott. After dreaming for such a long time that Logan would propose and he hadn't, she now had photographic proof that a proposal including her could happen.

She needed to post at least one of these on her social media and her website. And she could put another in the newspaper. Her discomfort with the situation grew as she flipped through the pictures. Since she'd been at this for over a half hour, she decided it was time to get up and pack up for the day. This would all be waiting for her tomorrow.

Remembering that her refrigerator was dangerously low on food she actually wanted to eat, she headed south to the grocery store. She got a cart and pushed it around, stopping at the vegetables and choosing things that looked good. Her brother was many things. Kind. Generous. And she'd been told handsome. It was difficult for a sister to know that because she thought all her siblings were amazing. But he also was a junk food addict.

She'd managed to carve out a cupboard for herself that included things like oatmeal, cereals that didn't have sugar in them, nuts, and pasta that wasn't white flour. The other cupboards in the kitchen contained her brother's abundant supply of chips, pre-made meals with a laundry list of difficult-to-pronounce ingredients, and other items she tried to avoid. The lettuces and herbs caught her attention as she wheeled past. She knew rabbits loved lettuce and some herbs too. When she'd gone through her stage of wanting a rabbit, she'd done research.

Amy brought up her phone to double-check and make sure she remembered correctly and that no new research showed otherwise. Then she decided to buy some green leaf lettuce and some parsley for Nosey the rabbit. She may have never gotten her own rabbit, but maybe she'd make up for it by visiting one.

Especially one that belonged to an older woman who clearly loved having company.

She had second thoughts when she pulled up in front of the house. They'd only met the one time when her rabbit was loose, so maybe Mrs. Robinson was only happy to have them around because they'd returned her pet.

Amy got out of the car with the rabbit treat bag in hand. Nosey would appreciate the gift. Simone had once mentioned that she dropped off meals and herbs to Mrs. Robinson when she had a chance. The herbs part had seemed odd, but now Amy understood.

And maybe she'd get to pet the rabbit.

Once she rang the bell, Mrs. Robinson called out from inside, "Come in! It's open."

For a moment, Amy wanted to caution her, but then she remembered that they were in a small town that seemed pretty safe. There were probably still people here who didn't lock their doors. She wasn't one of them, though, due to years of living in places that weren't as safe.

When she opened the door, she found Mrs. Robinson in her recliner.

The old lady put her hands on her cheeks. "Oh, my goodness! Did you stop by just to visit me?"

Amy made a note to visit as often as she could. This woman was obviously starved for company. But then, who wouldn't be if you were home alone all day?

"I hope you don't mind that I dropped by to visit with you and Nosey."

Amy held up the bag of produce. "I bought some treats for Nosey. Some green leaf lettuce and parsley."

Mrs. Robinson, her face alight with joy, said, "You already know he loves parsley, but lettuce is another favorite. You instinctively chose his favorite things." She looked over to her left. "Isn't that right, sweetie!"

Since there was no reply, Amy was sure she'd been talking to the rabbit. "Can I give him a bite?"

Mrs. Robinson nodded. Amy knelt beside the rabbit, moving slowly since he didn't know her. She pulled a rabbit-sized piece —or at least what she thought might be a rabbit-sized piece—of lettuce out of the bag and set it in front of him. He checked it out for a moment, gobbled it up, and looked at her.

"He likes you."

Amy thought a rabbit would like everybody who fed them.

"He doesn't like everyone. He's never been in love with my son." She sighed. "Whenever he visits, Nosey spends all day in his own room. It's almost as if he can tell that Cameron owns dogs, and Nosey doesn't get along with dogs."

Amy sat on the floor in front of the rabbit. "Can I feed him a few more bites?"

"Certainly. Nosey's good at knowing when to stop. If he doesn't want anymore—" She shrugged. "He just won't eat it. Or he'll walk away. I guess I should say hop." The older woman laughed. Mrs. Robinson's mobility might be challenged, but her mind was clearly sharp.

"Does your son come to visit often?"

As soon as the words were out of her mouth, Amy thought perhaps she shouldn't have asked. If they didn't get along, it might be a sore spot.

"As often as he can. He lives in Houston. There weren't any opportunities for young people when he lived here, so he went off to Texas, and he's done quite well for himself."

Mrs. Robinson spoke about him with true love and affection. "His children are long-grown and have children of their own. Some even have grandchildren." She beamed. "I have four great-grandchildren."

Amy handed the rabbit some of the parsley. That went down even faster than the lettuce.

"He keeps asking me to come live with him." She looked

down at her rabbit and sighed. "I'd love to. He even has a section of the house that he said could be mine. A bedroom that has its own little sitting area and an attached bathroom. I've stayed there a few times when he's taken me to visit, but it's been a while. I don't get around as easily as I used to."

Amy wanted to help her in some way. But maybe being kind to the rabbit was enough. As Amy sat there, the bunny drew closer and closer to her, finally getting up and hopping around to sit beside her, leaning on her leg. When that happened, Mrs. Robinson gasped. Amy looked up with shock. "Did I do something wrong? Do you want me to move away from Nosey?"

"No, my dear. You've done exactly the right thing." She stared Amy in the eye with a serious expression. "Tell me about yourself. You said your name is Amy?"

"Yes, ma'am. I was born here in Two Hearts. But my father passed away when I was a kid."

"What's your last name?"

"I was born a Barton."

"I know your people! Are you kin to Nick?"

"Yes, ma'am. We're cousins. My name is Marchant now, though. My mother remarried, and my stepfather adopted all of us. He was in the military, so we left town."

"And you're just visiting?"

"No, I'm staying. I bought the *Two Hearts Times*. I'm doing my best to bring it back to life." When the rabbit moved away, Amy stood. "I'm sure I've taken up too much of your time. I'd better go home and get dinner going."

"Will you be back to visit Nosey again?"

Amy perked up. "Would you mind?"

"You visit as often as you like, young lady. Do you have a young man in your life?"

Only someone her age would word it quite that way, but

Amy found it endearing. She thought of Scott immediately. "I don't."

"What about that handsome young man I saw with you the day you helped save my Nosey?"

"He's a . . . friend." Oddly enough, he did seem to be a friend, even though they'd just met.

"A pretty girl like you should have a beau. But you can stop by whenever you want. It's nice to have company. That lovely Simone and Nick visit sometimes. She told me the other day that she was very busy right now with cakes for weddings and a baby shower."

"I'll bet she brings you cake samples, doesn't she?"

Mrs. Robinson's eyes twinkled. "That she does. I only allow myself small bites because the doctor wants me to take good care of myself. But she does make a fine cake." She leaned in conspiratorially as she said those words.

Amy replied, "She certainly does. I'd take one of Simone's cakes over almost anyone else's."

After saying goodbye, Amy went out the door, being careful not to let the rabbit out. When she had stood, he'd hopped back into his rabbit bed. Just petting his silky fur had made her long for one of her own. Once she had her own place to live in, maybe she'd get one.

CHAPTER THIRTEEN

Scott stepped through a doorway into heaven. Also known as Mrs. Brantley's Kitchen. "That smells great!" The woman might try to plan everything within an inch of its life, but she was a great person and one of the best cooks he'd ever known.

Mrs. Brantley turned toward him with a smile. Her husband, James, was seated at the small kitchen table with a mug of what looked to be coffee in his hands.

"I thought omelets and coffee cake would be a good start for the day."

Scott inhaled deeply and breathed out slowly. "I don't think anyone can argue with that logic."

James laughed. "I must agree. When I first met Emmaline, I wasn't sure what to think. Then, when she helped nurse me back to health with her food, I may have fallen in love a tiny bit with it at first." He winked at her and she blushed. "Of course, the woman herself was quickly behind that."

Yes, she had a clipboard. Yes, it seemed as if she wanted to control his day. But she really wanted to give a visitor the best possible view of Two Hearts and make sure he wasn't bored.

That alone made staying with her a little challenging.

What really bothered Scott was that he was in the same room as a pair of newlyweds. He felt they would be better left alone. His big sister would describe them as adorable, but he felt slightly embarrassed every time they did one of these *adorable* things.

Before he could take more than two steps toward the coffeepot, Mrs. Brantley had turned from the stove, poured him a cup of coffee, and added what he was certain was the exact amount of creamer he would have added himself. Then she turned around and held it out to him.

Cup of perfect coffee in hand, he sat at the table.

"Do you have a role in the shenanigans about Cassie and Greg's wedding?" James asked.

Scott stared at him for a moment as he tried to process everything he'd heard while he'd been here. There had been talk of Greg wanting to get married.

"James! That's supposed to be a secret."

James whipped around to face her. "I thought it was only a secret from Cassie and Greg."

His wife sighed. "It's fine to tell Scott, I suppose. He'll be involved with this. He just may not know it yet."

Scott shook his head dumbly. "I have no idea what you're talking about." And he wondered again what he'd gotten himself into when he'd made the simple decision to take Greg up on his invitation to visit Two Hearts.

Emmaline plopped an omelet in front of each of them that appeared to be filled with ham, cheese, onions, and peppers. He loved Denver omelets, so his taste buds went into full action. She added a coffee cake. "Serve yourselves."

"So, what am I involved in that I don't know I'm involved in?" Scott put a square of coffee cake on his plate.

Mrs. Brantley brought an omelet for herself, sat down, and added coffee cake to her plate. "I can sum it up in a nutshell.

Cassie wants to marry Greg."

"I know Greg wants to marry Cassie. I've heard him say that several times since I've been here."

Mrs. Brantley gave a single nod. "And that's only a week."

Had it really been that short of a time? He almost felt like a local.

"The problem is that Cassie was traumatized by a jerk of a first fiancé. She's a wedding planner who doesn't want to plan her wedding." Mrs. Brantley shrugged, then took a bite of her coffee cake.

Scott waited for her to say more. "And?"

"Oh, I thought it was obvious. We're going to plan the wedding for her. A surprise wedding."

Scott waited for the punchline. This was a joke, right? "Is there such a thing as a surprise wedding? Aren't the bride and groom both supposed to be ready for the day?" He asked the question tentatively, not wanting to offend anyone.

Mrs. Brantley grinned. "Cassie can decide not to marry Greg at the last minute. She still has an out, you know?" She paused. "I know there's a risk of Cassie breaking Greg's heart by running away, but I'm almost certain she'll only be glad we've done this for her."

He and James both nodded. The *almost* concerned Scott, but it did seem like a good idea when he went over what he knew about the situation from Greg's side.

"So we're providing them with the opportunity to get married. Cassie has said so many times that she wants to do this." Mrs. Brantley beamed. "The wedding is scheduled for three weeks from tomorrow."

In Chicago, one day more or less blended into the next. Sure, he had different assignments at work. Some of them were quite exciting. His skills had helped bring in criminals and put them behind bars. But it still felt, somehow, it was all the same. He got up, he went to work, he came home. Every once in a while, he thought about getting a cat or a dog. Something that would be excited when he walked in the door in the evening. But it didn't seem fair to leave an animal alone all day.

In Two Hearts, things moved quickly. They didn't wait for things to happen here. They made them happen.

"That all makes sense the way that you worded it." He continued eating. The omelet and coffee cake were delicious. When he finished, he got up to pour himself another cup of coffee.

Mrs. Brantley said, "I'll get that for you, dear."

"No, please, stay seated. I need to move around a little bit." As he did, he realized he was missing a massive piece of what they'd said earlier. Scott whirled around with his empty cup in his hand, glad he hadn't filled it up. "You said I was somehow involved in this. What could a computer geek like me do to help a wedding come together?"

"Amy has some ideas. She's working on a project and thought you'd be able to help her with it."

At the mention of Amy's name, a warm feeling stole through him. He told himself that's what it was like with friends. They made you smile. That's why life back in Chicago beckoned to him. He had siblings, parents, grandparents, cousins, aunts, and uncles, not to mention friends. Besides, he loved his job.

"Scott, are you okay?" Mrs. Brantley was watching him carefully.

"I'm fine. I'm just going to head over to Amy's now." He gestured in the direction of her newspaper office. Mrs. Brantley muttered something under her breath as she took a sip of her coffee. He had a feeling he didn't want to know what the words were.

～

Scott stood outside the newspaper office. He could see Amy through the front window, bent over her laptop, working. When he opened the door, she looked up, and instead of the smile he'd expected, she had a frown. She'd been nice up to now, so he turned and looked over his shoulder to make sure there was no one behind him. Nope. She was frowning at *him*.

"Would it be better if I didn't come in today?"

She stared at him for a moment with a puzzled expression on her face. "It's fine if you come in. Why would you ask that question?"

"The expression on your face when I walked in the door." His sarcastic tone made her smile.

"I was in the midst of uploading a picture to my website."

He walked over and peered over her shoulder. "You know how to do this, so why look unhappy?"

She pointed at the screen. He saw himself kneeling in front of her with a ring box open and winced. "Ah! You don't love the photo? Are there any you like?"

She blew out a breath in frustration. "It's a proposal."

Scott stared at her as he tried to figure out what was going on. He'd always heard things about a woman's mind being different from a man's. Sometimes, they saw things men didn't. This instance had him completely baffled.

When no apparent light dawned over his head, she said, "It isn't real. If I was going to get proposed to, I'd like it to be real." She turned her chair to face him.

The defeated sound in her voice surprised him. There had to be a story here she hadn't talked about.

"Something happened. What was it?"

She closed her eyes and sighed before continuing. "I dated a guy for a while. We dodged around the question of a future, but I thought it was understood." She opened her eyes and looked up at him again. "I was alone in that assumption."

He went through everything that they were doing with these

fake proposals and reached one conclusion. "Why on earth are you doing fake proposals if you hate proposals?"

Amy groaned. "I keep asking myself the same question. In a nutshell, I'm trying to keep the newspaper not just alive but vibrant. I need it to support me here. I can't stay if it doesn't pay."

He sat in what he'd come to think of as his chair and faced her.

"Instead of this craziness, is there something else you can do on the side? I'm fortunate because I can technically work from anywhere. At least in general in my line of work. I don't know how the Chicago PD would think of me working remotely." He had some idea that it wouldn't be received well. "A beach. A mountaintop. As long as I have internet, I can work. But you?"

She brightened up a little. "I used to freelance articles and content for businesses. I've even thought about writing a book. In the end, I just love words."

He nodded. "I understand." She squinted as she stared at him, as though she was trying to see into his soul.

"You don't have to say that just to be nice. I know not everyone loves books like I do."

"No. I really mean it. Bookstores are one of my favorite places to be. Libraries. There's the smell of a brand new book when you crack it open for the first time or the fun of discovering a new author and immediately downloading the book and diving in."

Her smile lit her face. "You do understand. The thing is that I want to not just survive in Two Hearts. I want to thrive. The town is coming back to life, and somehow, I want to be part of that. But I'm not a wedding expert in any way. I know words and some graphic design. The town only seems to need that in a newspaper."

"Let's back up. Why are you in Two Hearts? I know that you're from here, but you've lived in lots of different places."

"Five states and three countries."

"You see? You could live in so many other places."

"This place. This town. Two Hearts was in my mind the whole time growing up. Moving from place to place, memories of being here are what kept me glued together. The people are kind. You know your neighbors. Are there mean people? There must be because a certain percentage of the world isn't pleasant. But everyone I've spent time with here is nice."

Amy smiled. "Until last year, I knew I couldn't come back. Oh, I could have just freelanced from a little house here. But, even as a child, I knew the town felt dead. It was as though it had been boarded up, and the life had been sucked out of it."

He thought about everything he'd seen and done since he'd arrived and found that hard to imagine. "I feel hope here."

"And that's why I came home. I was talking to my brother one night over the Christmas holidays and found out he felt the same way. He'd already rented a little house in town. He said I could move into the spare room, and here I am." She blew out another frustrated breath. "But now I can't support myself enough to get a place of my own. I've lived on my own for almost a decade, so my time here has been . . . interesting."

She swiveled around to face her computer screen again. Then she moved the cursor over the publish button. He put his hand on hers and scooted it off.

"Are you sure you want to do that? Once it's out there, there's no turning back."

She hesitated for a moment. "I'm positive." She clicked publish. "Thank you for helping me and letting me talk it out. If this proposal thing draws attention to the newspaper in our little town, awesome. But I don't see how it can actually earn me enough to do what I want and need to do."

"Then it looks like you need a *Plan B*."

He watched her mouth twitch. Then she brushed her hand

across one cheek and the other. He'd made her cry. He hated it when his sister cried.

"I'm sorry, Amy." Scott stood and moved behind her chair, wanting to do something to fix this. To make her happy again. A smiling Amy was a wonderful thing. She was one of those people who made him happy when she smiled.

She sniffed and reached for a Kleenex, wiping her eyes first, and then blowing her nose loudly. "I'm the one who's sorry," she said between gasps.

The woman was sobbing now. Who could he get to help her? As he reached for his phone to call Cassie, she stood up and held out her arms.

Scott stepped into her open arms and pulled her in tightly for a hug. He could feel her body shaking against his as she cried. He rubbed his hand on her back to try to comfort her.

Finally, she quieted down and sniffed a few more times. Against his shoulder, she said, "Scott, I have never been this humiliated in my entire life. I am so sorry for crying on you. For even letting you be within ten miles of me when that happened. I'm not normally a sad crier. Only a happy one."

He leaned back to look at her face. "It's okay." He brushed a strand of hair off her face. "I'm glad I was here and that you weren't alone."

She nodded.

And then he felt electricity crackling between the two of them. He glanced down at her lips and started to lean down for a kiss.

When he realized what he was doing, he let go of her and stepped back. "Gee. Would you look at the time? I think I'm going to go take a walk. Yes, a walk is exactly what I need right now."

Amy nodded her head vigorously.

"Okay. I think I'll go over to the diner and get a cup of coffee. Maybe some pie." He hurried out the door with barely a glance over his shoulder back toward her. If his face was anywhere near as red as hers, they both looked as if they needed some sunburn cream.

That had been an accident. Romance between the two of them was completely out of the question. She wasn't ready, and he was leaving town.

CHAPTER FOURTEEN

Amy sighed in frustration and scooted back from her desk. She'd spent the morning alone in this oversized room. The newspaper was done—but not right. She wanted to swap out a couple of articles for something different.

She stood and stared down at her open laptop. The screen showed a page of the paper and a blinking cursor.

Unfortunately, staring at that cursor had done nothing to create an article that would fill the space.

Purse in hand, she headed for the door. In the past, she might have gone to a coffee shop and sat with her laptop, absorbing the energy of the room and the people around her. That somehow fed her creativity. Being alone didn't always cut it. Not when she needed to have a fertile mind filled with ideas to choose from. Her mind was currently blank.

She locked the door behind her, a regular occurrence since that first night when Scott had snuck up on her. Then she headed for the restaurant. Just thinking about Scott made her smile. It had been nice having someone in her office for a couple of days. He wouldn't be here forever, but it was nice to have someone to talk to while she worked. If he were here, he could turn into a good friend. That's all she had room for in her life right now.

She opened the door to Dinah's Place, and wonderful scents wafted out. Her cup of coffee just became coffee *and* lunch. Today's special smelled great, so she decided to order whatever it was.

"By yourself today, Amy?" Michelle asked with a lift of her eyebrow.

Amy stared at her for a moment as she tried to figure out the subtext. Then it dawned on her. She'd been in here the last two days with Scott. If Michelle thought they had a romance going on, that probably meant the whole town did. She needed to nip that in the bud.

"Scott was helping me with a couple of things to do with the newspaper. He's amazing with computers if you need any help." Then Amy gestured toward a couple of empty tables against the wall. "Is it okay if I take one of those?"

Michelle sighed. Her apparently expected juicy news had fizzled to nothing. Just as Amy wanted it to. The good thing about understanding reporting and writing was that you sometimes got it right and could change opinions based on words.

"Sure." Michelle followed her over to the table then pulled her pad out to take the order. "Coffee?" Michelle wrote the word on her pad without Amy replying. She did love being a regular in a place where they knew what she wanted. "And today's special is meatloaf, mashed potatoes, and glazed carrots."

She'd planned on the special but changed her mind. "I'm not a huge fan of glazed carrots. I think I'll take a bowl of soup and a chicken salad sandwich."

After Michelle walked away, a voice from the neighboring table said, "Dinah does a good job on everything. Her chicken salad is excellent, but if you ever want the best, you need some of Mrs. Barton's."

Startled, Amy turned toward the familiar voice. "Mrs. Robinson! It's always nice to see you."

"And you too. This is Elaine. Micah's grandmother."

Amy had seen the other woman around town a few times but hadn't realized who she was.

A kind older woman with a great tan sat at the table. "I'm happy to finally meet you, Amy. I've been enjoying the newspaper when I'm in town. I remember it from years ago, and it had gotten rather dull. You're bringing a fresh breath of life to it."

Amy felt those words to her soul. That was exactly what she was trying to do. "Thank you."

At that moment, Michelle came over with her coffee, along with the creamer and sugar she always took in it. She'd tried to break herself from the habit of adding sugar to coffee, but she couldn't drink the brew without some. Michelle followed her beverage with minestrone soup and the sandwich. One of the best things about this restaurant was that the bread was homemade and fresh.

Before she'd taken a bite, Mrs. Robinson asked, "Where's your young man today?"

Amy wanted to bury her face in her soup bowl.

Did everyone think she and Scott were an item? "Scott was just helping me with my computer. He's visiting Greg from out of town, and he's very, very good with computers."

Mrs. Robinson stared at her for just a moment too long— long enough that Amy wondered what she was thinking.

"If you say so, my dear."

Elaine asked, "Are you working on any interesting articles right now?"

Amy sighed again, but at least this had nothing to do with Scott. But for some reason, she felt a little stuck right now. "The newspaper is almost done. It just needs something interesting, maybe a human interest story."

And then she realized what her answer would be. "Mrs. Robinson, would you allow me to do an article about Nosey?"

The older woman smiled so widely and brightly that it dropped at least ten years from her age. "Oh my goodness, Amy. Nosey and I would love that. And you know, he's rather a ham when someone's taking photos."

Amy chuckled. "Then I will be by later today. Is there a time that works best for you?"

They scheduled the meeting for four o'clock.

Then Elaine, checking her watch, said, "And that is my reminder that I need to get going."

As though on cue, Michelle came over with a to-go bag and set it in front of Mrs. Robinson. "One meatloaf special to go for your dinner."

Amy waved goodbye as the two of them made their way toward the door. Mrs. Robinson seemed a little more wobbly today. That concerned Amy. People in Two Hearts would need to visit her more, especially late in the day and on Sunday when the diner wasn't open, so she wasn't alone.

With her story idea in mind, Amy smiled as she made notes in a small notebook she always carried in her purse. Nosey would be just what the newspaper needed. He would give it warmth and interest.

Everyone loved a rabbit.

Amy had debated asking Paige to come to take pictures for the article, but then she remembered Mrs. Robinson saying that Nosey didn't take to just anyone. Since he seemed to like her, she'd take her own pictures. She'd done that many times for articles in the past.

When she arrived, she found Mrs. Robinson waiting at her door. As usual, Nosey was at her side. When Mrs. Robinson started to open the storm door, Amy called out to her, "Don't open it. I'll be right there." When she got closer, she added, "I want to make sure Nosey doesn't get out again."

Mrs. Robinson looked down at her side. "Oh, my goodness. I didn't even realize he was here." She moved toward her chair and Nosey followed. Then Amy went inside.

"I used to be so observant. Do you think I'm getting slow?"

Amy could honestly answer. "I don't see that in any way. You seem sharp to me."

Mrs. Robinson smiled slightly. "Well, what would you like to know about Nosey?"

Amy had been thinking about that on and off throughout the day. "Can you tell me about how you got him?"

"I'd be delighted to."

Amy let her talk as she recorded the conversation. "I was sad after I lost my husband. The house became lonely. When a friend suggested I get a pet, that sounded like a great idea. Every cat or dog we'd had over the years had been a stray, so I asked the vet to let me know when he had a cat or a kitten that needed a home. I thought I could take care of a cat better than a dog that needed to be walked. And cats are smart enough to move out of the way. Sometimes, dogs just want to lie where they want to lie." She chuckled.

"So I got a call one day. Someone had found a domestic rabbit, and they hadn't been able to learn who the owners were. The vet said some people get bunnies as Easter gifts for their children and then let them go into the wild, thinking they can take care of themselves. But they're just as much a house pet as a cat or a dog, and they don't know how to do that. He brought Nosey over to me, and we took to each other right away." She looked down at her rabbit, now curled up in his bed. "And after that, the house didn't feel lonely anymore."

Amy stared at her, caught up in the story. "That feeling is what I always thought I'd get if I had a rabbit."

"You want a pet rabbit?"

"Yes, ma'am. I'm not even sure where the idea came from. I've always been a big reader, so maybe someone had a pet rabbit in a book. It may just be that since we were never allowed to have a pet—Mom said we moved too much with our stepdad in the military and it just wouldn't be fair to have a pet—that a rabbit sounded fun and different."

Mrs. Robinson said, "A rabbit definitely is something special. They may not curl up in your lap like a cat or a dog, but they love you just the same. And there have been a few times when Nosey has taken to my lap. Those moments are always special to me. I don't play with him as much as I used to. But he does like it when I roll this ball."

She pointed to a toy Amy hadn't noticed before. Amy picked up the long stick and dangled it in front of the rabbit she'd thought had been sleeping. He bopped it with his nose. Laughing, Amy did it again. "He is fun, isn't he?"

Mrs. Robinson watched her in a way that made Amy wonder if she'd crossed a line somehow. She carefully set down the toy and went back to asking questions. "Is there anything else you can think of about Nosey?"

She laughed. "Well, you've already discovered he loves parsley."

Amy reached into her purse and pulled out a little packet she'd brought. "Parsley and basil?"

Mrs. Robinson sat back in her chair and folded her hands over her lap. "He would love that. Your visit is exactly what we needed today." Then Mrs. Robinson switched the conversation. "Are you planning to stay in Two Hearts?"

"If I can."

Mrs. Robinson frowned. "I thought you'd bought the newspaper?"

"A small town newspaper doesn't bring in as much income as I'd hoped. I'm still living with my brother." Amy sighed. Every time she said those words or thought about it, she caught herself sighing. "I love my brother, but it has been really hard sharing a space with someone who thinks watching sports and eating pizza are the ultimate activities."

"That sounds exactly like my Ken. Sports and pizza were his favorite things on a Sunday afternoon. There must be a place in this town to rent, though. So many places have been empty for a long time."

"Honestly, I haven't searched as much as I should because I've been focusing everything on the newspaper." After a moment, she added, "And right now, I'm taking out enough money for food each month, but everything else is going right back into the business."

Mrs. Robinson made a tsk-tsk sound. "You need to take care of yourself, my dear." She glanced lovingly around her room. "I've had a great place to spend my life. You know, Two Hearts was really something when I was a kid. It's good to see it coming back to life. I've been in this house through good times and not, but I think it's still in pretty good shape."

Other than being a little dated, Amy had to agree. "Yes, ma'am. The rooms are a good size. And the kitchen is bright and sunny." She'd been in there one time to get a glass of water for Mrs. Robinson.

Under her breath, Amy heard Mrs. Robinson mutter something like, "Sometimes you have to know when it's time." She didn't know what that meant, and the comment seemed personal, so she didn't ask.

Mrs. Robinson seemed to shake herself out of her unrest. "When will Nosey's article be out?"

Amy was happy the conversation circled back to business. "Monday afternoon. I'll bring you a few copies."

"That's wonderful. And maybe some parsley for Nosey?"

Amy laughed. "Definitely some parsley for Nosey." That meant she'd get more time with the rabbit. She needed to get a place of her own and a pet. It felt as if those things would help Two Hearts feel even more like home.

Her life had been torn apart when Logan had broken up with her. It had been devastating when, less than two months later, he'd become engaged to his new girlfriend.

She needed to build a new home and life here in Two Hearts.

CHAPTER FIFTEEN

Scott typed away at the laptop in front of him. "What page do you want the engagement photo on?"

A moment of pure terror ripped through Amy at the word "engagement." She took a deep breath before replying. "*Proposal.* You proposed. We aren't engaged."

He turned to her, grinning. "Technically, you said yes to my proposal, so I think that makes us engaged."

When her usual panic at the word "engaged" quickly faded, relief washed over her. Maybe she could heal from her past. "I concede. Had that been an actual proposal, and had I said yes, we would be engaged. But it wasn't, and I didn't, and we aren't." Amy sat back with her arms folded over her chest and watched him as he processed her words.

"You're right. I proposed, and you didn't answer."

She turned back to her computer. "Told you."

"But you did hug me. I think a hug implies a yes. Don't you?"

Amy felt heat rising on her face. She cleared her throat. "What it implies is that I'm a great actress."

He chuckled. "I won't argue that point. I do have a question.

Is this the front page story, or is it going to be buried on page four? You've left openings on both of those pages."

"I'm going to put the story about Nosey on page one."

He laughed. "Are you so afraid of showing the world the proposal photos that you'd rather feature a rabbit as your lead story?"

Under her breath, she said, "He's a cute rabbit. A *really* cute rabbit."

He shrugged. "It's your newspaper. I'll get to work on it." A few minutes later, he said, "I think the layout is done. If you want to look it over."

Amy checked her watch. He'd finished the job a full three hours ahead of the time it took her. Having Scott around had helped her feel as if she was on top of things. Not that the newspaper took so much time that she couldn't get the job done. It was actually the opposite. But this part wasn't her favorite. Now she had time to think about other projects, and more than that, spare time freed her thinking up to consider other projects that could bring in extra income.

But that thought also built up stress. A different perspective could be helpful. "Do you have any ideas that could help me bring in extra income?"

He turned to her with a smile. "You mean other than pretending to propose to you over and over?"

She laughed. Scott had a way of slicing through her stress and bringing out happiness. "Yes. I'm still waiting to see if that helps. And I keep considering other ideas, but nothing seems to be a good fit."

"Could you write articles for another publication?"

Her blood pressure rose. "I did that for years. It's a lot of work and often for very little money. Plus, I'm working on someone else's schedule. That's the biggest thing. Working at midnight to meet a deadline. No, I need to figure out something else."

"Maybe wait and see how the proposals do? You're hoping they will bring in subscribers and advertising, right?"

"Yes. It feels like a long shot, though. What about—" She blew out of breath. "Never mind. I could recognize that as a bad idea from a mile away."

She brought up the completed newspaper on her computer. When she flipped through and saw the placement of the articles, she knew immediately she'd been wrong. "Uh, Scott, could I get you to flip those two articles? Or I can do it. I was wrong, and you were right. I need to focus on the thing we're doing to try to bring in money. And I'll put our proposal photo and the one of Nosey on my website and social media. I think I'll get a fair number of views on each, but my money's on the engagement photo as the big winner."

He typed a moment, then said, "I just shared a new file with you."

She opened that up and gave the top half of the front page a quick glance. He'd already swapped the two photos. "How did you do this so quickly?"

Scott grinned. "I had already done it both ways. I had a feeling you were going to change your mind when you saw the finished project."

When Scott left town, she was going to have to get an assistant. Maybe she could offer a small amount of money to a student intern who'd work here because they wanted to learn how to do this. Amy certainly couldn't pay somebody enough to live on since she wasn't even doing that for herself. *Yet.* She had to keep telling herself she would succeed.

They both stood. "I'm going to send this off right now. And on Monday, I'll go pick up the completed newspapers to distribute. I think I should probably wait until then to put up the social media and everything. Don't you agree?"

"Yes. I think you'll lose interest in the newspaper itself if you give away too much before then."

She loved having somebody to bounce ideas off of. Dexter was an awesome human being, but to say he had an interest in anything like this would be a massive overstatement. Scott fit in well with her business and maybe her life.

CHAPTER SIXTEEN

Amy slapped her hand on the nightstand beside her bed, trying to turn off the ringing alarm. Then she remembered she didn't have an alarm anymore. She grabbed her phone. "Hello?" Her gravelly voice barely sounded like her own.

"Amy?"

She nodded and realized the caller couldn't see her, so she replied, "It's me. Bella?" She was pretty sure she recognized the voice on the other end. "Are you okay? Is the baby okay?" Amy sat up in bed.

"We're both fine. Everybody's fine. I woke you up, didn't I?"

Amy held the phone away from her face and squinted at it, trying to read the time on it. Before she could focus enough to read, Bella said, "I don't sleep much right now, so I forget that other people aren't awake at 6:00 a.m. I'm sorry. I'll call you back later."

"No! I'm awake." Now. She probably wouldn't get back to sleep, so she may as well help her friend.

"Cassie said that you drive to Nashville every Monday to get your newspapers. Is that right?"

"It is. Some days later than others." This had been one of those days when she planned to leave about noon and take her time. As long as she made it back before rush hour traffic heated up in the city, she knew she'd have a nice trip.

"I have a doctor's appointment at 10:00 a.m. They're really hard to schedule with this woman. Micah was supposed to take me, but a court case was just rescheduled. He has to spend his entire day in research. Micah tried to tell me it would be okay if he took time off, but I've been around him long enough to know that isn't true. So I called Cassie." Bella paused for a moment. "She wasn't awake either. I have to look at the clock before I call anyone from now on."

Amy chuckled. If she didn't say yes, Simone, Paige, or someone else in town would be next. "I'd be happy to head into town early so we can get you to your appointment on time."

Bella released an audible breath. "Thank you! Such a relief. I still have a couple of months until the baby arrives, but it's close enough that I want to make sure I keep all of my appointments. I'll buy us lunch."

"It's a deal. I still haven't had a chance to eat at Nick's restaurant. Is that okay with you?"

"Better than okay. The food at Southern Somethings is delicious. Then I'll see you about 8:00 a.m.? To make sure we have enough time to arrive on time."

Amy held back laughter. Bella was very exacting about things like this. They needed nowhere near two hours, but it would be a good buffer, just in case.

"I only say that because if I'm more than ten minutes late, they cancel my appointment and charge me anyway."

"I'll be there."

After they ended the call, Amy got up and opened her door, ramming into her brother as he came out of the kitchen. "Oof."

The cup of coffee in his hand sloshed from side to side. "Careful, sis. What are you in such a hurry about this morning?"

"Absolutely nothing. I opened the door, and there you were. You need a roommate who sleeps in."

"I already have one of those."

She smacked him on his shoulder playfully. "I get my work done. Is there a game on later today?"

"I can always find a game on the sports channels."

She sighed. She knew that to be true.

"Or I can work. I have a new client's financials to go through."

"You work so much. Have you met many of the guys in town?"

He shrugged. "I have met some of them, but I haven't taken the time I should to get to know them."

Amy put her hand on his cheek in a way she'd done since he was little. She'd played a bit of mother to him because she'd been eight when he'd been born. "Take the time, bro. If this is going to be your home . . ."

"It is. I like my house. I like the people I have met. It feels good to be home in Two Hearts."

She couldn't argue with that. Dexter had few memories of being here as a kid. She had more. He'd been so young that he didn't have many connections with people from that time.

"You have a good day of work. I'm heading into the city. Do you want anything special?"

"Nothing comes to mind, but I'll let you know if something does."

Amy poured coffee down her throat, feeling increasingly alert with every gulp. Then she headed to the shower and finished getting ready.

By the scheduled time to leave, she'd made a list of articles she'd like to have in this week's edition, had gone through her email, and prepared the social media she'd post later this afternoon when the newspaper was ready to be distributed. Every time she looked at the proposal photos, she broke out in a cold sweat. Was this really better than freelancing, than writing for someone else? She knew in her heart that it was if it helped her succeed with her own business.

Bella slowly climbed into the passenger seat, buckled herself in, and leaned back. "I am so excited about being a mother, but there are some steps on the path that I'm not as crazy about as I probably should be."

Amy pulled away. "I can't share any tips."

"That's part of the problem. My close friends here are childless. The only people who can share tips had children decades ago. Things have changed."

Amy laughed. "I'm willing to bet that the basics are the same. You're still going into labor to have a baby, right?"

Bella grinned. "That's what I hear."

For a second, Amy wondered if she should do a pregnancy and childcare column in the paper, but she definitely couldn't write that without a lot of research. They rode along in silence for a few minutes.

Then Bella asked, "What about you? Do you want a family someday?"

Amy processed the question for a moment before replying. "I need a man first, but I probably won't find one here. Many of the guys are taken. By women from other places, I understand." Amy grinned.

Bella laughed. "Believe me when I say that I had zero intentions of moving away from cities. I would have happily moved to another city, mind you. Not that I don't love Nashville, but any city would have worked over a small town."

This opened up a subject that Amy had wondered about for a while. "Then why did you marry a man from a small town?" The two of them were clearly in love.

"Are you telling me that you, as a newspaper reporter, have been here for months and have never heard our story?"

Had she? She'd heard about Cassie and the motorcycle. Then

Simone and Nick finally spent quality time together because of an alpaca. "I only know you got married quickly."

Bella laughed. "Ours was a classic marriage of convenience."

"A what?" Amy shouted. Then, in a lower voice, she said, "Sorry. You caught me off-guard there."

"I was having business troubles. Micah's grandfather was trying to con him into working for the family legal firm instead of staying a small-town lawyer. He'd set everything in motion to make things go his way."

Amy slowed for traffic as they approached the city. "And?"

"If Micah didn't get married within ten days, he had to come to work for the firm—and the next part wasn't nice of him—or his sisters were going to have to put themselves through college." Bella shifted in her seat slightly so she was better facing Amy. "Now, I know a lot of people pay for their own college, but these girls had been promised from birth that they were going to have that money. Both of them were going into careers that would need years of education. One a doctor and one an engineer. They'd have been paying off debt for years."

"So you agreed to marry him?"

"I thought it was temporary. Up until that time, we hadn't gotten along. Oh, he was easy on the eyes, but it definitely was not love at first sight."

The city started coming into focus, and the roads became busier. Amy focused on her driving and making the turns to arrive at Bella's doctor's office, a place she'd never been before.

"We're a half hour early. And I'm okay with that." Bella patted her purse. "I have my ebook reader in here and a book I will be happy to spend time with until they call me back."

"I need to hear the rest of your story."

Bella opened the door. "Remind me on the drive home."

Amy pulled away as Bella went inside the building. Bella's story was entertaining. Maybe she should consider doing a feature every week for a month about how her friends had come to Two Hearts. That might bring more people to visit and maybe even move here. At the very least, it should make them curious about the following week's newspaper. The love interest certainly tied in with her proposal photos—and the town's wedding theme.

As she pulled up to the printer, the thought flashed into her head that she might be able to skip additional proposal photos if she found a better option. But, until then, she needed to keep doing those. If they were what it took to succeed, she'd be proposed to again. And again. Scott was certainly easy on the eyes and was super nice too. If she were going to be interested in someone—and she certainly was not at this point in her life— he would be a good option.

As always, the *Two Hearts Times* newspapers were stacked in bundles and tied up with string. She had ten bundles. Everything above the fold on the front page could be seen, and normally, she'd take a moment to glance at it.

Today, she struggled with that because the proposal photo would be there.

With everything stowed in the back of her vehicle, Amy headed over to the doctor's office to pick up Bella. Since she hadn't received a text saying her passenger was ready, she sat in her vehicle, tapping her fingers on the steering wheel as she tried to focus on more ideas for articles.

Finally, after ten minutes of wondering if she should look at this issue, she got out and opened one of the stacks. Newspaper in hand, she sat down. Amy closed her eyes for a moment and then opened them, took a deep breath, and stared at the newspaper in front of her.

It was every bit as bad as she had expected it to be.

Oh, the layout was wonderful. Scott had done a job at least

as good as she would have, and she'd avoided the annoyance of doing it herself. She still hoped one of these days, she'd grow to love that part of the process. It hadn't happened yet.

There they were, him kneeling with the ring box, her staring at him with open-mouthed surprise and delight. If only that had been what Logan had done. She'd worked at forgetting him and thought she had.

Until this proposal situation arose, she *had* moved on. When she stared at the photo of Scott, she realized she wasn't pining for Logan so much as wondering about what might have been. Just when tears started to prick her eyes, her phone buzzed with a text.

Her passenger was soon climbing in. "I always feel so much better when I get a good report from the doctor. I know everything feels fine, but I've never done this before." Bella turned to her. "Can you keep a secret?"

"Always. You'd be amazed at some of the secrets I've had to keep over the years as a journalist."

"Rose."

Amy wasn't sure what she was talking about. The plant? A scent?

"Rose what?"

"Rose Elaine."

Now Amy understood. She'd just been told the baby's name. "It's a girl?"

"Only Micah and I know, but I think you're entitled to the secret since you drove me all the way here. And I woke you up this morning."

Amy chuckled. "You didn't owe me anything, but I feel privileged to know. When are you going to share the news?"

"We were still debating the name until just a few days ago. The first name is just a name we liked. The middle name is Micah's grandmother's first name, so we wanted to tell her first. She just came home from a Caribbean cruise, and we're planning dinner for tomorrow night. Simone's making a cake with the baby's name on it."

"Any grandmother-to-be would be thrilled!"

Bella glanced to her side. "Is that this week's issue?"

Amy nodded. Keeping her eyes on the road. "Tell me what you think."

Bella opened the paper. "I think Paige took some amazing photos. You guys look great. And you're a better actress than you let on because you look truly delighted."

That made Amy smile in spite of the situation. "I *was* Juliet."

Bella laughed as she opened the paper. Amy still hadn't looked at anything below the fold.

"This other photo is fabulous. How did you make the cow do that?"

Amy whipped into the parking lot of the grocery store they were about to pass and into a parking space. She threw the car into park and said, "One of the cow pictures is in there?"

Bella turned the paper so that Amy could see it. Sure enough, he hadn't inserted just one photo of the proposal. Scott had also added one with the cow pushing between the two of them. She had to admit it was cute. But she also knew it hadn't been there when she'd seen the first layout.

"You didn't know this was in the paper? Don't you do this by yourself?"

Amy bit her lip for a second as she thought about how to explain this. She had a feeling Bella was going to read more into it than she or Scott intended. "I'll trade you a secret for a secret. Mrs. Brantley had been planning Scott's schedule down to the second. It drove him nuts, so a few hours into her plan, I said I would show him around town. I felt sorry for him. And he's a computer geek, so he helped me with my website and said he would lay out the newspaper this week."

Bella's eyes grew wider as Amy explained the situation. Then she nodded slowly. "He's just helping you?"

"Of course. What else would it be?"

Bella grinned. "He's a guy. You're a girl."

Amy shook her head vigorously from side to side. "I am definitely not looking right now. He's a friend. Besides, he's leaving town in a few weeks. He has an entire life back in Chicago that doesn't include anything in the state of Tennessee other than his friendship with Greg Brantley."

Bella sat back in her seat with a smirk. "If you say so."

Amy pulled back on the road and pointed the car toward Nick's restaurant. A few minutes later, she realized Bella had fallen asleep, probably because she was up so early. This whole pregnancy thing seemed to take energy. Amy turned the car in the direction of Two Hearts. They could eat at Dinah's after Bella's nap.

Unfortunately, she realized in hindsight a lot of people were going to think she and Scott were an item. And everyone who only looked at the pictures and didn't read the story would think they were actually engaged.

Amy gulped. At least next week, when the next photo came out, it wouldn't involve an animal in a photo bomb, and everyone would realize it was just for the newspaper and not real.

Because as awesome as Scott was, she truly wasn't looking for anything more.

Scott headed away from his temporary home, debating the direction to go this morning. Breakfast had been great, as usual, but subtle questions about his plans for the day had caused him to rush out the door with the dog on the leash.

Amy had said she'd be in Nashville picking up the newspaper, so he couldn't go to her office. She gave him an excuse and as much as he wanted to avoid a holiday romance, he found himself wanting to spend time with her more every day.

Even if it meant another one of those proposals.

Cookie turned toward the park, so he let her lead him there. As the park came into view, his phone rang. He held the leash in one hand and dug his phone out of his pocket. He just hoped it wasn't work. They'd left him alone so far, and the break had been wonderful.

A familiar face peered up from his screen. With a smile, he answered, "Mom! How's everything in Chicago?"

"*I'm* fine."

Scott's heartbeat picked up a notch. "Is everyone else in the family okay?"

"Don't worry. We're all fine." Her tone of voice was off somehow. "I wondered about you. I checked with your dad, brothers, and sister. No one has heard from you since you packed a bag and drove away."

He chuckled. "You make me sound like a criminal escaping the scene of a crime. I sent a message to let you know I'd arrived safely."

"Weeks ago. I'd started to wonder about this town in Tennessee you'd gone to. I know Greg is from there and is the sheriff, so I thought you must be safe."

"Right. I'm safe here. I'm staying with Greg's mother."

"That's nice. Now, tell me about the woman."

"Mrs. Brantley?"

She gave an exasperated sigh. "The pretty blonde woman."

An image of Amy came to mind, but his mother couldn't be asking about someone she didn't know existed.

"The words with the photograph say it's a pretend proposal."

Scott knew better than most how the internet worked, but it hadn't occurred to him that anyone in Chicago would see the photos he'd put in the newspaper and helped Amy load onto her website.

"I'm helping her." He could hear the nervousness in his voice. This could turn out to be even more embarrassing than he'd expected. "Amy needed someone to pose with her for the photos. She owns the town's newspaper and hopes the photos will be a fun way to boost interest in the paper."

He sat at one of the pink picnic tables, doing his best to ignore the color.

"You're telling me you're helping with fake proposals? That's silly. Next, you'll be a fake groom."

He laughed. "Not a chance of my being any kind of groom. The proposals are because Two Hearts is wedding crazy." He explained what he knew about the town's rebirth through weddings.

His mother laughed when he told her about Cassie arriving in town wearing a wedding dress. "You sound different. Happier."

Was he? He'd been here a short time, and it had been interesting. So far, he'd been hit with a stuffed fish, helped with a wedding, made a fake proposal, worked on the newspaper . . . and enjoyed himself. "I like Two Hearts. It's the vacation I needed."

"From what you've told me about Greg since he left Chicago, he seems glad he moved." She paused, and then her voice grew more serious. "Are you considering a move there? Amy—is that what you said her name was?—seems to be happy you're giving her a ring."

"Mom! It's pretend. Fake. *Not real.* And my job is in Chicago. My house. Everything is there."

"Remember that Archer keeps asking you to go into business with him. You'd be able to work from anywhere then."

Scott closed his eyes and leaned forward, his elbows on his thighs. "Mom, please. I'm on vacation. I'll be home soon." And back to everything in Chicago he'd just outlined. Why wasn't he as happy about that as he should be?

"We'd come visit you."

"What?"

"Your dad and I would visit you in Tennessee."

The absurdity of her statement made him chuckle. "That's good to know." He stood. "I'm out walking Greg's mother's dog. I'd better head back."

"One last comment about your time there."

"Okay. One." He started across the park, Cookie leading the way but moving more slowly than he had when they'd started.

"Amy looked like she meant the hug."

"She's acting." Silence greeted him. "Mom?" She'd hung up. His mother had meant it when she'd said one comment, and she'd gotten in the last word.

As he walked, her words replayed in his mind. Was she right? Had Amy meant the hug? He'd almost kissed her but had thought that would be a mistake. Was she interested in him as more than a friend?

Thank you, Mom. Now I don't know what to think.

CHAPTER SEVENTEEN

Amy made herself a quick slice of toast and poured a cup of coffee before heading to the newspaper.

She'd received a text from Cassie this morning asking if she *and* Scott would like to come to dinner one night. People were starting to see them as a couple, which wasn't acceptable. Even though she liked hanging out with him, and he'd been undeniably helpful with her business, she'd have to avoid him for a few days. Then everybody would forget about it, and maybe she'd once again be considered as just the host of a Two Hearts visitor.

She had barely opened up her laptop when her phone rang.

Mrs. Brantley was calling. "I know it's early, Amy, but I wanted to make sure I got to you before you've scheduled your whole day. We're going to have a meeting here at 10 a.m. to discuss Cassie's wedding."

"Do I need to have anything prepared in advance?"

"You're working on the invitations, so maybe gather a few ideas together before then. Is Scott helping you this morning?" The tone of her voice in the last sentence, to Amy's suspicious mind, implied an interest in her love life.

"I haven't heard from him. I'm sure he's off doing other things. Maybe Greg knows." Amy was proud of that last touch. She'd put it back on Mrs. Brantley's own son to know where the visitor was.

"If you see him, please let him know about the meeting." And then she hung up.

Amy stared at her phone. Scott was living there. Had he left already?

As if an answer to the question, he walked in her door. "I thought I'd stop by to see if you needed anything. I know the newspaper is done, but I thought maybe you had something else going on."

She stared at him for a beat too long. Pulling herself away from her focus, she said, "I'm glad you stopped by."

He seemed to perk up at her words. With a smile, he asked, "What do you need?"

"My focus is shifting to the wedding. Mrs. Brantley just called. There's a meeting about the preparations at 10:00 a.m."

His smile faded. "Someone needs to tell Greg about this. I know he hasn't yet heard."

"How do *you* know?"

"James gave it away at breakfast one morning."

"Emmaline Brantley is exacting in all details. I wouldn't be surprised if she had a plan for telling her son. Actually, I'd be surprised if she didn't. Unless you want to go with me to interview a farmer, I don't have much going on today. After that, I'm researching online wedding invitations."

He hesitated a moment. "Are you sure you don't have anything *I* could do?" He glanced over his shoulder and out the front window as though he expected someone to come after him and drag him somewhere he didn't want to be.

"Were there suggestions for another tour this morning?"

"There was a schedule on the refrigerator. It was a backup

plan in case you were too busy to have me help or didn't need my assistance."

Amy grinned. "Having her as mayor is the best thing that ever happened to this town. At least in my lifetime." She thought of the dusty books in the back room that needed to be organized by date. "I do have a job, but I don't think it'll be fun."

"Unless it involves a hazmat suit and a mask to filter out toxins, I'm willing."

"A dust mask could be helpful." Amy stood and waved him toward the back.

As they entered the back room, he said, "Last time I was here, you were wielding a fish and wearing bunny slippers."

That caught Amy off guard. "I may love rabbits. And my family knows it."

"Oh, now I see your interest in Nosey," he teased.

"He's a very cute rabbit. I've been stopping by and taking him treats. I also feel sorry for Mrs. Robinson sitting there alone all day."

He stared at her for a moment as though he wanted to say something, and then he seemed to change his mind and focused on the room around him. "This is a mess."

Amy laughed. "Which also explains why I've brought you here. I'd love to have all of these books arranged in date order. Most of these were here when I arrived, and I've had a couple of people offer up old issues that were stacked in a barn, but I'm not sure what I have and don't have. I seem to be the repository for the town's historical archives."

"That would be an interesting thing to check on. Maybe you could write about it. See if anybody else has historical items and try to gather them all in one place."

Amy nodded. "I've always loved history, so I like that idea. Once I get settled in, I'll put that on my list of things to do."

She went back to her desk and finalized her list of articles for next week's paper. Interest in Mabel the cow had soared since she'd photo-bombed them. Maybe a follow-up article on her with a bunch of photos would be a hit.

When the time for the meeting arrived, she called out, "I'm ready to go. Want to tag along? Mrs. Brantley made it sound as if the invitation was for you too."

Scott stepped out, brushing dust off his shirt. "I may as well. As long as I'm with you, she'll know I'm taken care of." He paused, his face reddening under her scrutiny. "I mean that she won't invoke her schedule."

His first words had made them sound like a couple, and that was far more togetherness than she wanted.

Scott rode beside Amy over to Mrs. Brantley's, the place he had been trying to avoid but instead found himself brought back to like an escaped convict. Actually, being in the house was fine. He just wanted to avoid the bridal shop tour. He didn't think most men *would* want one.

When they walked in the back door, he smelled baking cookies. It seemed there was almost always something wonderful cooking in this house.

Simone, Paige, and Bella were already seated at the table. He was the only man in the room, which felt a little awkward.

Mrs. Brantley clapped her hands together to gather everyone's attention. "We need to make this fast. Cassie could drop in at any time and would be startled to find everyone here and her not invited. To begin with, we need to ensure Greg is informed of the details."

"Maybe we should change *informed* to *ask*. It may seem better to him," Bella said. "We aren't saying he has to do it our way. Just asking if he likes the plan." With a smile, she added, "But we're hoping he likes it because we're doing very well with that plan."

"Good point. No man likes to be told what to do." Mrs.

Brantley looked at Scott. "Am I right?" There seemed to be humor behind her words, humor he didn't understand because she'd made a true statement.

"Correct. But in this case, I think Greg will happily marry Cassie no matter what—as long as she's willing."

"Good point. I'm sure she is," Bella added. "I'll go first. I have a design for the dress I believe Cassie will love. Paige, you're about the same size. If you could come over to my shop, I'll have you slip it on. Not so much for an exact fit, but just to see how it hangs on an actual human."

"Happy to do it. As to my assignment, I don't have anything to report on the photos because I don't have much to do until the actual day of the wedding. It isn't as though we can run an engagement photo of them in the newspaper along with the ceremony date."

Mrs. Brantley nodded. "Good point. Simone?"

"I've known in my head all along what to make for Cassie. She has repeatedly exclaimed over the same types of floral decorations. I'll do a three-tier cake, along with a single-layer groom's cake, all decorated in that style. I know her flavor preferences, too, but I haven't settled on anything yet."

"It sounds like you're on track. Amy?"

"I did as you asked earlier, and I have some ideas for the invitations."

Mrs. Brantley turned to Scott. "And that's why you're here this morning. Well, one of the reasons you're here. Will you be able to work with Amy on the digital invitations?"

"I'm happy to help. It's quite simple to do. I just need to know what the invitation should look like and have a list of email addresses."

"We're working on that. Those addresses are now on the top of my list." She made a note on her list. "The closer we get to the wedding date, the less time someone will have to leak the surprise to Cassie."

Bella frowned. "You're right. I hope they notice that it's secret."

"Scott and I will try to make that obvious."

Mrs. Brantley continued, "On my end, I've contacted the different vendors, and it appears everyone is on board. As long as we have this wedding shortly before one that's already scheduled, they're just leaving things here for another couple of days. They're weekdays, too, so the items probably wouldn't be needed elsewhere."

Scott thought everything seemed to be running smoothly, so he wondered why they needed this meeting when it seemed like such a risk. If Cassie showed up, their plan could be exposed. At least, his part of the job would be easy.

Then Mrs. Brantley spoke again. "Scott, I have another assignment for you. I think Greg may receive the news about the wedding best if he's told at a guys' evening, and he has time to process it all away from Cassie. I don't want him to find out here and five minutes later see her. He'd look like the cat that just swallowed the canary."

Where did the men get together here? There was one restaurant and no bowling alley or other traditional hangout space. "I'm glad to help, but I'm not sure how to plan something like this in Two Hearts."

Bella spoke up. "Micah can help. He said he didn't have any appointments and that he'd be in his office all day. If you want to stop by?"

"Sounds good to me. I'll get directions from you before we leave."

With all of that settled, they broke up the meeting. Mrs. Brantley had each of them leave five minutes apart with Scott last, she said, since he was the only one who was actually supposed to be in her house.

CHAPTER EIGHTEEN

Scott found Micah's office with Bella's directions. Like so much of the town, it was in an older building with historic charm. Nothing in Two Hearts was like the five-year-old house in the Chicago suburbs he owned. Everything in his home was new, modern, and up-to-date.

At first, having everything older had been unsettling, as if he'd stepped back in time and was missing modern conveniences. But the history of the place was growing on him.

After a walk down a wood-floored hallway, he found the office door with a sign that announced Micah's legal practice and knocked on the door.

"Come on in," a voice replied.

By this time, he'd met all the guys, but he knew Bella better than he knew her husband. Micah stood when he entered.

"Bella texted that you'd be stopping by but that it wasn't about a legal matter. Since that's my whole reason for being in this office and my specialty . . ."

Scott laughed. "That may be easier than what we have to do. We're supposed to work together to get Greg to attend a guys' meeting tonight."

"Sit down." Micah pointed to the chair in front of his desk. "You sure you don't have any legal needs while you're here?" He chuckled.

"None that I'm aware of."

"This must be about the wedding the women have started planning." He shook his head. "It's ambitious."

"Do you think it will work? "

"Yes, but the hard part will be keeping Cassie in the dark. She usually has her finger in the town's events."

Scott hadn't thought about that.

"Pizza night would be common enough that Cassie wouldn't bat an eye. The guys get together maybe once a month, sometimes more, to have pizza. I can run over and get a stack and bring them back to town. We often squeeze into Greg's place because he's a bachelor, and we aren't displacing anyone. When Nick is in town, and he is, we're wall to wall humans. We need a larger space for this."

Scott looked around. "You definitely don't have enough room here, and I don't have a place to offer." He considered Amy's newspaper office, but they wouldn't have enough seats.

"Let me make a couple of calls. Nick's commercial kitchen doesn't have enough chairs. But CJ and Paige have the largest house with plenty of room for all of us."

Scott leaned back in his seat and waited while Micah called Paige first to make sure they could go there tonight. With that confirmed, he dialed CJ.

"I already talked to your other half. She said we could use your house tonight for a guys' meeting to tell Greg about the wedding." After a few seconds pause, Micah said, "*Ask*, right."

Scott chuckled as he realized Paige had told CJ to use different wording.

Micah furrowed his brow and held the phone closer to his ear. "Six o'clock." He glanced over at Scott, who nodded in agreement. "What? It's getting noisy there." He raised his voice. "I'll reach out to the rest of the guys. See you tonight."

He hung up. "Whew! CJ was at a noisy construction site. I could barely hear him after a saw fired up at the end." Micah made a few other calls, and everything had soon been planned for the men they knew well to show up at Paige and CJ's house, which Scott was informed sat on the lake. He must have driven by with Greg, but he hadn't pointed it out to Scott.

"GPS doesn't always work here, but it will be easy to find. Have you been to the park on the lake?"

Scott nodded. He remembered that one because he'd wondered if it would be a good place for one of those proposals.

"They're just a few houses down from that. Can't miss it because it's the pink one."

Scott cringed. "Pink?"

"That was the same reaction CJ had when Paige told him she wanted to keep the color it had been in the past. He seems to have gotten used to it, though."

Scott didn't think he could ever get used to a pink house. The amount of pink in this town was unnerving.

Instead of going to Amy's office this afternoon, he went for a long walk around the town. He passed by the veterinarian. When he reached the hardware store, he went inside to browse. He saw a couple of women buying things, but the place oozed testosterone.

Mid-afternoon, he called Mrs. Brantley when he remembered he needed to tell her he wouldn't be home for dinner. She already knew they'd been able to plan the guys' pizza dinner for tonight. Of course she did.

When it was almost 6:00 p.m., he got in his truck and found the pink house on the lake. He vaguely remembered noticing it when he'd done the rounds with Greg.

Still wearing his sheriff's uniform from the day, Greg was walking up to the house as Scott pulled in.

His friend waited for him mid-sidewalk. "This is a last-minute get-together. Do you know what's going on?"

Scott did but didn't want to spill the news. "Let's go in and find out." He thought he'd nicely evaded the question, but Greg stared at him a beat too long. Scott may have been on the streets for a year before moving to computers, but Greg had been out there a lot longer, and he was street savvy.

"Everyone isn't going to jump out from behind furniture and shout Happy Birthday, are they?"

Scott patted him on the shoulder. "If I remember correctly, we're nowhere near your birthday."

"That's true, but it feels as if something is going on, and I don't know what it is." His eyes widened. "Someone's not sick or dying, are they?"

"No! If anything is going on here—and I'm not saying there is—I'm sure it's good news."

Greg opened his mouth to speak, then seemed to think better of it and turned toward the door again. "You're not completely off the hook yet. But I'll wait and see before I ask you again."

Cassie was going to have her hands full being married to this guy. If she tried hiding Christmas presents in the house, he'd ferret the secret out of her over breakfast.

Scott smelled the pizza through the screen door. Inside, they found the guys gathered around a big dining room table.

"Now that everybody's here, let's dig in," Micah said.

Greg took a seat but watched them, still seeming to want information no one was offering. As he opened one of the cardboard pizza boxes and reached for a slice, he said, "Anybody want to tell me what's going on?"

The five men around the table froze.

CJ and Scott had each taken a bite of pizza, so they stayed mum. Micah was only pulling a couple of slices out of a box, so he had no excuse not to speak up.

"There's something we wanted to . . . *ask* you, Greg." Micah had caught himself as he was about to say the word tell, and Scott almost burst out laughing. "If, hypothetically, a wedding were to be completely planned, and all you and Cassie needed to do was show up to say I do, would that be something you'd be interested in?" Micah's lawyer persona had come to life. Scott could see him in front of a jury, making his point. He'd said nothing, but he'd said everything.

Greg put his piece of pizza on his plate and brushed off his hands. "So, hypothetically, there could be a wedding being planned in which I showed up and didn't have to do anything except say I do?"

"If there was such a thing, would you be interested?" Micah leaned forward and focused on Greg as if he was the only one in the room.

"Are you kidding? I'd be there in a heartbeat." He looked around the room as the situation seemed to dawn on him. "Are you guys telling me a wedding is being planned right now?" The excitement and happiness in his voice were contagious.

All the guys grinned.

"So you would definitely think that was a good idea?" CJ asked.

"Absolutely. Tell me when and where to show up. But how'd you get Cassie on board with this? She plans everything with infinite detail. That's really what's been the holdup for us getting married. She has struggled to plan her wedding after the last fiasco."

The tone in the room shifted dramatically.

"Let me rephrase my earlier question," Micah said. "If *you* were to know about the wedding and you just needed to show up, would that be acceptable?"

"And Cassie doesn't know," Greg said the words slowly. He processed the idea for a moment before responding.

Scott said, "It would be a complete secret to Cassie until the day of the wedding."

"My first thought was that she would be upset because she hadn't been part of the process," Greg said thoughtfully.

That was what Scott had wondered.

"I realized that she's said over and over again that she wants to marry me, but she freezes every time she even thinks about making the plans. She even hinted at a possibility of an elopement but knew her mother would freak out and never speak to her again." He looked around the room at the guys. "Honestly, I didn't see the flaw in that." He shuddered. "Even though her mother's a handful, Cassie loves her, so she wants her to be there when she gets married."

Scott processed everything his friend had said. "So you believe Cassie will be okay with this?"

Greg nodded. "I believe she will. It has to be beautiful, of course. Like something Cassie would plan. But I know that's exactly what her friends here would do."

"The women have planned it well so far. Bella says she has Cassie's measurements so she can make a dress with no problem." Micah took a bite of his pizza, seeming to consider his part in the conversation over.

"Paige is going to take the photos, and James is going to help her so they know they've gotten every possible picture Cassie would request from a photographer." CJ pulled another piece out of a box.

"Simone is making a cake that she assures everyone Cassie will love." Nick grabbed a slice of pizza but was stopped midway back to his plate when Greg put his hand on Nick's arm. "It can't be a regular cake."

Everyone stared at him.

Nick asked, "What's a *regular* cake?"

Greg sliced across the air in front of him several times with his hand. "She's tired of those cakes with many layers. Just the other day, she said she'd seen a million of them, and she'd like to see something different."

Nick reached for his phone, and Simone was on the line seconds later. He held his phone out for Greg to repeat what he'd just said. Nick asked his fiancée, "What would be different than a wedding cake for a wedding? I know you can come up with something, Simone."

Without missing a beat, she said, "How about cupcakes? Then I could do a couple of flavors."

Greg grinned. "That sounds perfect."

Nick set his phone on the table. "As long as I have you on the phone, why don't you give details to Greg."

Simone continued. "We've got everything covered. For the venues, the ceremony will be in the church, and the reception will be in Cherry and Levi's barn. Does that sound like something that will work?"

"It sounds perfect. One other thing Cassie has mentioned is that she wants casual elegance. I'm glad you guys are on this because I don't know what that means."

"That's where we were going with it. You'll need a suit, Greg. You know Cassie and details, so you'd better go to Nashville and get something tailored to fit you. The tie needs to be in the wedding's colors of yellow and pink. Oh, and Scott's working on the invitations, so he can probably tell you more about those."

After they'd hung up, Scott did as Simone had asked.

Still grinning, Greg leaned back in his chair. "When is this wedding of mine?"

Everyone laughed.

"Two weeks from last Thursday," Micah said.

The groom-to-be picked up a piece of pizza, and they all went back to their meal. Between mouthfuls, Greg said, "Cassie and I have been saving money for our wedding. You can't go wild and have ice carvings of swans—not that I'd want those, but we can pay for some things. It's in a joint account we set up for this purpose, so I think I can sneak the money out without her noticing."

"Amy told me that your mother is in charge of the show." Scott reached for another piece of pizza. When he looked up, all eyes were on him.

Greg smiled. "First, the invitations and now inside information from her. Is there something going on between you and Amy?"

Micah added, "I was wondering the same thing."

The other men nodded.

Scott felt like he was being interrogated. "Not that I know of. To escape the mayor's detailed plans for my—" He looked at Greg. For a second, he'd forgotten that his host was also his friend's mother. "You know how she can plan."

"Oh, I definitely do. So you escaped to the newspaper and have been helping Amy, I understand?"

"That's all it is. I've been helping Amy."

The men all grinned as though they knew something Scott didn't. He had to admit that it was a little unnerving.

CHAPTER NINETEEN

Amy returned to her newspaper office after delivering the week's edition to houses and businesses in town. She sold them everywhere she could. When she opened the door, she was stopped in her tracks by the pile of boxes that now lined the room to her right.

What on earth had happened while she'd been out?

When she got closer to the boxes, she recognized the handwriting on them. Hers. Most said "books." A couple said "summer clothes." And she spotted one with the word "kitchen" written on the side in bold, black marker with a drawing of a cup and saucer. Her artistic mother had clearly packed that one.

These were her boxes. The ones she'd stored in her parents' garage in St. Louis.

But how—

Then she remembered that Dexter had made a quick trip there. She'd expected him back sometime this afternoon, so this timed out right.

Phone in hand, she dialed him. Unsurprisingly, he didn't answer as he often didn't when he was working. *Or when he was avoiding her.* Next on the list was her mother.

She answered with the same words she'd used every time since Amy had moved here. "Hi, sweetie. How's life in Two Hearts?"

Amy hesitated for a second too long before replying with, "Good." Maybe her mother wouldn't notice her less-than-stellar response.

"But?"

Not a chance. She may as well get it off her chest. "I'm struggling a little to make a real home here."

"I sensed that. I knew it was time for you to have your things around you."

Amy rubbed the bridge of her nose. "But, Mom, I'm living with Dexter. I don't have a place to put all these boxes." She'd tried to shine a professional light on her newspaper business. She hadn't even wanted to threaten her credibility with a retraction about her cousin Nick's engagement to Simone that, at the time, had just been what his grandmother wanted and not a reality.

Of course, she was now posing with cows in staged proposal photos, so maybe the professionalism had slipped a bit. Still, what would she do with these boxes that were cluttering up her business space?

Her mom's gentle voice broke through Amy's annoyance. "Do you have somewhere to store everything until you're ready? I *could* get Dexter to bring them back."

Amy stared at the tower of cardboard.

"Your father would like to turn that side of the garage into a workshop."

Amy blew out a breath. A corner of her office filled with boxes wasn't ideal, but it was going to have to be fine for now. She loved the man she'd come to think of as Dad.

"Okay, Mom. I understand. This is all of it, right?"

"It's everything out of the garage. Dexter brought back some of his things, too, so we just loaded it all up in his truck."

So, on top of this, he'd added more to the already crowded house? She had to find a home of her own—and soon.

They chatted about her sisters and other brother for a few more minutes. By the time they ended the call, Amy was smiling at the family stories about her siblings that her mother had shared with her. Her sister Della lived near their parents, and her sister's son Gavin had just started walking. As soon as she hung up, Amy knew she needed to make a trip home herself. She could use one of her mom's awesome hugs, and she'd love to watch Gavin toddle across the room. She'd pencil in a visit— just as soon as life quieted down. St. Louis was in the four- to five-hour driving range, so definitely doable over a weekend.

As she tried to push boxes out of the way to make them a little less obvious—if possible—the door opened behind her.

She whirled around to find Scott. "I came back to see if everything was okay. When I was walking by earlier, your brother was unloading the boxes, so I helped him stack everything here." He studied her for just a moment before continuing. "It *is* okay that they're stored here, right?"

Amy turned back to the mess. "It's okay. That's what I'm rolling with right now. *It's okay,*" she repeated with a sigh. "There don't seem to be many large garages around here, so I don't think I can beg to use part of someone's."

"I noticed you had a lot of boxes of books. And not just by the writing on them. Those suckers are heavy."

That made her laugh. Scott had a way of making her smile.

"Yeah. I do love books. I've missed some of them, but I've collected these over time, and I may not need all of them. I always thought I would be able to sort through them and get rid of some *before* they were dragged over here."

Scott walked down the row of boxes. He turned around and said, "You know, it looks as if you have enough books to open a bookstore."

She laughed again. When he didn't crack a smile, she

realized he wasn't kidding. Amy stared at the boxes. Could he be right? As she counted up the boxes, knowing how many books must be in each, she realized she had even more than she'd thought. "That's an interesting idea." For a few seconds, happiness bubbled up inside her. Then reality hit. "Bookstores struggle to make money, don't they?" She already had one struggling business.

"But if you already had the inventory . . ." He let the words hang in the air. After a moment of silence with her staring at the books, he said, "I'm going to finish up organizing the newspaper archive in the back." He looked at his feet for a moment, almost seeming nervous, which was out of character. "I've been told we're having meatloaf for dinner tonight at Mrs. Brantley's house. I'm certain this is the world's best meatloaf because everything she cooks is outstanding." He hesitated for a moment. "But I *hate* meatloaf."

Was he fishing for an offer from her? She liked being around him, and she'd come to think of him as a friend. "I have some canned soup I'd split with you."

His grimace said it all. "Not much better. I was wondering if you'd want to grab a bite to eat somewhere?"

She processed that for a moment. Was this a date? She didn't want to go on a date anytime soon.

As though he could read her mind, he added, "You're just helping out a friend."

That sounded reasonable to her. Before she could talk herself out of it, Amy said, "If you help me go over ideas for a possible bookstore, I'll buy you dinner in the next town."

As soon as the words left her mouth, she wanted to take them back. She could say that she suddenly realized she was too busy. *Anything* to get out of what he might see as a date.

Before she could do that, Scott replied, "Deal," and she was committed.

He headed toward the back room, whistling.

Would a bookstore bring in the extra income she needed now? Or was this just another thing she should add to her list of great ideas for the future?

After some time spent pulling together her outline for the next newspaper issue, she pushed back from her desk and stood, bending her back as she stretched.

"Scott? Are you ready to head out?"

He appeared from the back room with his hair disheveled and his shirt partly untucked. He still looked great.

Scott grinned. "I'm very ready. What kind of food are you taking me out for?"

"Let's get some pizza."

She grabbed her purse, and they headed for the door. "It isn't too far. Just the next town over. Maybe someday soon, Two Hearts can get its own pizza place."

"The pizza we had last night was good, so I'm looking forward to it." He used the restroom and returned with his shirt back in place and his hair combed.

As she locked the front door with Scott at her side, she realized they were going on what would appear to anyone else to be a date and at one of the most popular dinner spots for Two Hearts' residents. Rumors would fly like wildfire through the town. She started to turn toward her car when he pointed toward his vehicle. "Let's take mine."

She liked to drive, but she didn't see any harm in giving in this time. She stowed her backpack in her car's trunk, and then they took off in his vehicle.

As they drove through town, Amy realized that even seeing them together in his truck in the evening would add fuel to the fire if someone spotted them. She could pass it off as newspaper business during the day. And she could shout from the rooftops that the pictures in the newspaper were fake, and they might even believe it. But once gossip got around that the two of them were alone having dinner together, nothing she said would stop that freight train of information.

As they drove out of town, her with her hand beside her face to make it more difficult to see, she asked, "How would you feel about having Chinese instead?"

He glanced in her direction. "That's fine with me too. I'll eat almost anything."

"Except meatloaf."

He grimaced. "I'm not sure what it is about meatloaf that crosses a line for me."

Amy directed him as they drove north out of town, but instead of heading for the next town over where Two Hearts' favorite pizza parlor was located, she was sending them a bit farther out. The more distance she had between herself and Two Hearts, the less likely she'd find someone from this town over there.

She glanced at Scott as they rode along in silence together. He did quiet time well, and she appreciated that. But she couldn't turn off the bookstore idea that kept running through her mind and needed input.

"I have a question for you. Can you think of any way to make a bookstore sell more? I'm afraid this town can't support one. If they struggle in big cities, what would happen in Two Hearts?"

The truck ate up the miles as he seemed to be considering her question. Finally, he said, "The town is all about weddings. Is there any way you can make your bookstore more about weddings?"

Could she? She thought out loud as she spoke. "None of the books I have are about weddings." She'd put those in the trash before she'd moved here. "There may be a mystery or romance with a wedding in it, but certainly not anything focused on weddings."

"But what if you added some?"

Amy frowned as she considered his suggestion. Purposefully

adding more about weddings to her life felt out of the question. But here she was with a man who'd just fake proposed to her.

"I'll think about it." Amy sighed as the uncertainty about her next steps in life piled up. Her newspaper, her living quarters, and now a bookstore. She blew out a breath and tried to relax. "Right now, we only need to have a great dinner. Turn left here." A couple of minutes later, he pulled into the side parking lot of the Chinese restaurant. "I've eaten here several times and liked it every time."

"I trust you."

The odd thing was that she trusted him too. That must be why his business idea had stuck in her mind.

There was an awkward moment when he held the door open for her. That was great because it showed he had some chivalry in him. But just that little touch made this feel even more like a date. That must have thrown her off because, as they walked into the building, she stumbled. Scott put his arm around hers to support her and kept it there.

The hostess came over and said, "A table for two?"

Scott nodded, and the woman directed them to a nice, intimate table for two in the corner.

It isn't a date, Amy.

"Have you gotten any response to your newspaper photos?"

The newspaper. She could talk about that all day long, and this definitely wasn't a date conversation. They were two friends having dinner together. Coworkers, even. Then she remembered that the photos were about his proposal, and she flipped right back into date mode.

Focus, Amy. "Let me check."

As she did that, he added. "One of those clicks on your website will be my mother."

Startled, Amy looked up at him.

"I hadn't checked in other than to say I'd arrived safely. She wondered what was going on here that had made me forget about my family in Chicago." He shook his head. "We often get together for barbeques in the summer, so I've been missed." He moved his hand around in a flipping motion. "I'm good with burgers."

Amy grinned.

She flipped through her social media accounts. "The pictures are getting some interest. Not a flood, but I'll take it. There are some cute comments on the cow picture."

"Do you have ideas for the next photo session?"

For just a second, Amy wondered what he was talking about. Then, the whole proposal thing came back. "I want to show them different places around town that would be interesting venues. The city park would be easiest but doesn't seem unique."

He nodded slowly as he considered that. "Good point. So something more uniquely small town or country?"

He seemed to be able to read her mind. "I had a very thorough tour of the McDonald Farm."

"That could work. What do you think?" She realized she really was interested in his opinion. Up until now, she'd been flying solo on this.

"I think it's a great idea. But maybe we should avoid anything to do with cows?"

She laughed. "That's my plan."

"Would it work to get your brother involved?"

Amy shook her head. "Dexter would hate being part of the proposals. He's in his mid-twenties and has avoided commitment. The Two Hearts wedding obsession hasn't touched him."

Scott grinned and his eyes crinkled in the corners. Amy stared at him for a beat too long.

Thankfully, the server took that moment to return to their table for their orders. Amy chose a vegetable stir-fry and Scott selected the sweet and sour pork. When they were alone again,

Scott picked up the conversation with the neutral subject of family.

"I helped unload the boxes, but I barely know Dexter. Does he work at one of the wedding businesses?"

"Definitely not. We both ended up as writers. He writes articles about small-town life for his own blog and others. On his off time, he hangs out with some of the guys. He knew a couple of them when he was younger."

"I keep forgetting you're from Two Hearts. Are you glad you came back?"

"Very. Though I'm still working on how to build up my business enough to be able to stay here."

"You're smart. You'll figure it out."

That sent a warm feeling through her. She thought of herself as industrious and maybe even ambitious. Logan hadn't appreciated those qualities or her intelligence.

Amy sighed. "I hope you're right about my succeeding. I'm trying. I've got a list of ideas. Every time somebody suggests something, I add to that list. So far, nothing seems to be a winner for Two Hearts. If I was in Nashville or some other city of a good size, I could do a lot of things and be okay."

"But Two Hearts is different, right? You have all these weddings, and it seems like people are starting to come here as tourists."

"That's all true. But there are only so many people who live here who would subscribe to the newspaper or advertise."

"That's why we're doing proposal photos to drive up interest outside Two Hearts."

She nodded. As she was about to add more, the food arrived. They were quiet for a few minutes as they dove in.

Scott paused after a few bites. "This is delicious. Thank you for saving me from that meatloaf fate."

Amy chuckled. "The evening worked out fine. I like to eat a

lot of different kinds of foods. There aren't many choices in Two Hearts, but this wasn't too bad of a drive, was it?"

"Nope. And my guess is that you moved us away from prying eyes who might think we were a couple if they spotted us out together too close to town."

Amy gasped and started choking.

Scott patted her on the back as she reached for her water. "Sorry! I think I caught you off-guard."

Once Amy could breathe again, she said, "I didn't think you'd know why we'd come here."

"Because I'm a computer geek, so I don't notice details?" He grinned as he spoke, softening the words.

"Not details. Things about people. I know you'd catch every detail in a computer code. So, tell me about yourself, Scott Miller." She settled into her meal as she waited for him to share his story.

After another bite, he said, "There isn't much to tell. I was a cop for a year. Working on the street wasn't for me. I always enjoyed computers, so that's what I do now, but still with the police department."

"You have a sister and nephew?" She was trying to remember what he'd said about the situation at his house.

"My sister has three boys, including a set of twins who are two and a four-year-old. Their daughter just turned three. I love them. I would run into a burning building to rescue them. But two days in my house with them drove me crazy. I don't know how parents do this."

Amy grinned. "My sister told me it's different when they're your kids."

"That must be true, or people wouldn't keep reproducing. But I also have a brother. I'm the oldest, then it's the sister who's in my house, and Steve is the youngest."

"Everyone's in the Chicago area?"

"Everyone's in Illinois. Steve lives further out in the country."

After a couple bites, he asked, "What about you? Just you and your brother?"

"I have two brothers and two sisters. We're scattered all over the country. My stepdad was in the military, so we moved around a lot."

"It must be hard to get everybody together then."

"Everybody always comes home for Christmas. My parents' house bulges at the seams then, but we make it work. Only my oldest sister has two kids—a toddler boy and a baby girl. If my other siblings have children, my parents may need to add an annex to their house." She laughed. "But it's always so much fun when we're all around the tree and in one room together."

"I feel the same way. I can see why a sense of family roots brought you back to Two Hearts. That's how I feel about Chicago."

She had to remember that Scott was a visitor to Two Hearts. He wouldn't be staying, so unless they were going to be pen pals, this would be a holiday-only friendship.

CHAPTER TWENTY

Amy walked up the driveway to Mrs. Brantley's house. She'd been told to arrive at 10:40 a.m. and not to park her car within a block of the house. With that in mind, walking from her office made more sense than driving, and she'd managed to time it just right.

She wasn't sure why she had such a specific time for her arrival, but she knew it must have something to do with Cassie's wedding. That seemed to be the only thing on everyone's mind right now.

As she entered the gate to the backyard, several female voices came through the screen door. When she stepped inside, Mrs. Brantley clapped her hands to get everyone's attention. Paige, Bella, and Simone were here. She knew Michelle wanted to participate in these meetings but had to work.

"Ladies, this is the last time before the wedding that we'll all meet together. Cassie mentioned last night that she'd heard several of us had gotten together over here. She wondered if she had somehow missed the invitation."

A collective gasp went around the room.

"We cannot risk that happening again. I don't need to tell

you all that if Cassie learns about this wedding, she will try to manage it because that's what she does. She plans weddings, and she's brilliant at it."

Bella spoke up. "But she can't take this one over because she'll immediately get stressed out, maybe even call it off."

"Exactly. So from now on, we will have secrecy the CIA would be proud of."

"So we all send text messages? Or emails?" Simone asked.

"No!" Mrs. Brantley shouted.

Amy jumped.

Then Mrs. Brantley added in a lower voice, "Sorry about that. I've given this situation a lot of thought, and even messages and emails have potential issues. What if Cassie were near you when you checked an incoming text? Or worse, what if you accidentally sent the message to a group that included Cassie?"

"That could easily happen," Bella said. "I often send messages that include everyone at this table."

"So what do you have in mind?" Amy asked.

Mrs. Brantley turned toward her with a smile that felt both welcoming and unnerving.

"I think we need someone to act as the go-between. That would seem more natural to an onlooker. To exchange information as we plan and work, one *woman* visits each person involved in planning Cassie and Greg's wedding."

Paige said, "I see your point. It would look much worse if Greg or one of the other guys was dropping in on each of the women."

Bella chuckled. "That could start World War III if Cassie got the wrong idea. Greg would never be unfaithful, but it could look that way."

Mrs. Brantley blanched at the suggestion. "So we need someone who could legitimately go to each house or business. Someone who could talk to every person in a day and not draw any suspicion whatsoever from Cassie."

Amy went through the list of women. They were all friends, but it might still look odd if Bella visited Simone, Paige, her, and Michelle within a few hours.

It seemed her thoughts and Paige's were in alignment. "I've gone through the list of the people involved, and I don't see anyone who could do that."

Mrs. Brantley focused on Amy. "The woman who owns the newspaper could."

Amy considered that for a moment. "Hmm. You may be right. But I'd need a good reason for suddenly becoming so social."

"Write an article?" Simone suggested.

"I did articles on each of the businesses when I started the newspaper, but the town could be due for an update because very few people were reading the paper at the time. Maybe I could talk about summer weddings and interview everyone."

"Perfect," Bella said. Then, she looked toward Mrs. Brantley for confirmation.

Simone grinned. "I couldn't have come up with a better idea myself."

For a moment, Amy felt as if she'd done something quite good. Then she realized that she had simply been the one Mrs. Brantley had chosen and would now have a lot more to do.

Mrs. Brantley glanced at the table they were seated around. Then she got up and came back with the coffee pot to top off some mugs. "Let's have a quick discussion, and then we need to break up in case Cassie decides to drop by. And ladies, please try to act normal around her. If you usually get together and hang out once a week, don't stop."

Bella frowned. "I just realized I didn't reach out to her last week like I normally would. I'll take care of that as soon as we end here."

Mrs. Brantley set a plate filled with brownies in the center of the table. "Everything is in good shape as far as plans go. We have the venue scheduled. The portable bathrooms will be delivered on time."

Simone grabbed a brownie. "You need to sell these in addition to the cookies I've already been telling you to sell." After a bite, she gave her meeting report. "Nick is going to do the food. Greg gave him a budget, and he will work within that."

Amy reached for her purse. "If you think we have time, I have samples of wedding invitations. I know that we need to get these few mailed out ASAP."

Mrs. Brantley shook her head. "Let's not stay long enough to discuss that. If you want to hand them to one of the ladies, then we can work on passing them around."

"As for my task, I have shades of pinks and yellows to go through for the wedding colors." Paige tapped a folder on the table in front of her. "I don't know if that will help, but I didn't mind looking."

Before Paige could present those, Simone said, "I have ideas for cupcake flavors. Let me know when you'll need them, and I'll have an assortment of cupcakes ready for her. In whatever shades we choose."

They heard something outside, and everyone stilled. The side gate opened and closed with a slight clatter.

Mrs. Brantley pointed to the doorway that led from the kitchen to the living room. Everyone rose as quietly as they could and hustled out. They went down the hallway, into the bedroom at the end of the hall, and clustered together without a word. Simone left the door open enough to hear the conversation.

"No one was in their shops, so I thought I'd stop in to see if they were visiting you," Cassie said from the kitchen. "You're always the destination."

Amy hid a gasp with her hand.

"You just missed Bella. I invited her over for tea and to chat about babies. It's been a while, but I still remember enough to share."

Cassie laughed.

Then Mrs. Brantley said, "I was just thinking about going over to the diner for lunch. Would you like to go with me?"

"It's a little earlier than I usually eat, but sure, let's go. And if I decide I'm not hungry—"

"You'll get a piece of pie and coffee."

Cassie laughed. "Exactly. It's always the right time for Dinah's pie."

Amy heard the screen door close, and the voices faded away as they left. They all waited another minute before Bella released a big breath. "That was close."

Paige said in a low voice, "I'd like to get through this without having to lie all over the place. I'm sorry Mrs. Brantley had to do that."

Bella whispered, "I *was* the first one here. Mrs. Brantley assigned me that time. And she made a point of giving me advice about babies. I didn't think anything about the conversation at the time, but now I know she was setting everything up, just in case."

Simone inched open the bedroom door. Silence greeted them. Then the sound of toenails skittering down a wood floor approached them. Cookie came to the door and nosed his way inside. She reached down to rub behind the dog's ears. "It's a good thing he didn't come here and rat us out by barking."

Bella stepped into the hall and paused for a moment, listening. She whispered, "I think the coast is clear. Let me sneak out first." She tiptoed up the hallway and peered around the corner into the kitchen. When her shoulders relaxed, Amy knew Cassie had indeed left. Bella returned to the group. "Give it ten minutes just like we did coming in."

Amy thrust the invitation samples at Bella. "Let's give her what we have right now. She can be the first to review everything. Then I'll start with her interview and move from person to person."

Paige handed Bella the color swatches.

Simone shrugged with her hands up. "I will only have samples to taste. Those aren't on me."

Amy outlined their plan. "I'll first set up the article idea with Cassie. On that day, I can pick up cake samples and take them to her. Could you have a set of samples for me *and* her? I'll tell her we're having each person give input on all aspects of the article."

Simone grinned. "That's a genius idea. I certainly can. Remember, you're asking about flavor and decoration. Decor colors too."

Bella disappeared down the hall. By unspoken agreement, the four remaining women sat on the edge of the bed. When only she and Simone were left, Amy checked her watch.

"I really need to get back. I need to plan another—" Amy breathed deeply before finishing the sentence. "Proposal. Hopefully for today or tomorrow."

Simone grinned. "The last one came out great. Are you getting more interest on the website?"

"I checked right before I came here. Interest is growing, and readers are loving it. I haven't had more subscriptions, but people have been visiting my website. That gives the ads you guys run increased exposure."

Simone said, "Why don't you get out of here next? I've already been proposed to and accepted." She grinned. "I'd rather not stay in this room, though. I think I'll sit in the kitchen and have a cup of coffee as if I'm waiting for Mrs. Brantley to return. I've actually done that before. She's told me to go right in and have a seat."

In the kitchen, the only activity was Cookie getting a bite to eat from his bowl.

Simone poured herself a cup of coffee, served herself a brownie from the plate, and placed it on a napkin in front of her. "I want to make sure I have the whole picture set in case someone stops by. Almost no one would come here and not have something sweet." She grinned cheekily.

Amy chuckled as she headed out the door. She knew Mrs. Brantley was busy, but she really should consider opening a cookie bakery. Simone could add cookies to her lineup, but she'd said multiple times that she really loved making cakes.

Amy didn't blame her. When you were good at doing something, why add something you didn't enjoy? The town already had a cake bakery and a place that made the world's best pies, so they probably didn't need anything else sweet. Then again, she could promote Two Hearts in the newspaper as a sweet place to visit. Tourists would probably love that.

Now that she was the courier for their operation, she needed to think through the plans. Everything for the wedding that hadn't been ordered yet had to be ordered this week.

Their aces in the hole were that Simone could make the cake and Bella the bride and bridesmaids' dresses. Almost anyone else would have a hard time pulling that off.

Who was she kidding? This would be a phenomenal amount of work in a short time, no matter what. She hoped they'd succeed in giving Cassie and Greg the wedding of their dreams.

Amy made a quick stop at the newspaper, jotted down a few ideas about the article she had to do as their cover story, and then went to Dinah's. After all the talk about lunch, she was hungry now too. She found Simone walking in the same direction. After Simone had crossed the street to reach her, she said, "You too?"

"If you mean being ready to eat now, yes."

They both laughed.

Simone nudged her with her arm. "I feel like we shouldn't be seen together, as if that alone would seem suspicious."

Amy looked around carefully before she answered.

"Remember, we're not supposed to speak about such things outside."

Simone nodded. "You're right. Let me say that I'll be glad when this *situation* is taken care of."

Spoken like a true spy.

They entered Dinah's and found Mrs. Brantley with Cassie, Bella, and Paige.

"We all got hungry at the same time!" Bella said, and she looked directly at them, challenging them not to say anything about having just overheard a conversation about eating.

When they reached the others, Amy completely ignored the subjects of weddings and meetings. She inhaled deeply. "The special smells wonderful! Could two more squeeze in at your table, or should Simone and I take a two-top?" The four already seated scooted around, moving their plates and drink glasses with them.

Michelle came over. "Let me get a menu for you two."

Amy stopped her. "Don't bother for me. I'll take the special."

Simone sniffed the air. "Chicken noodle soup?"

"Chicken and dumplings."

"Sold. I'll have that and a cup of coffee. I'm sure I'll want pie at the end too."

Murmurs went around the table that everybody would be having pie.

After lunch and that pie, Cassie pushed back from the table. "I have a bride coming this afternoon for a new client appointment, so I'd better get over to my office to start preparing."

Even after she'd left, they stayed on neutral topics. Amy questioned the group. "Does anyone have a phone number for Mr. McDonald? I was told he'd be good to ask about as a possible site for the next proposal photo."

Michelle brought over a coffee pot for refills. "I overheard you. I loved those photos with the cow! If you need goats, you can use my backyard. I'm a little closer to town, and you only have to deal with four goats."

Mrs. Brantley held out her cup, and Michelle poured. "I thought you had two."

Michelle grinned. "They're so much fun that we got two more." Then she frowned. "They're also mischievous. We had to add a fence in the middle of our yard to give us a private area. The goats were eating the flowers, and one of them took a liking to the laundry hanging on the line. I love to sleep on sheets that I've hung outside to dry."

Amy's mother had done that when they were young. They'd smelled wonderful.

"To make up for their lost space, we expanded their fenced area. Now, I get to have flowers and sheets that aren't nibbled on, and the goats have more room to run."

Amy looked at the group. "Do you all think that would be a good place to take pictures? I've never been to Michelle's."

Mrs. Brantley said, "I think it would be great. They have a pretty yard and a charming house if that ends up in the photos."

"Then I accept your offer, Michelle. Is tomorrow too soon?"

Michelle laughed. "Anytime from now on is fine with me."

Amy thought through her day. "I need Paige to take the pictures."

Paige said, "This afternoon is better for me than tomorrow."

"Then I guess we can do it."

Bella tapped her on the arm. "I think you may be forgetting one important detail?"

Amy stared at her, nothing coming to mind.

"You'd better check with Scott to make sure he's available."

They all laughed.

"That's probably a good idea," Bella said, chuckling.

Amy shot off a text to Scott. He responded immediately, saying he was available, and he would get photo-ready.

"It's all set. I'm going to go change for my photo shoot and meet you out there, Paige, in…" Amy checked her watch, "about an hour? Does that work for you?"

"That's perfect. I'll do a quick bit of research to see if I get any ideas for the photos to make these different from last time."

"At least there's no danger of a cow wanting to be part of it. Michelle, could I get a cup of coffee to go? I think I'll need caffeine for this."

Michelle grinned. "Give me just a sec. And I'll tell you where I leave the goat treats. They're quiet and happy when they're eating. Mostly." She shrugged. "If you're among the goats and not just in my little backyard, I can't guarantee you won't have a goat nosing in between the two of you. Oh, and watch out for Bernie. He likes to butt into people. But Sally is sweet."

They all broke apart, and Amy went on her way. She had just enough time to change. She texted Scott, asking him to pick her up at her house. As soon as she sent it, she realized he didn't know where she lived, so she sent off the address, along with directions in case GPS didn't find it. One of the questionable joys of living in a small town was sometimes technology didn't work right.

CHAPTER TWENTY-ONE

Scott was parked in his truck in front of Amy's home when she looked out the window a short time later. Since their dinner out together—definitely not a date—he'd driven them a couple of times. He had a pickup that would certainly make picking up her newspapers easier. Maybe she could talk him into driving with her next Monday. It was kind of nice having company as you drove too.

She found him dressed in the same tan pants he'd worn last time and a deeper blue dress shirt. "You look great!" That sounded over the top. She cleared her throat. "I mean, you look great for a proposal. Not that you're going to an actual proposal." Amy sighed with frustration. "I mean—"

Scott laughed. "I'll just say thank you."

"That's probably best."

"I'll return the compliment. You look very proposable."

His quirky compliment warmed her. She'd chosen a pink and blue floral-print dress that flowed to mid-calf with blue sandals on her feet. She saw it as feminine, and it appeared Scott did too. Amy switched to what she hoped would turn into a more professional conversation. "Do you have any innovative ideas for this proposal?"

"Because I'm the expert, right?" He chuckled. "I admit I watched some more proposals last night. The elements hold true, though. The guy gets down on his knee. The girl looks surprised. She says yes." He glanced her way. "There was one where she said, 'No way!'"

"Seriously? And they put that out for the world to see?"

"It's amazing what you can find online."

Amy fidgeted with the fabric of her dress. Once they'd done the first proposal, how did they make it look fresh and new for the next one? The same image of him kneeling in front of her with only a different background wouldn't work. "Paige is so used to setting people up for photo sessions that she may have ideas."

The photographer's vehicle was already parked to the side when they pulled into Michelle's long driveway.

As soon as they exited the truck, Paige called, "Come see the goats! They're adorable!"

Amy had to agree. Just as Michelle had described, a fenced-in area near the back door contained the clothesline and flowers, and a big fenced area behind that held four goats, three of them white, one of them black and white. They wandered over to the gate to greet the visitors. "Michelle sent a text that said they were all friendly, and that we could pet them. And she reminded me that they love treats."

Amy entered that fenced-in area and found a tin filled with treats, just as Michelle had described.

Paige glanced around. "I think we should go toward the back of their yard. The woods behind their property should make a pretty backdrop."

The four animals watched them with curiosity. "Do you think it's safe to be in with the goats?" She remembered visiting a farm when they lived here years ago, but she wasn't sure who that was now. Other than the cow she knew by name, she'd mostly watched farm animals from a distance.

Paige laughed. "I've seen videos of people doing goat yoga."

Amy and Scott stared at her.

"It's a thing." When they continued to stare at her with what Amy knew was a questioning gaze, she added, "It really is. These people do all their regular yoga stretches. When they get on all fours for a pose, the goats jump on their backs. It's so cute!"

Amy shrugged. "If that's safe, I guess goats are friendly."

They all entered the goat area. Amy brought the treat can with her in case their four-legged friends needed a bribe.

Paige posed her and Scott as she had at Cherry and Levi's. "Maybe this time, Amy, lean down and hug Scott around the neck when he's on one knee. That's your yes. Shout yes, lean down, and hug him."

Amy stared at Scott like a deer in the headlights. She'd been avoiding any form of contact with him. A hug had almost led to a kiss, and she definitely didn't want that to happen. Amy shook out her arms to loosen up. But Paige had a good idea that Amy couldn't refuse without an embarrassing explanation, so she had to get on board. "Do you have any other ideas to make this proposal slightly different?"

"I'm going to try some other angles. But there isn't much other than that to try. Unless you want to go with a hot air balloon like Michelle's proposal or a boat like Simone's, a proposal is a proposal. And before you get too many ideas, photos like you want would be harder for either of those. I don't think a picture from the shore like I got for Simone is what you need."

"It might not be ideal, but let's keep it in mind as a possibility. I do think that a closer photo makes readers feel as if they're part of the story, so that would be better." They needed new ideas. And fast.

When Scott and Amy stood posed in front of each other, one

of the goats came over and nudged her with his head, but she scooted him away. When he came right back, she realized he was after the treats she'd dropped in her pocket. "I'll give you one when we're done. Is that a deal?"

He watched her closely for a moment before moving out of sight behind her.

Paige waved at them. "I'm ready. It's go time."

Scott pulled the ring box out of his pocket as before. He was getting to be a better actor because she didn't even doubt the sincerity on his face. He knelt on the ground they had once again protected with a piece of plastic and said, "Will you marry me, Amy?"

Amy stared at him for a beat. The moment almost felt real, which was very strange. The man should be on Broadway. When she realized she hadn't said anything, she brightened up her expression, leaned down, and hugged him as she'd been told to do. As soon as she touched Scott, warmth flooded her body.

As she reluctantly let go and started to stand, something slammed into her from behind. She flew through the air, landing face-first in the grass next to Scott.

Chaos swarmed around her. She heard Scott and Paige speaking from far away.

A warm, wet nose nuzzled her cheek. Then another on her other side.

When she flipped over, she tugged her dress down from its position around her knees. Then she tried to move her arms and legs to check for broken bones. Once assured she'd survived unscathed, she croaked, "What happened?"

Scott crouched beside her. "I think we now understand what Michelle's warning meant."

Amy nodded, then regretted the move when her shoulder ached.

"Are you okay?" He put his hand on her arm. "Bernie likes to push against people. He came at you like a freight train, and you were airborne."

Amy sat up and brushed off the front of her dress. "I think I'm fine. But I can't do more photos at this point. I have grass stains on this dress."

Paige held up her camera triumphantly. "Don't worry about the photos. I got the proposal with you hugging Scott. Those came out great." She grinned. "And I have the goat beside you before that, you getting hit from behind, and your flight through the air. Oh, and the goat nuzzling you afterward. Lots of great goat photos."

Perfect. Just perfect.

"I'm slightly annoyed by goats right now." Amy stood on shaky legs. "And here I thought the cow was a problem."

Scott chuckled. "The cow was easy compared to Bernie the head-butter."

As the three of them walked toward the gate, Amy kept a watchful eye on the goats. They had to prevent escapees when they went out, and she desperately wanted to avoid any more up close moments with Bernie.

Once they'd closed the gate after exiting, Amy stopped for a moment, leaning against a fence post to steady herself. "This is at the top of my list for worst things to happen at a photo shoot. The good news is I won't mess up your truck seat, Scott, because it's only the front of me that is filthy."

"I don't care. I can clean it later." After waiting a few more seconds for her to continue walking, he startled her by picking her up and carrying her toward his truck.

She held herself stiffly for a few seconds, then rested her head against his shoulder. Not walking right now was a good thing, and she had to admit that being in his arms wasn't a hardship.

"I got more photos just now," Paige called from behind them.

Just what she needed. More fake relationship photos.

Scott gently placed her on the seat. When he started to reach for her seatbelt, she put her hand on his arm. "Thank you for the lift, but I can do this."

"Do you want to stop for lunch on the way back?"

"Not wearing this. I think I need to go home and change."

He gave a single nod and went around to get in the driver's seat. As they drove, he said, "Start thinking of places we can go for fake proposals that don't involve animals."

"My thought exactly. The way it's been going with us, as long as we're outside, we'll at least end up with birds or squirrels or something else that wants to be in the photos." She chuckled.

As they drove back to town, Amy felt a little bruised but overall fine. Unfortunately, the cow photo had been really popular both in town and on the internet, so she might have to make the decision to use the goat one. She'd have to swallow her pride to save her business. She had to silence the thought that maybe—if she was lucky—she'd get another ride in Scott's arms.

CHAPTER TWENTY-TWO

Amy paced across her newspaper office, turned, and crossed again. After several trips each way, she sat on one of her boxes to think about this. How could she go from person to person and have it look purposeful? She needed to be able to spend time with Cassie with the top goal of prying information out of her about the wedding of her dreams, which they were all hoping they were about to deliver.

She leaned forward and rested her elbows on her knees. Then she stood again. "Okay, think of this as if it was an ordinary article. You're going to pitch the idea to an editor. It's all about being sneaky to figure out what someone wants for their special occasion."

She nodded as she thought about it. "I just have to ask questions." And then she perked up. "I'm a reporter. Reporters ask questions."

She picked up her phone and called Cassie. "I'm going to do an article—really a series of articles—about the wedding businesses in Two Hearts."

Silence met her. "I appreciate this, but didn't you already do that?"

In her excitement, she had forgotten she *had* done that. And in the first month she'd been open. *Think. Think!*

"I am actually switching this up a bit. I want to write about the businesses, but this time in a way that doesn't seem quite so promotional." She loved the words coming out of her mouth and hoped her good ideas continued. "I could ask you about wedding trends for the summer. I know it's the last minute if someone's planning their summer wedding, but I think more people than we realize wait until now. And it may help someone who's actually planning a year ahead. What do you think?"

"I love publicity. And I like your idea of not having it seem so much like an advertising campaign."

Now Amy felt like she was on a roll. "It may be fun, too, if each of you comments on the others. That probably only made sense in my mind."

Cassie laughed. "You're right."

"Bella could indicate her choices for wedding dress styles for a summer wedding, and you can comment and say which one you loved most. Simone shares cake flavors and decorating for a summer wedding, and you comment. Not just you but each of you for the other's trend suggestions. Does that make sense now, Cassie?"

"I love it! And each time you write an article, it promotes the rest of us too. But don't forget Paige and her photography."

Amy chewed on her lip for a second. "I'm never sure when it comes to photography how something would change for the season. But you're a wedding planner, so please clue me in."

"Paige would take more outside photos if the background was green, beautiful, and not cold, as long as it wasn't one of our ridiculously hot and humid summer days."

Amy laughed. "I think I'd choose more inside photos then. But I do see your point. I'll get Paige on board with this too. I may as well get started right away. Are you available tomorrow morning for an initial chat?"

She heard rustling as Cassie seemed to be checking a schedule.

"I can do any time from 11:00 a.m. to 2:30 p.m. Your price of admission is a piece of pie."

Amy laughed. "I should be there at 11:00 a.m. I'll see what I can do about the pie."

As soon as she had ended the call, Amy raced out the newspaper office door to get to Simone. A few minutes later and out of breath, Amy burst through the door and startled a woman inside buying a cake.

"Sorry. Forgive me. I'll just sit over here at this little table. You take your time."

The woman, whom Amy did not recognize turned back to complete her order. From her interaction with Simone, she seemed to be a town resident. Amy knew she needed to get out more in the town and meet people, and this confirmed it. She should know everyone in Two Hearts by now. But in reality, she only knew the people she'd interviewed or spent time with. Even in church on Sunday morning, there were quite a few people she couldn't address by name.

When the woman left, Simone said, "What was so urgent that you looked like you were about to pass out when you flew through my door?"

Amy approached the glass counter that held the few cakes Simone had made in advance. "I have an appointment to talk to Cassie tomorrow morning. I'm not allowed to call you, so I'm here to see if you can put together samples by then. I could pick them up and take them over for her to taste as part of the article." She explained the idea she'd come up with as she'd been talking to Cassie.

"I love it!" Simone giggled. "We may just pull this off yet. And to answer your question, yes, I can have three or four samples ready. Stop by after 9:00 a.m. tomorrow."

The door opened to another customer. Simone's business

really was taking off. Amy was glad for her because she knew she had been concerned when she'd moved here as to whether or not she'd be able to survive in the small town. As the town began to prosper, though, people had money in their budget for special birthday, anniversary, or graduation cakes. Amy heard the order begin for the last one as she was leaving.

Amy had the rest of the day before her and wondered what she should do with it. She knew enough about the town and the businesses that she probably didn't need to do any more research for tomorrow's interview with Cassie. Standing in front of Simone's bakery, she looked directly at Bella's Brides. But she did need Bella's info, so she crossed the street and went in. Amy quietly wove her way through the dress displays to peer into the center area and ensure she wasn't interrupting a bridal party.

"Amy?"

Amy jumped, her hand on her racing heart. "You scared me!"

"What's with the subterfuge? I saw you skulking through the shop." Bella watched her with a questioning expression.

"I'm the courier, remember?"

Bella grinned. "If this has something to do with Project Wedding, come toward the back with me. Then no one will see us together. Well, no one outside my employees, and they know not to say anything about anything."

"Are there many secrets shared in here?"

Bella's grin widened. "So many things. What spills out of someone's mouth when they're about to get married is amazing. It must be the pressure."

Amy explained her idea for the article. Then she added, "I'm going to see Cassie tomorrow. If you have anything ready, I could take it over to get the ball rolling."

Bella shook her head. "I need a little longer for the dress sketches, so please come to get them right before your interview with Cassie. I had a plan but changed my mind. What I really need—like *desperately* need—is the color or colors she wants. I know it's pink and yellow, but which pinks and yellows? I have to get going on the matron of honor dress."

Amy didn't know how long that would take, but it must be more than a couple days.

Bella went over to her check out desk, retrieved her purse from underneath, and pulled something out. "I also have the color swatches Paige gave me yesterday." She passed both to Amy. "Once the design and colors are confirmed, I'll be able to ramp up production."

Amy felt a little fidgety when she thought about the role she would have to play with Cassie. "I certainly hope this works. I've never played a role like this."

"Just consider it a new role for the stage. Like your proposals."

Amy laughed. "Hopefully not like the proposal photos." She gave a brief summary of the goat experience that had Bella laughing by the end.

As Amy tucked the items in her purse, Bella said, "I hope we are able to pull this off. Cassie isn't stupid, so it's game over if she catches a whiff of anything that doesn't feel right."

Amy's nerves ramped up. "Thanks for calming me down."

"It wouldn't be the end of the world." Bella put her hand on Amy's shoulder. "They'll get married. It just could be a lot longer before she can do this on her own. One thing did occur to me. What about the marriage license?"

Amy gasped. "I've never gotten married. Do you need to have one of those *before* you get married?"

"You definitely do. I'm surprised Mrs. Brantley hasn't thought of it, but she's probably been so busy with her tasks and being mayor that it hasn't occurred to her." Bella stood, tapping her ballet-flat-covered foot as she considered it. When Amy had arrived in town, Bella's feet had often been clad in high heels. Now that she was far into her pregnancy, Bella only wore flats.

"We may have to talk to Micah about this to see how we can get it to work. As a lawyer, even if he doesn't know, he'll know who to ask."

"I'll add him to my list. Maybe I'll stop by right after this."

Bella grabbed her arm as she turned to leave. "Remember, *you* can't go to Micah. We don't want you going anywhere that wouldn't make sense to Cassie if she happened to see you there."

"Right. *Everything* is much more complicated right now. I could come up with a legal matter to talk to him about or even put him in the article I'm supposed to be writing. A lawyer in it would be a stretch, though." Amy blew out a breath. "I'll put Scott on it."

"I'd talk to my husband for you, but I'm so exhausted by the time I get home from work that I can't guarantee I will do anything except collapse on the couch. Micah's even trying to learn to cook for me."

"How are the results?"

Bella made a fake, toothy smile. "You see this?" She pointed to her mouth. "This is the expression I give him when he asks if I enjoyed a meal. I appreciate Micah's attempts in the kitchen, but he needs to stick to lawyering."

Amy laughed. "Maybe we should let people in town know you would love some meals when you got home from work. There's nothing some of these older ladies enjoy more than sharing their love of cooking with someone."

"We received some meals when we were first married. I loved having great readymade food. I'm kind of counting on that again after the baby's born, so I'll put up with Micah's meals for now."

Amy laughed again. "Then I'm going to be on my way." As she started toward the door, she realized she had one more question. "What do you know, Bella, about the empty stores on Main Street? There are a lot of them."

"I know the owners would be thrilled to either sell or rent

them. I've been in every one of them at this point. The one next door to me used to be some sort of general store or sold fabric. It has shelves."

"It has shelves?"

"They go all the way up one wall. In the old days, you walked up to a counter, and then they got whatever you wanted."

"Are they wood shelves?" Having those already there would be a big help.

"Yes, they are, but why are you interested? You have a big place for your newspaper."

Amy looked at the floor and then at the ceiling. "I love books. I have so many of them that it's been suggested—multiple times—that I open a bookstore."

Bella's eyes lit up. "Another business on Main Street would be fabulous! Now, we don't have many options for visitors. Paige's place is cute inside, but visitors don't browse at a photo studio. They go there intentionally for a photo session or to talk to her about getting wedding photos done. It's kind of the same with my shop. Simone is really the only one who draws people in just to buy. It would be great to have a business like a bookstore to bring foot traffic to Main Street."

"The problem is that I don't think I'd be able to afford the rent. You already know my struggles with finances and the newspaper."

"Has anything changed after the proposal photos went out?"

"Yes. Well, sort of. A few people have written to say they're enjoying the small-town feeling." The weight that had settled on her shoulders lifted slightly as she thought about new possibilities. "I keep hoping that will translate into new subscriptions. That the newspaper makes them happy." She needed to remember those words. The increase may be tiny, but it was also a move in the right direction.

"As to the cost, the owners are so thrilled to get someone into their shops that they will give it to you for almost nothing.

As long as they don't have to pay any property tax on it, they're already ahead."

Excitement was starting to build in Amy. What if she *could* have a bookstore?

"Do you think I could see inside the building sometime soon?"

Bella gestured around her. "I don't have an appointment for hours. Would now work?"

Amy thought over the rest of her afternoon. She wasn't on a deadline crunch for next week yet. "Are you going to call the owner now?"

"I have a key. When I had some work done in the upstairs bathroom, the contractor said he could work on it more easily from the other side. Don't ask me about the logistics of these things because I don't know. Don't worry, though, because I know it was completely patched up, whatever they did."

Was she ready to do this?

"I can read your mind. Looking at a building isn't buying or renting it. It's not even fixing it up. It's just looking at it."

"Kind of like window shopping. I do love window shopping."

"Exactly. I need to do some shopping in the city for the baby. Maybe we could get together for that one day. It worked out well when I rode with you the last time. Except we missed lunch out there."

"But you had a good nap."

Bella rolled her eyes. "I seem to be doing that a lot."

"I go into the city every Monday. You're welcome to ride along anytime you want."

Amy waited while Bella went back and got the key. Her mind said *this is completely wrong.* She shouldn't even consider looking to start another business in Two Hearts when she was already struggling with the first one.

Bella returned, and they started for the door again. "Why are you looking for a new place, though, when you already have one? You could easily fit a bookstore inside your newspaper office. And you own that building outright, don't you?"

"I do, but because of where it's located, I get close to zero foot traffic. Just dog walkers and things like that. I know having a bookstore in a small town probably isn't going to bring in a bunch of money to start with, anyway. Reducing my chances of success by having it on a side street doesn't seem like a good plan."

"You're definitely right. But it seems kind of a shame to have two buildings."

When they arrived in front of the neighboring building, Amy realized she hadn't paid much attention to the individual buildings on the street. She should write about the history of each one sometime.

This one was another one of the closed-up shops on Main Street. She'd seen a photo from a year before, and at that time, there'd been boarded-up windows instead of what they had now. It had looked completely abandoned. The weddings in town led the townspeople to remove the boards and occasionally clean the outside windows on the buildings to make the town feel lived in. Even if parts of it weren't. At least not yet.

Bella opened the door and stood to the side. Dank air rushed out at them, and Amy wondered what she'd gotten herself into. "Maybe this is a bad idea."

Bella laughed. "When these buildings are closed up, they feel lifeless. Now that the door is open, though, it will be fine. My building felt so abandoned when I first went inside. Look at it now."

She had a point. Amy followed Bella inside. As she'd said, one wall was lined with wooden shelves. It was better than she could have asked for. They were spaced apart, just as she would have chosen for books. The other side had wood paneling on it, which she was pretty sure was called beadboard. At various points in history, there had been coats of turquoise, white and olive green because hints of each came through the peeling mess. Even so, she could feel the potential of the place as she surveyed the room.

"It sucks you in with possibilities, doesn't it?"

Amy had almost forgotten Bella was with her. "It does. Is this how you felt when you got your shop?"

"Frankly, I was marrying a man to save my finances. No, I take that back. We were already married. My life was being uprooted in big ways. But when I saw my shop, I immediately envisioned my business there, and it gave me hope."

Amy definitely wanted more hope. The building was deeper than she'd realized from the front, and as she compared it to Bella's, she realized a lot had been done there in the same amount of space, so much that she couldn't tell what the space must have looked like empty.

A long counter stood in front of the shelves. "This counter is awesome, but I wonder if it will cut off people trying to see the books?"

"I was wondering that too."

Amy moved to the back of the room. "The flow would be better if the counter was portable and could be relocated here. I wonder where I would store other books and office supplies?"

Bella pointed upward. "The second floor."

Amy gazed upward. "I didn't even realize there was one. Do you have a second story?"

"That's where we make the dresses."

"I've never been in that part of your business. I've only seen the finished dresses."

"You're welcome to have a tour anytime you want. You may find something useful for the new article you'll be writing."

Amy started for the back of the building. "Great idea! Let's head upstairs here."

Bella stepped in front of her. "Be ready for anything. I've

never been upstairs here. If you had seen mine when I went there the first time . . ." Bella shuddered then moved to the side so Amy could pass.

How bad could it be? Amy stopped at a closed door and pulled it open slowly. It creaked, ratcheting up her concern. Then she laughed. "I was starting to let this get to me. Let's see what's up there."

Amy slowly crept up the dimly lit stairs. A window somewhere was allowing in enough light that she could see where she was going, but nothing more. Bella lumbered up the stairs behind her. When Amy reached the top, she realized the room was cleaner than she'd expected.

A couple of minutes later, Bella was beside her. "I just remembered Mrs. Brantley stored some boxes of ornaments and lights here for the Christmas tree lighting ceremony we had last December. Dinah ordered everything, but it was stowed here. I'm not sure where they're keeping everything now."

Bella waved her hand at the room. "So what do you think?"

Amy wandered over to the window and rubbed an area clean with her hand. Her hand came back dirty, but enough light entered through the semi-clean spot that she had an idea of the bright space this room could be.

"This reminds me of my second floor." Bella looked around. "I have a bathroom on both floors." She walked over and opened up a door. "I think this is where yours is. I didn't notice a door downstairs, did you?"

"Nope. That's okay. Now that I see a room this size, I wonder what I'll do with all the space."

"You want storage, don't you?"

Amy laughed. "Yes. But I guess you can't have too much room, can you?" She could envision boxes of books, maybe shelves where neatly organized books waited to replace those that were sold.

"Are you going to sell other things? In other bookstores I've seen specialty items like stationery and chocolates."

"I can only picture books right now, but maybe I could add more items later. There's one wall of shelves, so maybe I should build another one on the opposite side."

"The room is wide enough to add shelving units down the center too."

The vision came more to life as they spoke.

"Will your store be special in some way? Unique?"

"Everything in this town has something to do with weddings."

Amy hadn't realized she'd spoken out loud until Bella said, "Are you thinking of a wedding bookstore? I get a lot of clients —even with the many information-packed websites available— who want a book about planning a wedding or choosing a wedding dress. I'll bet Simone has the same situation with cakes, Paige with wedding photos, and Cassie with the overall planning."

Amy's excitement built. "I'd only considered a small area for those, but I could have a whole section of the store with wedding books. A big how-to collection."

Bella grinned. "That would be so fun."

Amy heard someone calling from downstairs. A female voice she didn't recognize at first asked, "Can anyone join your party?"

When she realized it was Cassie's voice, Amy started to panic. Then she realized nothing she was doing right now had anything to do with Cassie's wedding. Bella's face showed a similar range of emotions.

Bella went to the top of the stairs and called down, "We're up here."

When Cassie got to the top of the stairs, she looked around. "I saw inside here a couple of times in December. It's funny how an empty room appears so big." Cassie walked around for a moment, and then she turned to the two of them. "Are you thinking of expanding, Bella?"

Amy raised her hand. "It's for me."

"Then I'll rephrase my question," Cassie said with a smile. "Are you thinking of expanding, Amy?"

They all laughed.

"Expanding isn't really the right word. I'm thinking of having a bookstore too."

Cassie lit up. "That sounds like a great addition to Main Street. What would you do with this space on the second floor? Storage?"

Amy looked around. "Seems like a lot of room for storage."

"She has great ideas." Bella explained the idea for the wedding section of the store.

"That's so good! I can give you the titles of the books I recommend to my clients when they ask. And almost all of them ask. I've even thought of putting together some sort of journal on my own so they can keep track of details, but I didn't want to go to all the trouble of trying to sell it myself. Would you sell my journal if I create it?"

Excitement rushed through Amy. "Absolutely! This store is feeling more real by the second. I'm both excited and terrified."

Bella laughed. "I can certainly relate to that. Cassie's fortunate because she didn't need a storefront, just her house."

Cassie looked around the room. "Every once in a while, I think about getting a space for meetings so I don't need to have somebody in my house if I'm not in the mood. Or if I didn't feel like vacuuming that morning."

Bella chuckled. "I'd have needed that space right away. I rarely feel like vacuuming in the morning."

After another chuckle, the women moved toward the stairway and back down. At the bottom of the stairs, Cassie said, "What have you decided, Amy? Are you going to check out some other places in town?"

Once again, Amy pictured her bookstore here and open with customers pulling books off the shelf and bringing them up to the register to buy. It felt so real. "I can't imagine another place that would have shelves like this. This seems like the perfect place for a bookstore to start. I can add more shelving later."

Bella nodded in agreement. "It certainly does. I know the owner, Harriet Tumwater, and she would love to have a tenant in here. It's been empty for decades."

Amy went toward the door. "I'm going to have to sleep on this. I'm not sure how I'm going to pay the rent when I already have one property. I'd try to sell it if I thought anyone would be interested, but two other nearby buildings with similar space are already available."

That evening, Amy ate a rare dinner with Dexter. She made spaghetti for them and a salad for herself. She would have happily made a salad for him, too, but he wasn't interested.

"So, Ames, how's the newspaper going?"

He never asked about her business. "Business has been okay." Make that stagnant. "How about you? How's the exciting world of blogging?"

He rolled his eyes. "I picked up a new sponsor. I'm happy about where it's going."

She pushed her pasta around on the plate. "Things have been slower than I'd like, but the proposals will help."

He laughed as he served himself a second portion. "What? You mean like a wedding proposal?"

"I guess I haven't talked to you about it, but I'm surprised you haven't heard. Scott and I have been doing engagement mock-ups. The readers liked the one I published."

"I wouldn't usually say a proposal would help with *anything*, but I see your point, especially where Two Hearts is concerned."

Dexter had a way of making her smile. "Spoken like a true bachelor. I do have one other thing I'm considering." She told him about the possible bookstore in her future.

"Great idea! I remember saying you should have a bookstore, bookworm that you are."

"Mom said something like that too. She got me thinking. But I'm not sure I can make it all work. Not yet, anyway."

They finished their dinner with family chitchat, Amy all the while trying to figure out how she could make a bookstore happen. She loved the idea. And it dovetailed nicely into her newspaper. She could even sell the newspaper there. Of course, she'd need to be in two places at one time to run both businesses. She'd have to sort out that issue when the time came.

CHAPTER TWENTY-THREE

It usually took a cup of coffee to get Amy feeling as if she could embrace the day. Today, she'd woken up energized. Today, she would be acting as a courier, giving Cassie information from each of the women. And she'd receive vital information from Cassie for her wedding.

But if she didn't do this right, the whole wedding could fall apart. She might accidentally give a clue that had Cassie asking what was going on. Or she might not remember the information correctly. As that thought came to mind, she decided to record what she would call an interview with Cassie. And it truly was an interview because she'd truly have to write an article about this.

A sound at the kitchen door startled her. *Tap.* A pause. *Tap, tap, tap.* A pause. Then, another *tap.* She slowly opened the door to see what was going on. Paige stood outside.

"What's with the weird knock?"

"I thought it sounded mysterious and in keeping with our spy mission."

Amy rolled her eyes. "Come on inside."

Paige glanced quickly to the left and then the right, now

seeming serious. "I don't think anyone saw me come here. I just wanted to drop off some ideas for wedding photos."

"Paige," Amy said in a low voice, "it's okay for us to be seen together. It would be really weird if we weren't seen together."

Paige stilled for a moment and then laughed. "You're so right." She thrust a folded paper at Amy. "Since James is in on this, I asked him for suggestions. It isn't much because so much happens on the wedding day, but it should give you something to talk about."

She leaned closer. "Now I'd better get over to my shop. I have someone coming in about forty-five minutes. A couple for an engagement photo. They're already engaged, but when they saw your article, they decided to have a more formal engagement photo taken. Her words were that they'd missed it with the proposal but could make up for it with the engagement." She turned to walk away but turned back. "And they're bringing her family dog with them. After seeing photos with animals, she said she wanted the dog in the picture. I hope that part goes well." Paige went on her way.

Amy slowly closed the door. She *had* seen an increase in her website traffic, but helping other businesses mattered a lot to her. This was awesome. Helping her town—and her friends— thrive would be fabulous.

As she carried her coffee into the living room to sit down for a moment, Dexter started on his first shower song of the morning.

She took a big swig of the coffee for strength. "I want to help my town. But I really need a place of my own."

The concert stopped, so she headed toward the bathroom. Now it was her turn to get ready—but music-free. As she approached her newspaper office an hour later, she found Scott standing outside. When she realized she was speeding up her pace to reach him, she forced herself to slow down.

He smiled widely at her. "I wanted to see if you needed anything today."

Amy put the key in the lock and opened the door. "Did our mayor have a tight schedule for you again today?"

"She's been busy working on things for the town and this wedding stuff. That's kind of let me off the hook. But there is still a daily schedule attached to the front of the refrigerator with a magnet. It's my *option* if I have nothing to do, so I always want to make sure I legitimately have something else to do. I'll admit, though, that she's started to put some things on there that are a little more interesting. She had a hike in the woods listed for today."

Amy sighed without meaning to.

"Not something you enjoy doing?"

"Huh?"

"You sighed when I mentioned hiking."

"I hadn't even realized I'd done that. I'd love to have time to do things like going for a hike, but I'm too busy right now. I don't mind, though. I love my work, and I'm enjoying being part of the wedding planning."

"Maybe you could take an afternoon off later this week to do something different."

Could she?

"I'll only be here for another two and a half weeks, so if I'm going to go on a hike, it will have to be soon."

His meaning reached her. Scott only wanted to hike with her. And . . . she loved the idea of spending that time with him. Amy felt as if a vice had clamped around her heart. She took a deep breath and then another to loosen up.

She hadn't fallen for him. She was just getting used to having Scott around.

She went back to her usual defense against emotion toward him. Business. "I don't have anything for you to do with the newspaper because I'm between issues. Maybe if you help me, we can go on that hike."

"I'm game. But you just said you didn't need help."

"Wedding help."

He took a step back. "What sort of wedding help?"

Amy laughed. "Don't worry. We're not looking for a substitute groom. We have a question about the marriage license, and we thought Micah could answer it."

"Do you need to have a marriage license in the state of Tennessee before you wed?"

"According to Bella and Paige, the only two among my close friends who are married, you do."

"Then I would be happy to help."

"We're in full spy mode here. Close the door when you enter to speak to Micah. No one else can be in the room. Not unless it's Greg or one of the people who you're certain is in on this. We can't let anything slip. Cassie is far too observant."

"Are you sure it's safe to talk in here?" he said in a suspicious voice. He dropped his volume a notch. "What if we're being . . . bugged?"

Amy grinned. "If someone has thought to bug my oh-so-boring newspaper office, they have far greater problems."

"Okay, I'll get right on the wedding license mission. Do you need me to do anything else?"

Did they? She did need to take care of cake flavor testing. "Do you know if Greg's working today?"

"He is. I think he said something about getting off at four this afternoon."

She explained about the cupcakes. "A taste test would probably be safest in his car. At home, Cassie could knock on his door and potentially overhear you. Especially if he left a window open. And this time of year is awesome for leaving windows open."

"I'll call him to set up a meeting."

"Before you do that, let me call Simone to make sure she can have another set of cupcakes ready. As to the other choices we're offering Cassie, I honestly don't think he will care about the colors, and he definitely can't see her wedding dress."

Scott got an impish—and adorable—expression.

Where did that thought come from?

"Could there possibly be two sets of these cupcakes? I may need samples so I understand the situation well and can report back correctly."

Amy laughed. "I hope Simone made enough. I'll call right now. No, wait. I can't call. That's against the rules." She paused. "But I'm asking about something I'm picking up today that Cassie will know about. That would be okay, wouldn't it?" She felt like the situation was spinning around her and becoming a complicated web.

Scott stared at her. "You do realize that this is a wedding and not an event about creating world peace?"

Amy took a deep breath and exhaled slowly. "You're right. It's just that I want the whole wedding to be perfect, and I don't want to be the one to blow the secret."

"It will be. You're doing a great job. All of you are. I've never seen anything like this, to be honest."

Amy picked up the phone and called Simone. When she answered, Amy said, "I'll be picking up those cupcakes for the tasting soon. I wondered if you could do another two sets for me to share with a couple of men I know."

Silence greeted her as Simone processed her words. Finally, she laughed. "I can see the need for that. I'd be happy to put together two more sets. I baked enough so that isn't a problem."

They ended the call. "Good news. I got you a sweet deal." Amy grinned. "I'll pick up enough for you two and drop them off here before I go to Cassie's house."

"Then I'm on my way to see a lawyer about a marriage

license. Words I hadn't expected to say today." Grinning, he left for his assignment.

～

With Scott now on assignment, the room felt empty. She pushed that thought out of her head because she didn't want to need anyone in the room with her. She was a one-woman show for the foreseeable future. And she ignored the voice that said it was Scott's presence she missed, not just another human's.

Amy checked her watch and saw she had an hour before she needed to be at Cassie's, so she gathered what she needed. Her digital recorder, a notebook and several pens, the fabric swatches, and the photo plan. A quick stop with Bella and then Simone would bring it all together. In short, she was a wedding planner today, a career she'd never anticipated and didn't particularly want. Amy put all those things in a tote bag she thought would also be large enough to hold the cupcakes and headed toward Bella's Brides.

When she arrived there, she found Bella busy with a bridal party, but her assistant April met Amy near the door and handed off a package to her with a questioning expression. Amy leaned closer and whispered, "It's for an article I'm writing. It's a secret, though."

April nodded. "That's what Bella said." Her confusion about the situation was apparent, but Amy couldn't explain it to her.

As Amy walked away, she thought about the current situation. She was now fully immersed in weddings. After her failed relationship, this would be laughable if it didn't come with so much stress.

She crossed the street to Simone's and went inside, thankfully finding the room empty of everyone except Simone. Even the door to Nick's kitchen next door was closed.

"I made sure I didn't have anyone else in here with me this

morning. I have found someone in town who is wonderful with decorating, and I'm training her. But not on the spy days." Simone grinned.

Amy couldn't help but smile back. "This is all very strange, isn't it?"

"Agreed, but we're going to make this happen for Cassie."

Simone set four plastic containers on the counter, each holding four cupcakes, with two decorated in shades of pink and yellow.

"Pretty!"

"Thank you. I wanted to do all of them in pink and yellow, but since those are Cassie's favorites, I thought it might tip her off. It would be helpful if you could take notes on the decor in addition to the flavors. Speaking of that, I think I have some she'll enjoy."

She tapped one container. "I labeled every flavor right above it. You have a raspberry cupcake with lemon frosting. There's white cake with lemon curd filling and raspberry frosting." She looked up at Amy. "Cassie loves the lemon raspberry combo, so I included options." She tapped the top of the container. "This one would be more difficult to do in her colors, but it's a chocolate cupcake with a toasted marshmallow frosting topped with crumbles of graham crackers."

"A s'mores cupcake!"

"Exactly. I have a feeling that will go over well with the guys."

"*I* love it."

"Last but certainly not least, because it's one of my personal favorites, is a chocolate cupcake with cream cheese filling and fudgy chocolate frosting."

Amy licked her lips. "They all sound fabulous. What if she doesn't like any of them, though? Do you have a *Plan B*?"

"I can always have more flavors, but we'd have to work to come up with a reason for you to be there again."

"You're right. Let's hope she chooses one of these."

Simone motioned to the end of the container with the raspberry-lemon duos. "I'm pretty sure we're going to have winners with these two." She shrugged. "But I've been wrong before. I was sure one couple would choose a strawberry filling for a cake based on everything they'd told me in advance and the paperwork I have all my couples fill out."

"Obviously, they didn't. What did they choose?"

"I'm still surprised by this one. Pralines and cream. The woman told me she didn't want a cake that was too sweet. But she chose what's basically pecans in crushed-up candy. And with chocolate frosting, no less."

"Is it hard to find flavors someone wants?" Amy wondered if her task was going to be more daunting than she'd first realized.

"Usually, it's simple." Simone snapped her fingers. "I listen, and I put the flavors in front of them. I know Cassie very well, and these are her favorite flavors. And the chocolate is for Greg because I've seen him eat a lot of chocolate cake."

Amy tucked the cupcakes into her tote bag. She'd need to get two of these to Scott. Avoiding texting after Mrs. Brantley's dire warnings, Amy called Scott instead.

"Amy?" He was justifiably surprised by her call since she had only texted him, never called.

"I wondered if you could come by the newspaper office." She checked her watch and picked up her pace when she saw she needed to arrive at Cassie's in the next ten minutes. "At about two." That would give her plenty of time for an interview that was sure to run long. They had a lot to talk about and cupcakes to eat.

"Sure. I'll meet you over there. Is this for the project we're working on?"

"Definitely. I have what we talked about earlier. I know you'll be able to help me with this."

"See you then."

She arrived at Cassie's house a couple of minutes early and went around to the back as everyone did in Two Hearts. She tapped on the screen door.

Cassie let her inside. "I'm excited about this new article. Even though you didn't have many subscribers when you started the paper, I think the first articles you did were helpful. The newspaper is doing better now, so we should see even bigger results."

Amy felt a moment of guilt because she wasn't here to help Cassie's business but instead to grill her for details about a wedding she wasn't expecting. Then she realized she'd be helping all the businesses she mentioned, which made her feel good. She wasn't just a spy—she was a spy with a purpose.

"Where do you want to sit? The kitchen table where we can have a cup of coffee? I have some cookies from Emmaline. Or the living room where it's more comfortable? We could even go into my office if you want more formality for an interview."

"I choose the kitchen. And I'll definitely take that cup of coffee, but you don't need to get the cookies out. Simone sent cake samples for you to test for her part of the article, so I have a snack for both of us." Amy pulled out the two containers and set them on the table.

Cassie stared at her sugary bounty. "I would have happily shared. You're leaving me with four whole cupcakes?"

"It is a bit much, isn't it?" Amy smiled. "Maybe you can have Bella come over later in the day. It seems baby likes sweets."

Cassie laughed. "I know she's trying to control that, but I have seen her with pie at Dinah's more than I usually would."

They sat down with coffee and forks.

"She must have chosen these colors because she knew you were coming here. They're my favorites."

Amy's heart threatened to beat out of her chest. "They are pretty."

Cassie seemed to have moved on from the colors to tasting,

so Amy willed her heartbeat to slow. Amy told her the first cupcake's flavor, and they each took a bite.

Amy sighed. "Mm. This is amazing. I love raspberry and lemon together." Remembering her job, she asked, "How about you, Cassie? And I want your own opinion. I know you're the wedding planner, but I also want this to have a personal touch."

Cassie savored the bite. "It's been one of my favorites forever, so I'm not surprised she sent that flavor. This one's the winner."

Amy laughed. "We better keep going. The next one is also raspberry and lemon."

Cassie raised an eyebrow as she stuck a fork into it and took a bite. "Oh my goodness!" she groaned around the bite. "This is probably the best thing I've ever tasted."

Amy had to agree. Simone was a master of flavors, and her cakes were always moist and wonderful. Amy got out her notepad and a pen. "I'd better take notes. I thought this would be simple, and I could say the first one would be the one everybody loves."

"It's never that easy with Simone. They'll all be amazing. But she outdid herself on the one with a lemon curd filling. It's such a bright pop of lemon with the raspberry." Cassie started to dip in her fork for another bite. Amy reached out and stopped her.

"We'd better wait and try all of them. Then you can go back for seconds."

"That's a good plan, or I may have so much sugar that I don't even want to taste the last one by the time we get there."

"The third one's a s'mores cupcake."

"Whenever there's a campfire, Greg is making s'mores, so this would be his pick. But I love chocolate too."

Amy had a hard time not saying anything or even making notes. Scott would take care of the Greg input.

"This cupcake is delicious. Simone toasted the marshmallow on top. And those graham cracker crumbs . . . This is one hundred percent a s'more. I can't believe how difficult she made this decision." They each drank a couple sips of coffee between bites. Amy pointed at the last one. "This one sounds crazy good. It's a chocolate cupcake with chocolate frosting and a cheesecake filling."

"Cheesecake? Simone's been holding out on me because I've never had this kind." They each put their fork in and took out a bite. Cassie closed her eyes, leaning back in her chair. "Oh, my goodness. Rich, dark chocolate with creaminess and a little tang from cheesecake. This is genius."

Cassie stared at the box in front of her. "And I'm supposed to choose *one* I love? Is that what everybody's going to do for the article?"

Amy quickly thought over her reply. "You're my first interview with the cupcakes. This is much more difficult than I expected. Why don't we choose two and call them the flavors of summer? How does that sound?"

"Still difficult." Cassie laughed. "I love them all. I would happily recommend any of these to a bride."

Amy hated to push in any way because she didn't want to give any signs to alert Cassie about their plans. "If I were to choose for my own wedding—not that I'm getting married anytime in the foreseeable future—I would pick the s'mores and the lemon curd."

Cassie laughed. "I know the article needs a choice." She bit her lip and stared at the baked good in front of her. "I think I would also pick the lemon curd one. And—ooh, this is hard. I love both the chocolate and s'mores. They're each a little bit different. I think maybe—ooh! I just don't know."

Grinning, Amy made a note. "That actually may be fun in the article. You nailed down the lemon between two that were similar, but the others were so awesome you couldn't choose."

"I like that. And it wasn't that there was anything wrong with the first lemon one. The second one edged it out slightly.

As a wedding planner, I might suggest either the chocolate or the s'mores and have a third flavor, something simple. Maybe white cake with vanilla frosting and sprinkles on top. Kids love plainer things like that. Some adults do too."

Amy made notes. "This is *exactly* what the article needs. Advice from an experienced wedding planner." And what the planners for Cassie's wedding needed even more.

"That would be lovely at any wedding." As Amy was about to ask about the decoration on the cupcakes, Cassie said, "And they're all pretty, but I think I'd personally avoid the one with the traditional rose on it. I prefer the other design. And I like the soft yellow and pink over the brighter version."

Perfect.

"What else do you have in store for us today? Cupcakes are going to be hard to top."

Amy had almost forgotten she had her other mission. "First, let's look at summery wedding dress sketches."

Cassie frowned. "But everyone will have already made plans for their summer weddings."

"It felt funny to mention fall or winter in an article when summer is just beginning. Do you know what I mean?" Amy thought she'd done an excellent job of subterfuge. In the end, maybe she had missed her calling and should look into espionage as a career.

"I see your point. As I think about it, wedding dresses can change somewhat by season, but someone might wear a sleeveless one in December or long sleeves in July."

"And you do get some elopements, don't you? People who come to you at the last minute for a wedding?"

"More than you would expect. Some people don't want the big fancy wedding with all the long planning involved. They just want a beautiful ceremony, and they don't want to wait. You're right. This could be great for bringing in business this summer."

Amy laughed. "Then here are Bella's sketches."

When Cassie saw the drawings her friend had done, she exclaimed, "These articles will be so much fun!"

Amy had to agree. The idea had been born out of a need to plan the wedding, but she had a feeling her readers would love this. It definitely would be something to put on her website that strangers could find and read. They may even need to do something like this seasonally.

Cassie flipped through the sketches. Bella had provided seven. "Just as with the cupcakes, I love everything Bella does. Going with the summer theme, I think I'd avoid the ball gown because that's too much fabric for a hot day, and we have a lot of people who come to Two Hearts for an outdoor wedding." She pushed aside the mermaid-style dress too.

"Not that one either?"

Cassie frowned and seemed distressed for the first time since they'd been talking. "I had that style before. I must tell you, it wasn't easy riding a motorcycle wearing that." Her smile returned. "I choose this one as a favorite." She tapped a fit and flare. It had narrow straps, a fitted bodice to the waist, and then it flared out to a flowing skirt. "That would be beautiful for a summer wedding."

"Can I say it's your personal favorite and not just the wedding planner speaking?" Amy held her breath, waiting for the reply. She hoped she hadn't pushed too much.

"Definitely my choice. And the same one I'd choose as the planner. Bella went over and above with these."

Amy agreed. And Cassie would be stunning in that design.

CHAPTER TWENTY-FOUR

Scott waited outside the newspaper office. Amy's earlier nervousness about their spy-like operation made him want to get off the sidewalk where someone might see him. And that was ridiculous. Anyone who saw him here would assume he was dating Amy.

Not that he'd mind that. He had to keep reminding himself that a vacation romance wasn't what he wanted. Amy deserved better than that.

She ran around the corner toward him. "Sorry I'm late! The interview with Cassie took longer than I expected." She unlocked the door.

Once she'd closed it behind them, he asked, "Do you think Cassie suspected anything?"

Amy grabbed his arm, bouncing on her feet.

Scott grinned at her contagious excitement and joy.

"I'm sure she didn't. And she gave me the answers we needed. I have flavors, colors, and approval of the dress and wedding photo ideas!" She glanced toward the front window and motioned him over to his desk. "I think we're in the clear for the cupcake handoff to Greg." Amy glanced back at the door.

"I wonder if I should lock that first so no one will walk in on us."

Scott fought laughter because she was completely serious. "Since I've only seen a few people walk in here, I'm sure we're fine." He didn't mention that the window would still be uncovered, anyway.

Amy opened the big side drawer on the old desk. Two clear plastic containers with four cupcakes each sat inside. She stood. "I just realized that I don't have anything for you to carry them in."

"What did you carry them in earlier? I'll use that."

Amy pointed to a fabric bag on her desk. "I don't think you want to carry this pink flowered tote."

He grimaced. "Not a lot of men of my acquaintance would."

"We also cannot have you going to Greg openly carrying the same cupcakes. That could blow this whole thing wide open."

Scott glanced around the room. "I guess I could wrap them in newspaper, but that would look strange too." Then his gaze landed on the pile of boxes. "Amy, could you unpack one of the smallest boxes? Then it would look like I was giving something to Greg. When we get to his car, I could casually put it in the trunk. We'll drive to someplace outside of the town to eat cupcakes."

Amy grinned, and a dimple appeared in her cheek.

Adorable.

Get that thought out of your head!

She'd had her heart broken by Logan. He didn't want to add even more heartache when he left. They had to be friends but no more.

He helped her move the boxes around to reach one that might work. She cut through the tape on a box and started unloading it, stacking the books on the pile of boxes beside her. "This project is getting more and more complicated, isn't it?"

"It's a good thing you chose a date with only three weeks' notice. I can't imagine six months of this."

"I agree. Cassie works on weddings sometimes a year or more in advance." Amy shuddered. "I wouldn't want to think about all these details for that long."

She paused with a book halfway to the pile. "Wow."

"Why *wow*?"

Amy blushed. "I didn't realize I'd said that out loud." She set the book down and continued her work without giving an answer. A moment later, she said, "Empty," as she picked up the box and handed it to him. He set the cupcakes in the box, but they only filled about a tenth of it. He'd have to be careful to keep the box upright and the cupcakes intact. Each one had been beautifully decorated.

Amy continued, still seeming to avoid his question. "I used to think a wedding was the most romantic thing in the world. That the longer I could plan it and the more involved it was, the better. But after living here in wedding town and now being part of Cassie's wedding myself, I think I'm all for a small wedding or eloping."

"I agree. I wouldn't want to do this for my own wedding." An image of him proposing to Amy came to mind, but he knew that had to be because he'd already done that twice. "To whoever that is in the far, far future."

When she tensed up and didn't smile at his comment, he wondered if he'd put his foot in it again. She was very sensitive about the subject of weddings and marriage. "Not that there's anything wrong with wedding planning. I think it's more of a girl thing than a guy thing."

Amy's shoulders relaxed. "Very true. I hate to admit it, but I even subscribed to a couple of bridal magazines. Whoever moved into my apartment is probably getting those now because I didn't forward them here."

That guy really had been a jerk to her. Scott would never

treat a woman that way. Especially not Amy. She deserved better. Scott went over to the stack of books from the box and flipped through them. "You have quite a variety just in this one box. I see a couple of romance novels. A few mysteries. Here's a motivational book and one about . . ." He looked up at her with a book about the perfect wedding on a budget in his hand.

"What?" She peered over his shoulder to look at the title. Then she grabbed it and threw it in the trash with a vengeance.

"Are you sure you want to get rid of a book about weddings in a town that loves them? I'll bet you could find someone who would pay for that."

She glared at the trash can, then with a sigh, she reached in and pulled the book out. "You may be right. No dents or scratches." She set it down gently on the stack and walked away, giving it one last glare as she did.

Scott chuckled at her expression. As soon as he did, he forced a serious expression. "Sorry. It's kind of funny."

Amy looked at the book and the trash can. Then she smiled, and he felt as if he'd been saved. "That's what made me say, wow. I thought I'd pitched all of those books. It was a stupid knee-jerk reaction." She focused on the box. "You'd better get out of here with these cupcakes. I wouldn't want you to miss Greg today because I doubt they'll taste as good tomorrow. Although I have had some of Simone's day-old baked goods, and they're still pretty fabulous."

She glanced over at her tote bag. "In fact, I have leftovers from today in there that I may be munching on tomorrow." Amy looked into the box he'd packed. She scurried away and returned with forks and napkins from the backroom. Finally, she grabbed a newspaper off a stack, crumpled it up, and stuffed it around the plastic containers. "Much better." He loved how she did everything with purpose and care.

"Maybe you should get coffee to go from Dinah's. These will be extra sweet if you don't have anything to drink between each flavor. Greg has to take at least one bite of all four. Don't let him gobble up the first one and ignore the others. I had to rein Cassie in."

"I have been known to eat a few donuts in one sitting, and I did have two slices of pie at Dinah's one day because I couldn't bring myself to choose. But this is a lot of cupcake."

She grinned. "Are you saying four cupcakes are doable for you or that you're going to have leftovers?"

"Definitely leftovers. Do you want to tell me which ones Cassie favored?"

Amy chewed on her lip for a moment. "I don't think I should. Don't you think that would skew his answer?"

"Knowing Greg as well as I do, I think he'll support whatever Cassie chooses for this wedding. He just wants to marry her."

"I want Greg to give his honest opinion so that he's represented at the wedding, but you're right." She pushed the newspaper in the box to the side so he could see the containers. "They're labeled on top. The two lemon raspberry ones were similar, but there was a clear winner with Cassie. The one with the lemon curd in the middle." She pointed. "She couldn't pick between the chocolate cupcakes. If Greg favors one of those, we can narrow it down that way. She also suggested the addition of a plain white one with sprinkles for kids." Amy shrugged. "Maybe we'll just have a bunch of cupcake flavors. I don't know if that's a hassle for Simone or it's just another day in the office."

Scott picked up the box. "I think this is probably the easiest wedding Simone has ever done. The bride isn't involved. The mother of the bride isn't directing anything. That alone sounds like a big win to me from everything I hear."

"I met her once and have to agree. She is a little intense."

Scott hesitated for a moment. He should just leave, but as foolish as it was with his short timeline here, he didn't want to walk away without plans for the next time he'd see her. "Are you doing anything special for dinner tonight?"

Amy stared up at him, this time without the deer-in-the-headlights expression. She seemed pleased by the offer. "I'm not. And I'll need something with a lot of protein in it to counteract all the sugar I consumed today. Maybe with some healthy veggies and fiber thrown in. I seem to have had cupcakes for lunch."

He grinned. "What if I stop by about five o'clock? We can head out to get a bite to eat?" He held his breath as he waited for her reply.

She seemed to be considering his offer. "I know I'd wanted to avoid even a hint of us being a couple—" She paused, and he wondered what she was thinking. "Now that we're working together on the wedding, and you're the go-between, there's a solid reason for our friends to see us together."

Did that mean she wanted to spend time with him, or was it only tied to the wedding? He waited, hoping she'd say more. As much as he'd thought he didn't want a relationship here, he knew he really did.

She added, "Dinner is a great idea. Let's make the connection obvious so no one suspects we're working on something together."

And his excitement faded. Amy wasn't willing to eat with him because she was interested in dating him. She was doing this to strengthen their cover story.

Scott walked into the small sheriff's department office with the box in his arms. He'd tucked the coffee from Dinah's inside with newspaper keeping it upright. Right now, he felt like a fool. He belonged behind a computer, not in a spy thriller.

He found Greg seated at his desk. The clerk tried to stop him, but Greg waved him back.

"He's okay, Maryanne."

Scott hovered next to Greg with the box, searching for a place to set it down on a desk filled with paperwork and files, not finding one. "I thought maybe you'd be going out for a drive around town before you ended your work day."

Greg looked at him with a confused expression. "I did earlier. What's in the box?"

This wasn't going well. "It has stuff from the newspaper office."

Scott could see the wheels turning in his friend's mind. Finally, everything clicked into place. Greg stood. "You're right. I should do another round through town. Let's put that in the trunk. And since you're here, do you want to ride around with me? It's been a while."

Scott hid a smile. They'd hung out together yesterday. "Let's do that."

When they got to the car, Greg motioned toward the back seat. "Would this box be good here?"

"It may be better there than the trunk." At least they could easily access it then.

They drove away from the office together. Thirty seconds into the trip, Greg asked, "What's in there?" He gestured toward the back seat.

"I brought you cupcake samples for the wedding."

Greg nodded slowly. "You aren't putting this completely on me, are you?" The big bad cop had terror written all over his face.

Scott laughed. "Don't worry. The ladies are smart enough not to ask you to make major decisions. You'd be riddled with guilt if you chose something Cassie disliked. Your fiancée has already tasted the cupcakes and put in her vote. They want your vote too."

"Cupcakes plural? I like that idea. I grabbed a sandwich at the diner hours ago, so I'm ready for a snack."

"Four cupcakes."

"It's a tough job, but someone has to do it." Greg took a left, and they curved around the lake, passing Paige and CJ's pink house and continuing around the lake, the water occasionally peeking through dense brush and trees.

It felt like they were miles from town instead of a block or two. "I've never been out here."

"Long before I was born, this was a popular area. There's an old inn around the bend. No one comes out here now."

Greg slowed the car, and they turned into a barely passable driveway. He wound along what was little more than a wide path at this point, with limbs brushing the sides of his car, and stopped. "Bring out the samples. I wish I'd known to grab some coffee to go with it." Greg said.

"Amy thought of it. I went to Dinah's on the way to your office."

"Smart woman."

"She is that and more."

Greg turned to him with a smirk.

"Don't start. I've just been impressed by her. And before you add a comment, I'm leaving town soon." Scott leaned over the backseat and reached into the box, pulling out the items one by one and passing them to Greg.

"Forks and napkins too. *Your Amy* is amazing."

"Don't start," Scott warned again.

When Greg chuckled, Scott rolled his eyes.

"She said to begin with the raspberry lemon cupcakes and leave the chocolate for last. She didn't want to overwhelm our taste buds early on."

Greg scooped out a forkful of the assigned cupcake. "I doubt that my taste buds care, but we'll do this as instructed."

Scott did his best to not make comments before Greg did to influence him, even though it was hard not to sigh with happiness at the first bite.

After the first cupcake, Greg said, "This is amazing. Plus,

every time Simone makes something with lemon and raspberry, Cassie says it's wonderful." He leaned down to inhale the scent of the next one. "This also smells like raspberry." He dug his fork in.

"Wow. Even better. Definitely a keeper for the wedding."

Scott checked the label. "That's the one Cassie chose."

"Excellent. We're on the right track."

They tried the two chocolate ones.

"Now, these are hard to choose between."

Scott laughed. "It's my understanding that Cassie couldn't. She picked the one with the lemon filling and said either of the two chocolates would work. She also suggested a plain white one for kids. Do you agree?"

"One hundred percent. Got to love that woman."

Scott grinned. "We get to keep the rest of these to snack on later."

Greg stared at the baked goods in front of him. "The problem is that I can't take them back to the office, and I can't leave them in the car in case Cassie sees them. I'd better eat what I want now."

Scott hadn't considered that. "I can't take mine to your mother's house, either, because Cassie visits so often. I'd have to hope she wasn't there. I think I'm in the same boat as you. Let's eat."

After a few minutes of silent cupcake consumption, Greg asked, "So, what's going on with you and Amy?"

Scott inhaled cupcake. Coughing, he reached for the cup of coffee beside him. "What do you mean?"

Greg turned toward Scott with an expression he couldn't figure out. "I know we're guys, and we don't do this touchy-feely, warm-and-fuzzy kind of thing, but you have an expression that reminds me of myself with Cassie when we first met."

Scott shook his head. "I think you're reading this wrong.

Amy and I have become friends. I'm the male courier in this weird espionage game we seem to be playing about your wedding."

"You're at her office almost every day. Why?"

Scott didn't want to say anything bad about Greg's mother.

"I know that Mom has you scheduled within an inch of your life, and you're running from that."

Scott turned to Greg and raised an eyebrow.

"She's been my mother for decades. I know how she is. But she means well. She wants you to have the best experience possible in Two Hearts."

"I know that. I'm just not used to having anyone control my schedule. And beyond that, she keeps wanting me to do things with the wedding stuff in this town."

Greg laughed. "The disgust in your voice at wedding stuff says it all, doesn't it? But seriously, are you sure there isn't more between you and Amy? I noticed the two of you driving out of town together the other day."

He was just starting to admit to himself that he might want more. Did he want to admit it to somebody else? "Maybe I'm interested in her beyond friendship."

"Aha! I thought so. I'm going to give you one small piece of advice, and then we can go back to being two guys sitting in a car stuffing ourselves with cupcakes with no more deep discussions of romance."

"That's a hard-to-pass-up deal," Scott said with a grin. "What's your advice?"

"If it starts to feel serious, do something about it. Don't let her get away."

"I'm stuck right now proposing to the woman over and over."

Greg chuckled. "That has to be the funniest thing I've heard. You had no interest in dating her, but you had to propose."

"You should have seen her when the goat butted her from

behind, and she flew through the air at the last one." Scott chuckled.

"Are there pictures of this? And the real question—is she going to publish them?"

"There are, but I'm not sure if she'll put any of them in the newspaper."

They continued eating cupcakes for another ten minutes in silence, just as Greg had promised. Unfortunately, the silence gave Scott time to think about what they'd discussed. He *was* interested in Amy. But she was still hung up on that loser she'd been dating before she moved here. Throwing that book in the trash earlier today had brought that point home.

CHAPTER TWENTY-FIVE

*N*ick, Simone's fiancé and a respected Nashville restaurant owner, surprised Amy with a visit to the newspaper the next morning.

"Simone offered for us to provide the food for the wedding next weekend. I had a menu in mind, but then Simone told me about the article."

"Do you have something to add? Or did we make a mistake?" She really hoped he hadn't spotted a flaw in the plan. There were probably massive holes in it, enough to drive a dump truck through.

"The only flaw is that I wasn't invited to be part of the article, and I'd love to get some feedback on the menu."

That had been an oversight on their part. "I can definitely include you in the article." In case he hadn't gotten the details from Simone, Amy explained their cover story.

Nick grinned. "That's genius. Then yes, I would like to be part of it. We can call my ideas appetizers for a summer wedding. In fact, I like that. Having the theme narrows down choices and helps me with the menu."

"The appetizers should go well with the cupcakes, don't you

think?" Amy asked. She knew nothing about event planning, but this made sense to her.

He nodded. "That won't be a problem. I've tasted the cupcakes, and they'll be easy to pair with savory food. And no matter which direction Cassie and Greg go in their selection, it's a win. Of course, I love everything my fiancée bakes." He leaned closer. "I'm supposed to."

Amy laughed. "That's definitely a good trait when you've got a cake maker and a chef together. When do you want to do this, Nick? The wedding is coming up soon, and I should probably get this article written in case Cassie asks about it."

He frowned as he stared straight ahead for a moment. "My schedule is open today, so I could do this quickly. A meal of appetizers in my commercial kitchen. Greg and Cassie, Paige and CJ, Bella and Micah, and you, of course. I know I've seen you with Scott. Do you want to bring him?"

People thought she was dating Scott. She'd pushed that intentionally yesterday, but it felt both odd and good to have them connected in her friends' minds. "He's just a friend. But he's deep in the heart of this wedding, so sure, we can invite him. And don't forget Simone."

He grinned. "I never forget about Simone. I guess I'd better get cooking. And if Simone isn't on a cake deadline, I'll reel her in to help. Tell everyone 6:00 p.m."

When the door closed behind him, Amy realized she'd just been nominated to contact everyone.

And that's when it hit her that she hadn't done the invitations for the wedding yet. Amy sat up straight in her chair and gasped. "Oh no! Oh no! Oh no!" They were now a week away from the day of the wedding.

With everything else going on, she'd forgotten about the invitations, and Scott hadn't brought them up. She'd handed the invitation samples to Bella ages ago. With everything else going on, she'd forgotten about them. She grabbed her phone and called Scott. "I need your help ASAP. What are you doing today?"

"I'm taking a long walk through town with Cookie. I left right after breakfast."

"What *was* planned for you today?"

"I was going to watch Paige at a wedding photo shoot."

Amy was sure there wasn't a wedding today. "Wedding?"

"In *Nashville*." He said the word with emphasis. "I was supposed to drive with her to the city where she is currently photographing a midweek morning wedding."

Amy smiled so widely her cheeks hurt. "That definitely wouldn't be my idea of a good time." Remembering why she'd called, she added, "Bring your laptop."

"I'll drop off the dog and be at the newspaper office in about fifteen minutes. See you then."

Her heart leaped in her chest when he said those words. She was looking forward to seeing him. Her heart needed to understand that Scott would be leaving soon and would not be looking back.

As to the invitations, they'd have to get them out today. Amy spent the time while she waited for Scott going through online invitation ideas, coming up with what she thought was a fairly good selection by the time Scott came through the door.

"What's the crisis? Because it feels like there is one."

"I forgot about the invitations."

She was certain his expression mirrored her own earlier. "How did we manage that? I guess it was all of the behind the scenes espionage, but I don't normally forget important things."

"Neither do I."

"Are we in trouble?"

"Definitely. But at least there aren't wedding police."

"Actually, there are. Everyone involved in this wedding is part of the Two Hearts wedding police force. So, I repeat, are we in trouble?"

Amy chewed on her lip. "Let's finish this project today and call it a win. Maybe it's for the best because fewer people will spill the news if they have just a week. Of course, on the downside, fewer people may come because it's short notice."

Scott sat at his desk and opened up his laptop.

Over a week ago, Mrs. Brantley suggested that they set up an email address to be used only for this list of guest email addresses. They had but that alone caused part of this problem because Amy had never thought to check the new account. She just hoped that email had arrived. He brought up that account, opened the one message in it, and Amy let out a breath.

Scott's thoughts mirrored her own. "The addresses are here, so we have everything we need. Except for the actual invitation to use."

Yet one more decision she had to make.

Scott tapped away on his keyboard as he went through the list and seemed to be organizing it.

"Do you go everywhere with your computer?"

"I only have one here. I usually have three monitors on my desk at work. And multiple computers in my house. For me, this is traveling light."

A geek was never without a computer. He didn't look or act like TV and movie versions of a geek—no dated clothes, too short pants, white socks, or pocket protector—but he truly was one. She forwarded him links to the wedding invitations. As soon as they arrived and he flipped through them, she asked, "Which one do you think we should base their invitation on, or do you think we ought to mix a couple of them together?"

He spun on his chair to face her. "Did you actually ask *me* for input on a wedding invitation?"

"Yes. I'm no more of an expert than you are. I have no idea what they should look like. I mean, I've received wedding invitations from friends and relatives in the past, but they've usually been the fancy ones on heavy cardstock and often with elegant calligraphy or using a formal font. What do we do for something digital?"

He pondered her question for a moment. "We have two options. We can go ahead and choose whatever we believe is best. Or we can put together several mock-ups, and you can walk around getting opinions. That will, of course, shine a light on the fact that they weren't sent earlier."

"More than that, it will take time we don't have. I'd rather just send them out, but I'm not sure I know what would be best."

"Simone knows cakes. Bella knows wedding dresses. Everybody has their own specialty. The town doesn't have anyone who's an expert with invitations. Maybe that could be you."

She thought about the idea. "I spend a lot of time with graphic design because of the newspaper. You're great at design. Maybe, between the two of us, we *can* figure this out." She leaned over his shoulder. "All the options I bookmarked are beautiful. We know the colors Cassie chose—soft yellow and pink. Why not use those colors with something similar to one of these?"

They worked together on the invitation for about an hour, coming up with several options. Finally, Amy said, "I know I talked big earlier, but I'm not willing to make this decision on my own. They're all going to know when these invitations go out because people will start sending in RSVPs. The biggest thing we need all over this invitation and in big letters at the top is, *This is a surprise.*"

Scott changed the text as she'd asked.

Amy sighed with frustration. "I was wrong. That takes away some of the elegance. This is the biggest flaw in our plan. Any one of these people could blow it. Can you save those to show the others?"

"Sure." He shrugged one shoulder. "Do you want to ask everyone? And do you need a legitimate excuse for going from place to place?" He closed his computer and waited for her reply.

"I'm doing additional research for my article?"

"But why am I tagging along?"

An idea came to her, but she knew she'd turn bright red when she said it aloud. Amy cleared her throat. "Because you want to spend time with me?" She was coming to realize that she wanted to spend as much time with him as she could before he left.

Scott stared at her, an expression on his face she couldn't read. "I like that. Let's run with it." He stood and put the computer back in his backpack, slipping the straps over his shoulders. "We may as well go now."

Before they left, Amy realized she had a mission, anyway. She was in charge of contacting everyone about Nick's event tonight.

"Hang on a sec." She brought up Cassie on her phone. When her friend answered, she said, "Hey, Nick stopped by this morning. We'd left him out of the article, but he wants to be in with appetizers for a summer wedding."

"That's a great idea! We never should have left out the food." Amy could hear the enthusiasm in Cassie's voice.

"Agreed. But this gets even better. He wants the whole group of us to come to his kitchen for a tasting tonight at 6:00. Can you make it?"

"I would rearrange my schedule to eat Nick's food. Of course, I'll be there. And I'll call Greg to make sure he can come. I know he's not working tonight."

Amy hadn't considered that, and she should have. What was distracting her so much from being orderly and in control? "I'll get the word around to everybody else. I need to work on the article more, anyway. Research."

"Is everything okay, Amy? You sound a little . . . nervous."

Amy closed her eyes and took a deep breath. Then she said

the first thing that came into her mind to push Cassie off the scent. "Scott will be hanging out with me today."

Cassie quickly asked, "And he's there with you right now?"

"Yes."

She laughed. "I'll see the two of you tonight then." Still laughing, she hung up the phone.

Now, everyone would think she was interested in Scott. He stood silently watching her. "You heard all of that, didn't you?"

He nodded.

"I had to come up with something in a hurry."

He didn't say anything for a second. "We'd better get going. I guess I'm having appetizers for dinner?"

"I hope you don't mind being my . . . date."

"Not at all."

Whew! "And if you haven't had Nick's cooking before, you're in for a treat."

Simone was decorating a baby shower cake when they walked in. Amy didn't think anything could be cuter than a cake decorated with sunflowers and baby booties.

Amy explained why she was there. Simone took a look at the pictures and pointed to the one Scott and Amy had both preferred.

Bella chose the same one, but not until after she'd asked questions. "Aren't we cutting things a little close on this?"

Amy nodded. "I'm going to be honest and say I forgot about this."

Bella said, "It's partly my fault. I'd wondered about the invitations but didn't mention them. This can't all be on you, Amy. You have the article and sneaking around to coordinate, as well. Don't worry." Bella checked her watch. "I'd better get ready for my next appointment. I don't move as quickly as I used to."

"We're on our way out."

Bella walked them to the door. "You know, in the end, it may be better to give guests shorter notice. People can come or not.

Even if we'd given them another week, that probably wouldn't change their availability much. And this is one less week for someone to goof up and tell Cassie."

"That's what I thought. But hearing you say that makes me feel a lot better." As she had with the others, she told Bella about the dinner.

"The three of us will be there." She put her hand on her stomach. "I've been *so* hungry lately."

They found Paige at her studio, adjusting a backdrop. She agreed with everyone's choice of invitation but stopped them as they were leaving. "I'm still waiting to see goat photos in the paper." She grinned.

Amy laughed. "Your photos were great, but I could barely look at the ones with the goats." She paused as she thought about that day. "Enough time has passed, though, that I'm feeling more charitable toward Bernie. Once this wedding is over, I may have to do an article on him and his four-legged friends. My readers loved everything I wrote about Mabel."

"I'm sure Michelle would be happy to have them featured." Paige pointed to her camera. "And I'm willing to take more photos of them. They really are cute."

She had thought the goats were cute—before she'd gone flying. "Bernie's an adorable menace. Okay, let's go ahead and do that next week. But now, we'd better get going."

Paige called out, "See the *two* of you tonight," as they exited. She'd put a bit too much emphasis on the word "two."

As they went down the sidewalk to the catering kitchen Nick had built next to Simone's bakery to give him his headcount for the evening, Scott said, "I noticed that none of your friends were surprised to see me with you, and yet you only decided to be seen with me on purpose last night and mentioned it to Cassie less than an hour ago."

Amy felt her face heat. "Everyone had seen us together anyway, so staying away from each other was pointless. I think that horse has left the barn." She used an expression her grandma had used when she was young.

"I get your point. Everyone thinks we're a couple, don't they? I got grilled by Greg yesterday."

Amy gasped. If the guys were doing it, what were the women thinking?

"I decided none of that mattered. What we think is our own business."

Yet one more reason to like this man. Even though they weren't dating.

Back at the newspaper office, Amy worked on the wedding article, and Scott worked on getting the invitations out. She rubbed her shoulder when it tensed from the combination of wedding planning stress and sitting.

Scott surprised her less than a half hour later when he said, "Done."

"What do you mean done? You haven't been working on the invitations very long."

"Once the invitation was chosen, there wasn't much left to do. Mrs. Brantley did the hard work with assembling the email addresses."

Amy pushed back from her desk. "Then I'm ready for a break. I didn't expect to finish this article today, especially with the invitation and dinner surprise. I'd like to take some treats to Nosey. And I'll get a few bananas for Mrs. Robinson. She seemed to enjoy those when I brought them before."

"Nosey is the rabbit we rescued?"

Amy nodded as she closed her computer. "I've become friends with a rabbit."

"Friends? With a rabbit?"

When she realized what she'd said, she turned to him. "He

doesn't like everyone, but he apparently likes me. I guess he runs and hides when it's somebody he doesn't know. Mrs. Robinson is all alone from midafternoon to the next morning when someone picks her up to return to Dinah's, where she stays for both breakfast and lunch. Since I found out about that, I've been buying herbs I know Nosey likes and dropping them off." She grabbed her purse and looked around to see if she needed to take anything else with her.

"I'll go along." Scott closed his laptop and put it in his backpack.

Mrs. Robinson's question about whether or not she had a young man in her life popped into Amy's head. When someone reached ninety-seven years old, they seemed to lose whatever filter they had. She just hoped Mrs. Robinson wouldn't say anything embarrassing. Amy couldn't find a way to tell Scott he couldn't come when they'd be going together to Nick's appetizer party in a couple of hours.

Outside, Amy started toward her car, and Scott walked toward his truck. Then they both stopped and turned to face each other.

Amy chuckled. "Which one of us is driving?"

"Why don't we both drive to your house where you can drop off your car. Then I can bring you home after dinner."

One more thing that made this feel a lot like a date. Her time with Scott had an increasing number of those moments.

Ten minutes later, they'd left her car at her brother's house and were having a very domestic moment at the grocery store together. Scott grabbed a jar of peanut butter for himself, telling Amy he enjoyed peanut butter on toast in the morning, and Mrs. Brantley didn't have any. If his host had known, Amy was certain it would have appeared in the cupboard within hours. She had to hand it to Scott for not bothering her with it. Amy grabbed parsley and bananas to take to Mrs. Robinson and bagels for her own breakfast. She'd have to remember to remove them from Scott's car.

Walking side by side up to the cash register, they passed two older ladies she knew from church but couldn't recall their names. "I don't recognize your date, Amy," one said as she passed. "Is this a boyfriend you brought with you when you moved here?"

As Amy tried to reply with her jaw wide open in shock, Scott said, "I'm visiting my friend Greg Brantley. Amy and I were just in the grocery store at the same time."

One of the women got a shrewd expression on her face as she looked at the two of them. "If it looks like a skunk and smells like a skunk, it's a skunk." With that, she turned and left.

Scott watched her go. "Do you know—"

"No idea. I hadn't noticed that either of us needed to bathe."

They made their way to the cash register, and as they were paying, she asked the woman if she knew what the expression meant.

"Sure do. It means that if it looks like it's something, it is. It doesn't matter if you tell somebody it's not."

Amy and Scott whipped around to look at each other, realizing the woman had been talking about their relationship.

Amy said, "I know some of the ladies enjoy spreading gossip around town."

The clerk sniffed. "It isn't gossip if it's sharing information about a fellow resident. Think of it like a telephone line that goes around the town communicating important things." The woman said it with such conviction that Amy believed for a moment that this was helpful. Then she realized it was still gossip.

"So does the woman who just left here participate in this service?"

The clerk stared at her for a few seconds, then started laughing, doubling over with her face turning bright red. She gasped for air. "I thought you were funning me for a second. Anything she knows will be spread around this town within three minutes. Maybe less."

Amy had decided yesterday that she didn't care as much what others thought of her relationship with Scott, but now she'd forever be connected to Scott in the town's eyes. He'd be long gone, and they'd ask about the handsome man she'd dated. Then again, did it really matter? He wouldn't care, though, because he'd be leaving soon. Her heart sank a little more than she thought it should.

As they drove from the grocery store to Mrs. Robinson's, Scott said, "I don't think the potential gossip about us matters. Do you?"

"Your thoughts echo my own. It doesn't." She thought about it for another few seconds before adding, "But it would be nice not to have everybody talking about us. Do you know what I mean?"

"Completely. There's good and bad in a small town and a big city. In the city, very few people care."

"That's true. I lived in an apartment in Denver for almost a year, and I didn't know who my next door neighbor was other than by sight because I'd passed his door when he stepped out to pay for pizza delivery. Here, everybody knows everybody."

Scott grinned. "But you heard what the clerk said. It's just information."

"If her words were true, then why does the juiciest *information* get the most attention?" she wondered aloud.

He laughed as they pulled up to Mrs. Robinson's house. "Good point. Should I wait in the car while you go in?"

Amy hated to have him do that. Leaving him behind seemed rude. Besides, Mrs. Robinson would probably be happy to have another person visit her. "Come on in with me. Let's see how Nosey feels about you."

She knocked on the door and, as always, heard, "Come in."

And as always, it unnerved her that Mrs. Robinson was inviting people in without knowing who they were. She pushed the door open and stood in the open entry for a moment. "Mrs. Robinson, it's me, Amy. And I brought a friend."

"Come in! Come in! I know Nosey is going to be thrilled to see you. Not that I'm not thrilled too."

Amy walked in with Scott behind her and went over to Nosey's bed. He hopped out of it when he spotted her, and she knelt to give him some fresh parsley. As he snacked, she ran her hand down his soft fur. "Could anything be softer than a rabbit?"

"This is mighty interesting. Nosey doesn't seem to be afraid of you either, young man."

"I'm Scott Miller, ma'am."

"Amy said she didn't have a young man."

This time, his face turned bright red. Amy had been prepared.

"We're just friends. We're going to a dinner with some friends tonight."

"When it looks like a skunk and smells like a skunk, it's a skunk."

Amy and Scott both grinned.

"We've heard that twice today," Amy admitted.

"That's probably because people don't believe your words. They're going with their eyes."

Amy turned to look at Scott. "He's just a friend, ma'am. He's visiting Greg Brantley. They knew each other back in Chicago."

"Uh-huh. Why don't you kneel down, Scott, to see if Nosey will allow you to pet him?"

Scott stared down at the rabbit. "I'm more of a dog or cat person."

"He's sweet. See?" Amy rubbed her hand down the rabbit's back again.

Scott knelt and did the same. "He does seem like a nice rabbit."

Mrs. Robinson sounded happy when she said, "He likes both of you. That's quite nice."

Amy ignored the comment, which hinted at matchmaking. "We don't have time to stay for long today. I got you some bananas that look like they'll probably be ready to eat tomorrow."

"Thank you. You've been a sweetheart to me. Could you stop by tomorrow afternoon? There's something I want to talk to you about."

Amy stood. "Is anything wrong?"

"I think everything's going to be great." She wore a satisfied smile.

They left with Amy wondering what Mrs. Robinson wanted to talk to her about. The older woman had talked about moving in with her son, but Amy wouldn't have anything to do with that. Randi, the local real estate agent, would take care of any real estate transactions when her new friend sold her home.

Scott and Amy went back out to his truck. Driving away, he asked, "Is it common for her to ask you to return the next day?"

Amy shook her head, "I've only known her since we rescued Nosey, but she's never asked me to return and especially not at a specific time. I hope everything's okay."

Tonight, she'd focus on having fun with friends and enjoying delicious food. In between being careful and sneaky and making sure she didn't say the wrong thing.

CHAPTER TWENTY-SIX

When Scott pulled onto Main Street, he felt a twinge of nervousness. The two of them had been invited as a couple. He knew Amy would have fought against that as few as two days ago, but last night, she'd loosened up. He didn't dare hope it was because she was interested in him.

He had to admit that he was more than a little interested in her. He had only a handful of days left to win her over. Then reason took over, and he asked himself if he should try. He'd be leaving town, and this was a woman with strong roots in Two Hearts, roots that were growing deeper every day. His entire life had been in the Chicago area.

They ended up being the second couple to arrive. Everyone milled around, talking, the volume of laughter and conversation increasing as each couple joined them. Bella and Micah arrived last and filled out the guest list.

Nick took charge of the chaotic situation. "Everyone!" he called out. "I have eight appetizers for you to test. I want your opinions on all of them. And if you think something needs to be changed a bit, tell me that too. I want to come up with a top-notch list for summer weddings. Maybe we can catch some of those elopements that will take place in the next few months. Right, Cassie?"

Cassie grinned. "I'm happy to pack the schedule with last-minute weddings."

Paige snapped photos of the food before they started eating, so Scott knew Amy would have good photos for the article.

Halfway through the tasting, Amy's hand brushed his. He wasn't sure if it had been an accident, but he rubbed his hand over hers. She stilled but didn't move away. The moment was broken when Nick announced the next appetizer.

He was sure that melted brie topped with what looked like strawberry preserves would be delicious, but he was so distracted with Amy at his side that he wasn't able to give an opinion as everyone around gave enthusiastic reviews. Scott took a bite. "This is really good."

After sampling six options and Cassie raving over all but one that Scott knew would be nixed from the menu, Greg said, "That was almost enough for dinner, but not quite. Would there be anything else at an actual wedding?" Greg asked.

Everyone but Cassie felt the undercurrent of his question. He really meant, would that be enough at his own wedding?

"You each only had one. At a normal event, we'd portion at least two per person."

Cassie spoke up, "I usually up that to two and a half each per person. That seems to round out for the people who don't want to eat much and those who eat more."

Amy asked, "Could I put that statistic in the article? It might be interesting to people. I can quote you saying it, Cassie."

"Please do. I'll see if I can come up with another tip or two about appetizers for the article."

"Perfect. I'm going to finish writing it in the next few days. You've all given me so much great information that I may need to turn it into a series of articles."

Nick brought the moment back to the food. "Now that you've all tasted one, there are more. Please come back for seconds." He turned toward Greg with a smirk. "I wouldn't want you leaving my establishment hungry."

After the laughter, they loaded their plates. Everyone treated Amy and him as part of the gang with no awkward moments. They also seemed to believe they were dating. Being together as a couple made his heart sing *and* filled him with uncertainty about his future plan.

After they'd been there a couple of hours, Amy yawned. "I can walk home if you'd like to stay."

He wasn't going to miss more time with her. "I'm ready to go whenever you're ready."

As they said their goodbyes, Greg made an odd comment. "There's a full moon tonight. It should be beautiful over at the lake park."

Then Scott realized he was giving him a romantic place for them to go. The men were as bad as the women when it came to matchmaking.

Amy beat him to a reply. "I'm sure it will be beautiful. But I have work to do. The rest of you can watch the moon."

Scott smiled as they went out the door. Her friends were trying to make romantic comments, and she just bounced them right back to them. While he drove her the short distance to her house, he tried to think of a way to end up at that park. Nothing short of the classic excuse of the truck running out of gas came to mind, so he dropped her off and continued on his way.

Amy arrived home after the appetizer party, walked in the back door as she often did, and discovered a kitchen sink full of dishes. Dexter was in the living room watching TV with a friend. Standing in the doorway, she could tell they were watching a movie. The dishes would have to wait until he was free.

In bed, she went over her long day. She hoped tomorrow would be simpler. And that whatever Mrs. Robinson was going to say turned out to be good news. With her living and business situations, she desperately needed good news.

Amy felt as if the weight of the world was pressing down on her. The fact that she was helping Cassie get married was a bright light in the confusion. But she felt responsible for it all going well.

The next morning, she found Dexter in the kitchen getting a cup of coffee. The dishes were still there.

"Hey, bro, we've talked about the dishes before. I hate having a cluttered kitchen." She hated a cluttered anything. Homey was fine, but stuff just sitting around didn't work for her. She'd started to notice that her brother's lifestyle leaned more heavily toward clutter than away from it.

After a big sigh, he set the cup of coffee to the side and filled up the sink with soapy water. But he didn't say a word.

"Dex—"

"I'm on it. I don't need any more reminders." As she started to leave, he said, "Amy, it seems to be getting harder for us to live together, doesn't it?"

She'd had the same thought. The most important thing to her was family, and it felt like they'd have a strained relationship if they didn't move apart. And quickly. "I agree. And I'm working on it. I'll be out of here soon."

"That's great!"

When she turned to look at him, he made a face and said, "That sounded as if I'm pretty happy that you're leaving, didn't it?"

He was hard to be mad at. "It did. What's with that?"

"The buddy I had over here last night is looking for a place to live. He was from Two Hearts and, like us, has just moved back. He's living with his folks now, but—"

"He wants to get out of there." Not for the first time, she wondered if she should just put a cot in the newspaper office. She had a full bathroom. If she added a hot plate and maybe a microwave, she could get by. There was no way to put a curtain on big storefront windows that wouldn't look odd, but maybe she could curtain off a corner of the room for privacy. With that plan in her pocket, she headed to the office.

CHAPTER TWENTY-SEVEN

Amy found herself restless, unable to focus on her writing or anything else to do with the newspaper. Scott worked quietly at the desk next to hers, but finally, after she'd fidgeted for what seemed like an hour but was probably only ten minutes, he spun his chair to face her and said, "What's wrong?"

She opened her mouth to deny anything was wrong but instead decided to open her heart to him and tell him the truth. "I have a big decision to make."

He waited patiently, not speaking but clearly paying attention.

"Both you and my mom said I should open a bookstore. I realized that sounded fun. Years ago when I was maybe twelve or thirteen, I went into a used bookstore. I think it was in Europe, probably Germany, because Dad was stationed there for a while. It felt magical. Shelves were stacked with used books, and the historic building was beautiful. At that moment, I said, 'Someday, I'm going to own a bookstore.'"

She sat back and blew out a breath.

"And? Are you going to open a bookstore?"

She jumped to her feet, her arms raised in frustration. "I'd like to. But I already have this building. And before you say I should make half of this a bookstore, picture that. It doesn't have a warmth that would envelop you because half the room would have desks. And I'm so far away from possible foot traffic and the other new businesses that it wouldn't have much of a chance."

"I wasn't going to say that. I *was* going to say I couldn't picture it being here."

A flicker of hope came alive in her. Maybe he would agree with her about the other building. Even if not, another opinion and fresh ideas from someone she trusted could help. Amy grabbed her purse and pulled out her keys. "Let's go."

He stared at her for about two seconds before he got to his feet. "I don't know where we're going, but I'll follow you wherever it is."

Amy stumbled a bit at his words. They sounded almost . . . romantic. Outside, she stood beside her car. "Drive or walk? We're going to Main Street."

"Walk. Is everything else okay? No crisis?"

"My brother has a friend looking for a place to live. Dexter thinks he'd make a great roommate."

Scott's brow wrinkled. "I thought you said it was a two-bedroom. Would he be sharing his room with him?"

Amy blew out a breath. "No, he wants me to find my own place because I said our arrangement would be temporary. We've agreed that we love each other, but we're two very different people and probably shouldn't be sharing a home."

"Is there somewhere for you to move? I know rent is cheap in this town. Two or three people have told me that." He chuckled. "They're probably trying to convince me to move here."

Everything kept coming back to the fact that Scott had come to Two Hearts as a visitor and would return to Chicago. He had a house there. Yes, it was currently overrun with his sister's family, but it would be his alone again.

When they arrived at the building, he said, "I'm uncertain about some things." He looked up at this two-story brick building in front of them. "Is this the place you see as a potential bookstore?"

She stared at it, hoping for an answer to leap out at her. A neon sign flashing *Rent Me.* "Wait here a second. I'm going to get the key from Bella."

"Don't worry about me following you in there."

Amy chuckled as she raced next door. She quietly approached Bella and what sounded like a bridal party, regretting coming here on a whim and interrupting them. Bella stepped away from the bride she was working with, pulled the key from her pocket, and handed it to Amy. "I had a feeling you'd be back soon."

It seemed everyone knew what she wanted more than she did. They were matchmakers and business enthusiasts.

Amy opened the door to the building, and they entered the large room. She'd been here once, but this time, she saw more details. The tin ceiling overhead would be perfect for a bookstore. The bow window had a wide windowsill she could use to display books.

She pulled out the tape measure she'd tucked in her purse a week ago. "Will you hold this at the end of the long counter for me? I want to see if this whole thing could be shifted down to the end of the room."

Scott did as she asked. Then he nudged the unit to the side, scooting it an inch on the floor. When she looked over at him with what she knew must be a question in her eyes, he said, "I wanted to make sure it wasn't attached to the floor. If it had been, you wouldn't be able to move it without leaving damaged floor behind. I think you can, though." He pointed to the wood floor that had been hidden under the unit. Scott turned in a circle, checking out the room. "I can see this as a bookstore. The big question is—can you?"

Amy nodded. "From the first moment I stepped in here. Perfection." She sighed. "I can see books lining the shelves. I can see another bookcase over here. And Bella had the idea—which I think is pretty genius—to have a section of new books about weddings. I could ship all over the country."

"Maybe have a Plan Your Wedding bundle. It would be fun if Cassie, Bella, Simone, and Paige wrote how-to books. You could sell those."

His vision lured her further into the dream. "You're going to make it a lot harder to say no to this."

"Why would you if you love this place and the idea?" After a second, he said, "Oh! I understand. Everything costs money."

"Exactly. I already have one building I'm paying utilities for and will owe property tax on. But let's pretend for just a minute that I find a solution to my problems. Let me show you the upstairs."

She led the way up the steps. Today, the sun was shining brightly, and even with the filthy windows, she could tell this would be a beautiful room to work in. "It's quite large here." He wandered around, opening the closet doors and looking inside. He closed one of them rather abruptly. "You may need to fumigate before you move in."

"I already figured that out. I don't even want to know what you spotted."

At the bathroom, which included a shower, he said, "This actually isn't too bad. I think it will clean up and be fine."

Amy kept trying to picture what she would use the upstairs room for. "I can envision the downstairs level being a bookstore, but this level is wasted space. Maybe I should look at a smaller building."

Scott faced her and put a hand on each of her shoulders. "I

just had an idea. You're either going to love it, or you're going to hate it."

"With an opening like that, I don't know how I can say no to hearing what you have to say."

He grinned, and her heart fluttered.

"I can picture the desks from your newspaper office over there." He pointed by the windows. "You could even have a couch or comfy chairs for people to sit on when you are interviewing them. There's a lot of built-in storage, so your newspaper archive books would easily fit in one of the cupboards."

She could see his vision. "I'd have plenty of room for storage here, wouldn't I?"

"So much. If you wanted, you could even wall off this back section behind the staircase and turn that into storage for the bookstore."

"I love it!" Amy felt like dancing around the room. The bubble burst when she remembered her situation. She sighed. "There's a glitch in your wonderful plan. I already have a building for the newspaper."

"Could you find someone to lease it from you?"

Her newspaper office currently held four desks, piles of boxes, and still had extra room. She might have a chance in a city to find someone who wanted that much space, but there weren't many businesses searching for a rental in Two Hearts.

Then she remembered her conversation with Cassie. Was she serious about wanting an office away from her home? Amy pulled out her phone and called. When Cassie answered, Amy said, "I want to bounce an idea off of you." She explained the concept of a bookstore and the newspaper together in the Main Street building.

"I love it. But you already have a newspaper office."

Everyone kept saying that. Amy bit her lip for a moment before continuing. "You mentioned that you'd thought about getting an office outside your home for your business. Would my current newspaper office work?"

Cassie laughed. "That's just a thought that comes to mind sometimes. I haven't seriously considered it."

Oh, well. She'd need a new plan. Maybe Dexter would like a permanent place to have interviews and write, but she doubted that.

To her surprise, Cassie continued. "Your newspaper office has decent light from the front windows and on-street parking. You've got me thinking more seriously about this. I must admit I'm getting tired of bringing clients through my living room to my office. After Greg and I get married—whenever that is—this will also be his home they're trudging through."

"I hadn't thought of that."

"Believe me when I say that I often think about life married to Greg. One day soon, we'll have that ceremony. But enough about my failure to commit to a wedding date. I *can* commit to this. I'll take the newspaper building off your hands. I wouldn't want walk-in traffic like I might get on Main Street. I like scheduling appointments so the client has my uninterrupted attention."

This was almost too good to be true. "You're sure?"

"Positive. I know this is right. I had an office in Nashville, and I have missed that privacy in my personal life. Now, if only my own wedding could come together this easily." Amy heard Cassie's frustration through the phone. She hoped her friend meant that because she was about to have a chance for that ceremony.

They ended the call after they'd agreed on a figure for Cassie to pay for the building, and Amy offered to contact Micah to draw up the papers.

"That all went well." Scott's deep voice startled her.

Amy jumped. "I got so wrapped up in the call that I forgot for a second you were there. This is monumental. I just sold the newspaper office to Cassie!" She hugged him, and he wrapped his arms around her, holding her close. "One problem solved." She still needed a place of her own to live.

And for Scott to stay here forever.

"Amy, I have another idea. A way to solve another problem you shared with me."

Her heart leaped so fast and hard that he must have felt it. Had he decided to stay?

"What if the couch I mentioned for your new newspaper office was a foldout bed? You could live here. I know it wouldn't be the same as a real house, but—"

She stepped away from him, immediately wishing she could have the warmth of his arms around her again. But when she turned and pictured what he'd said, she grabbed her phone to call her brother.

"Dex, I'm going to lease the building on Main Street and live upstairs here for a while. You can tell your friend he can move in anytime. Well, as soon as I get this place cleaned up. Give me a few days."

Silence greeted her. "I don't know, Sis. That sounds like something that'll get Mom and Dad over here as fast as their car will drive. And Mom will yell at me on the phone the whole time for kicking you out of my house."

As he spoke, Amy started smiling. That would probably happen, but everything felt right to her. "I'm certain. I'll even call Mom to place the blame for your lack of brotherly love on me."

He laughed. "Then let me know when you're ready to move." He hesitated for a moment before adding, "I'm happy to wait." His words said he could wait, but she knew him so well that she also knew he wanted to move forward with his own plans.

If her friends helped, they could clean everything before the wedding. She might be able to live with the current wall colors for a while to save on paint costs. "As soon as we've cleaned this place, I'll get out of there."

"You sure you want to do this?"

"Yes. You don't have to ask again. It's all good. I'll give you a heads-up if I find out Mom's in the car on her way here."

Dexter laughed. "I think you'll be fine if Mom knows you're happy." Then he surprised her by asking, "Can anyone else hear me speak?"

Amy glanced toward Scott. "Yes, Scott's here with me."

Silence greeted her.

"Dex?"

"Step away for a second. And Scott, it isn't anything bad. I just wanted to mention something personal."

She went downstairs. "Now, what's so secret?"

"We aren't usually touchy-feely. But I want to tell you that Logan was a jerk. I could never see what you liked about him."

Amy gasped. "I thought he fit in with the family." Had her whole relationship with him been in her imagination? She had thought she loved the man and had planned to spend her life with him.

"We all put up with him for your sake. When he broke your heart, we weren't surprised in the slightest. We just hated seeing you hurt."

Amy felt tears prickling her eyes. "Why didn't anybody say anything?" she whispered.

"Because you were head over heels for him. We all talked about it and decided you must have seen something in him we didn't. Turned out we were right, I guess."

Amy stared out the window toward the street. "Why are you telling me now?"

"Because Scott's a good guy. Don't judge all men by Logan."

"Scott?"

"I've seen you around town with him, and . . ." He paused for a moment, and she could see him pursing his lips as he thought about what to say next. "If he's the one for your future, figure it out. I'm worried you're still hurt about the past."

She and Scott had lives to live that didn't intersect, so she wasn't about to let him in to break her heart.

"Gotta go to work," Dex said. "See you later, sis."

Once she'd hung up, she went back upstairs to Scott, who had patiently waited through the call.

He cocked his head to the side as he watched her. "Everything okay?"

Amy nodded. "Fine." As she stared back at him, she wondered what Dexter had noticed when he'd seen them together. She shook off those questions and went back to business. "I finally feel as if I'm getting my footing here in Two Hearts. I think between the bookstore and the newspaper—and with both in one location—I'll be able to manage everything and do better financially."

"It's all turning out well."

They were standing in the messy building, so she wasn't sure why he'd said that. When she glanced up at his face, though, she realized he was looking at her. Amy sucked in her breath. "Thank you for coming over to check it out with me." She wanted to ask if he'd like to visit Two Hearts sometime in the future and sit at the desk he'd been using but in this new location. She just wasn't sure how to do that. Then she realized she might be able to move in while he was still here.

"You could try out your desk beside mine before you leave town."

Scott reached out and pressed his palm onto her cheek. Gently, he rubbed his thumb over her cheekbone. Somehow, the two of them moved closer together, but she didn't remember either of them taking a step.

When he leaned down to kiss her, alarm bells began clanging that she didn't want this in her life. Complications would arise. But in her heart, this was exactly what she wanted.

He kissed her, and she wrapped her arms around his waist, pulling him close. When they came up for air, Amy leaned her forehead against his chest. "Does that mean that you'll give the desk a test run before you head out of town?"

He wrapped his arms more snugly around her and didn't say a word.

❧

Amy worked on the wedding article. A few weeks ago, she might have done that from the kitchen table at home. Today, she found herself at the newspaper office. She caught herself glancing out the window for what must be the tenth time and realized she was waiting to see if Scott would stop by. Her heartbeat went into overdrive at the thought that she might see him soon.

She laid her head down on her desk. "I can't be falling for someone who's going to break my heart."

Pushing thoughts of Scott out of her head, Amy took a deep breath and focused on her article again. It had come together very well. She might be able to sell this article to other newspapers. She hadn't done that in the past because everything had been so focused on Two Hearts, but this was an article with known experts in the wedding industry giving their seasonal forecast. They'd all done weddings for celebrities, so they had already been in major publications and online in the past.

When a shadow passed her front window, she forced herself to stay focused on her computer screen and not look up, only to have her hopes dashed when someone continued down the sidewalk.

Much to her surprise, her door opened. She looked up with a smile, expecting to see Scott but instead finding Mrs. Brantley.

"I wanted to check on the progress of everything related to the wedding."

Amy did her best to hide her disappointment. She'd have to have a stern talk with herself after this because she couldn't be fixated on this man.

"Everything—much to my amazement—is on track." Other than the oversight with the invitations, Amy thought she'd done a decent job working behind the scenes on the event.

"I've spoken with Cassie's parents. I had to talk to her mother for close to forty-five minutes before she calmed down about the secret wedding. It didn't feel 'proper' to her." Mrs. Brantley used air quotes when she said proper. "I think she has accepted the situation. But after my conversation with her about the wedding's details, something seemed off. This morning, I realized I didn't know who was in charge of flowers. There's nothing about them on my task list. I stopped by to see if you knew something I didn't."

Amy brought out the list she'd made and kept in the bottom drawer under lock and key in case Cassie stopped by. "I'm sure we talked about flowers in at least one of our meetings. I made notes in case I needed information for the article." She tapped her finger on the spot on the pad. "Cassie wants a simple arrangement of flowers for her bouquet. She loves ribbon, so maybe something tied with ribbon." Amy looked up and down the list. "I don't see anything about buying the flowers, though."

She felt herself go faint. They were days from a wedding with no floral arrangements in sight. "We can't have a wedding without flowers," Amy breathed the words quietly.

"I woke up with that thought myself this morning. We've assigned everyone tasks except this one. I'll call Cassie's florist Henri to see if something can be done. I know they have a close relationship. Cassie has introduced me to him before."

"Cherry and Levi have a floral farm. If her florist can't help, maybe we can put something together with flowers they grow."

Mrs. Brantley's expression turned even more serious. "It's a good thought, but I don't know a single person who's done that before. Cassie is used to professional weddings."

"That's true, but she also loves less conventional things. Like the cupcakes and appetizers instead of a full-service dinner and tiered wedding cake."

Mrs. Brantley exhaled. "That is certainly a valid point and may help me sleep tonight if I can't get flowers from Henri. But those unconventional cupcakes will be the best of the best, not made by someone who's never picked up a mixer."

Amy saw her point. To her knowledge, none of them had done more than put flowers in a vase.

Mrs. Brantley patted her shoulder. "Please know that this wasn't your fault, dear. If anyone's to blame, it's me." She left just before it was time for Amy to leave for Mrs. Robinson's house.

As Amy walked over, she went through her current list of problems, which felt greater than her strength to solve them. She needed to resolve her business's financial issues. She did have a flicker of hope things there would improve. She also had to get through this wedding without any more mistakes. Or one of them blowing it with a single wrong word.

She wanted to get her new building cleaned up and livable so she could move into the upstairs. Her brother had been on a conference call around five o'clock this morning that had woken her up. He must have been speaking to someone in a much different time zone to find them available that early.

And last, but certainly not least, was the situation with Scott. What was she going to do about that? There was no question in her mind—or her heart—that she'd fallen for him.

She kicked a tiny pebble on the roadway. What *could* she do about it? An infatuation on her part didn't mean he felt anything permanent. Sure, they'd had a romantic moment last night, but she would still be watching his taillights as he drove out of town. She had too many connections to this town, especially with the signing of the new lease, to move and follow him. Besides, she'd done that once, and it hadn't gone well.

She arrived at Mrs. Robinson's and hesitantly went up the driveway. When people broke their pattern as much as the older woman had with this invitation, Amy didn't expect good news.

She tapped on the door and received her usual invitation to enter.

When she opened the door, Nosey was waiting for her a couple of feet inside. She edged the door open and quickly stepped inside, closing it behind her so the rabbit couldn't escape. It was easy to see how he'd gotten out because Mrs. Robinson didn't do anything quickly anymore.

"Come in! Please take a seat and join us."

For the first time, Amy realized a man who looked to be in his sixties or seventies was seated in a chair beside Mrs. Robinson. "I'm Cameron Robinson. Mavis is my mother."

Amy had never heard Mrs. Robinson's first name, but it suited her.

"I'm going to be moving in with my son. He's here to help me load everything up."

Amy glanced around the room. It was filled with a lifetime of treasures and furniture Mrs. Robinson must enjoy having around her.

"Will a moving truck be coming soon?"

Mrs. Robinson glanced over at her son. "Cameron bought me new everything. It's so exciting. A brand new recliner and other furniture. And a shower I step straight into. I won't have to climb into a bathtub anymore." Mrs. Robinson beamed.

"That's wonderful." They'd started to become friends. That must be why she'd been invited over here. "Are you leaving soon?"

Her son answered. "She'll be leaving in the morning. We're going to pack up the things she wants. But we have something to ask you." He turned toward his mother, clearly waiting for her to speak.

"I know you love Nosey."

Amy realized then that the rabbit would be leaving town too. She'd enjoyed finally having a rabbit to play with. She needed to get her own pet because it wasn't acceptable to fall in love with an animal and then have him leave town weeks later. "I do. I'm going to miss him."

Mrs. Brantley leaned forward in her chair, an earnest expression on her face. "Cameron has dogs. I think I told you that?"

Amy nodded. She remembered that discussion, so moving with the rabbit surprised her.

"I can't take Nosey with me there. Until I got to know you, that was a problem." Mrs. Robinson reached down and petted the rabbit in his bed beside her. "I wondered if you'd like to have him as a pet."

Amy's first thought was an affirmative *yes*. Her second one was that she couldn't. "I'm sorry, but I don't have a place of my own here yet. I don't think it would be fair to Nosey to be in a place with people coming and going."

"Oh my goodness, I realized that I skipped a question here. Would you like to live in my house?"

Amy stared at her and then turned her head to look at Cameron, who seemed fine with his mother's question if she read his expression right.

He said, "You could live here for the life of the rabbit and just pay utilities. If you'd like to buy the house at any point, I'd finance it for you with zero money down or interest."

Amy gazed at him with suspicion.

He smiled, and when he did so, she could see how much he resembled his mother. "I know the offer sounds too good to be true, but it is genuine. I've done well in life, and I know Mom would love to have this home go to somebody who truly wants it. Neither of us wants it to be unoccupied. I know Two Hearts is growing and changing, but there are still too many empty houses. Some of them are in great shape. Some have been empty far too long and will need a lot of work to bring them back to life."

"I'm going to need to think about this before I give you an answer." Amy stood. Then she realized there was nothing to think about. "You know, I take that back. I'm going to say yes."

Mrs. Robinson rubbed her hands together with glee. "I thought so. Nosey is going to be so excited to have you living here. And maybe your young man will come visit too."

Amy was certain that wouldn't be happening.

Her son pulled out a document. "We had an agreement drawn up, but you should run this through your lawyer."

She left with the legal document in her hand and shock in her heart. She had a place to live.

And a rabbit.

CHAPTER TWENTY-EIGHT

On the day before the wedding, Scott came into the newspaper office with trepidation. Amy would either like their new assignment or hate it. He knew she was busy working on both the wedding article and the next edition of the newspaper. "Mrs. Brantley would like you and me to go out to Cherry and Levi's place to scope it out and make sure everything for the wedding is in order. She's going to meet us there."

Amy stared at her computer screen for a moment, then said, "I hope it's all good. I've been dreading the moment when everything has to come together for their big day. There are so many things that could go wrong."

"But what if it's all good?"

She grinned. "I love an optimist. Let's do this."

Scott went toward his truck, and Amy followed him and climbed inside. When she didn't question who should drive, he knew she was distracted by something big. "Has your part in the wedding become overwhelming?"

"So much! That and . . . everything else going on in my life right now."

He knew she meant her business as part of that, but maybe it included their kiss and what that potentially meant for them. When she didn't offer more, he changed subjects to their upcoming farm visit. "Mrs. Brantley had one piece of advice for me."

Amy turned toward him with a slight smile. He could tell she was making an effort to be cheerful. "Just one?"

"Well, she worded it as having one, then gave me more." He chuckled. "She said that everything was fixable. Other than the portable bathrooms, we can make almost anything okay."

She sighed. "I know that's true, but I still had trouble falling asleep last night." After a couple of minutes of silence, she asked, "Have you talked to your boss since you've been gone?"

Her question surprised him since she'd never said anything about his job. Work was the last thing he wanted to think about right now. "I don't need to call. He would have called in a crisis. I do know I'll have a huge stack of work waiting when I get back." Then he knew why she'd asked. She wanted to know if he was returning to his old life. Since he didn't have an answer for her, he didn't say more.

They reached the farm and pulled up near the barn. Since he'd been here for the proposal photo, the flowers had come to life. Summer flowers were in full bloom. Mrs. Brantley was waiting outside the barn when they stepped out of his truck.

As soon as they got out, she approached them with her clipboard in hand. "Let's divide and conquer. Scott, if you wouldn't mind, please go to the portable bathrooms, flush every toilet, and test the faucets. Check to make sure there's plenty of toilet paper and paper towels."

That would be his least favorite job, but someone had to do it.

Mrs. Brantley directed Amy to go through the barn to make sure everything looked right. "We want it to be as clean as a barn can possibly be. The tables should be set up with the linens stacked on them, ready to be put out in the morning. There has to be a place for Simone's cupcakes and a staging area for Nick to set up his appetizers."

They went their separate directions. As he went in and out of the various stalls, Scott noticed Mrs. Brantley walking around the outside of the barn. He wasn't sure what she was doing, but he knew there must be something she needed to check off on that clipboard. After a few minutes of flushing and running, he was glad to have that job done and to be able to report back to her that all was well.

Mrs. Brantley glanced at the barn where Amy still worked on her assignment. He had a feeling Mrs. Brantley was about to say something she deemed important.

"You know Greg will be moving into Cassie's house immediately after the wedding."

"I do know that." He wasn't sure why she was telling him this.

"Have you been in Greg's apartment over the garage?"

"Yes, ma'am. It's nice." And he meant that. Greg's parents had fixed up the apartment for Greg's sister before she'd married, and they'd thought it out well. Then Greg had lived there since he returned to Two Hearts.

"It will be a shame not to have anybody living in it."

"I'm sure you won't have a problem finding a renter."

She turned to face him. "It's on my property, so I see it as different than a normal rental unit. James and I have bought a couple of those, and CJ is fixing them up as we speak." She turned back to face the barn. "No. I want someone I know living there. It's only been family thus far. I think I would need to feel as if the renter was family."

He still wasn't sure of the point of this conversation, but she seemed to have one. "Do you want me to help you find someone?" he asked tentatively.

"My goodness, for someone as smart as you are, you can be a little slow sometimes."

Scott took a step back. He'd clearly just been insulted. "I apologize?"

Mrs. Brantley patted him on the shoulder. "Scott, I'm saying that if you wanted to live there, I'd be open to that option."

Amy came out of the barn, stopped, and turned back toward it as though she was trying to sort something out.

Mrs. Brantley continued. "Amy's a great girl. Are you going to run away from here and go back to the life you had? Or are you going to embrace the possibilities of an amazing future?" Then she walked away from him and toward the barn, leaving him standing there dumbfounded.

He had avoided thinking about staying in Two Hearts. He had a life in Chicago. One he loved. He had a great job with excellent coworkers. He had his family all within an hour's drive, probably less if he took the time to add it up. He'd finally gotten his house fixed up how he liked it. He'd even been thinking about adopting a pet because that seemed to be what one did when they were settled.

And Mrs. Brantley had blown that up by making a future life in Two Hearts even more real.

Scott watched Amy move her hands in an animated way as she spoke to Mrs. Brantley. He liked her fire, her joy in simple things, and the way she cared about others. He loved everything about her. It wasn't the first time he'd entertained thoughts like that, though. The kiss they had shared had been special. He'd been trying to maneuver them together so that could happen again. She seemed to have stopped running too.

The two women walked toward Scott.

Mrs. Brantley ran her finger down the list on her clipboard. "Looks like everything is in good shape. Cassie's mother and father should be arriving in town any minute. Are you and your friends still taking Cassie out for a pampering day in the city?" she asked Amy.

"We are."

She checked her watch. "Oh my, I need to get back right away. I need to be ready to greet guests." Mrs. Brantley hurried to her vehicle. Before she stepped in, she turned back to them. "You understand what I meant earlier, right, Scott?"

"Yes, ma'am." He was coming to realize that Amy was the best thing that had ever happened to him. Now, he needed to figure out what to do about it.

Amy looked at her watch every few minutes as they drove back to town.

After more than a dozen time checks, Scott asked, "Am I missing something? Are you ready to get away from me?" He said it with a smile, but she thought he might actually mean it.

"It's what Mrs. Brantley mentioned. The girls' day in the city. I really do need to get back to town for that." Her phone rang with a call from Bella.

"I'm on my way to Cassie's house. You can pick us both up there."

This surprised Amy because she had to stop and get Paige and Simone on Main Street. Bella would be an easy addition.

Bella added, "I've noticed some visitors in town. It may be a busy couple of days in Two Hearts with the wedding this weekend."

Oh! Bella had seen some of the guests.

"I saw a car go by that held what must be guests of honor."

Amy tried to process that. Guests of honor would be . . . Cassie's parents! She turned toward Scott. "Can you get this going any faster—legally?"

He edged the truck forward.

"I'll make a stop on Main Street. Then we'll meet you at Cassie's house."

Bella giggled. "All this stuff makes me laugh. I'll see you there."

Scott eased off the gas when they arrived at the town limits. He pulled up in front of the newspaper office. "Is this all to get Cassie out of town?" When she looked up at him, he added, "I couldn't help but overhear the call."

She unbuckled her seatbelt and reached for the door handle. "We don't want Cassie to see wedding guests by accident. There is no reason for a college friend to be here, and her parents definitely wouldn't come without contacting her first."

"It's almost over, and you've all done a great job."

She hoped so. As she stepped out, she realized that Team Wedding needed him tomorrow. "Could you pick up Greg in the morning? I'll get Cassie. We can meet at city hall for the marriage license."

"That's already worked out. Greg is going to city hall by himself. I'm supposed to be out at the reception site working on anything that needs to be done."

A pang of disappointment went through her. She wouldn't be seeing Scott in the morning. But then she wouldn't be seeing him ever again once he left town.

Amy whipped out of her parking space on the street in front of the newspaper and around to Main Street, where she found Paige waiting at the curb. She hopped in the car and said, "I just got a text from Simone. She's too busy decorating the cupcakes to go with us today."

Amy drove past Simone's bakery and took a left toward Cassie's place. "That's too bad. I'd wanted her to come along, but I know there are a lot of cupcakes."

"I'm glad I don't have any prep work like that. And Bella has everything done by now." They pulled into Cassie's driveway and went around to the back. Bella and Cassie were outside, sitting in the garden.

Cassie helped Bella up from her chair. "We wanted to be ready. It looks like we might be cutting it close for our appointments?"

Amy checked her watch again. They had plenty of time to get to the spa—extra since she'd sped up—but they could be in trouble if they came upon a traffic stoppage.

When they were in the car, Bella said, "Let's go out the other side of town. I think it's a little shorter, and you may not know this way over to the highway yet, Amy." She gave a slow wink.

Amy played along. "I didn't realize there was another way out of town." That much was true. "Let's go." And there they were, hurtling away from Two Hearts at the maximum speed Amy felt comfortable with and that the law agreed upon.

"Anything interesting with you guys?"

Bella put her hand on her belly. "She's been kicking up a storm. Very active."

"She!" Cassie shouted.

"Yes." Bella grinned. "We're having the baby's room painted a soft pink. I found the cutest fabric with tiny pink roses on it for the curtain. And I can tell you that there's only one baby. There won't be any twin surprises." Amy knew the reason for the pattern on the fabric, but Bella still hadn't shared the baby's name with everyone else. Amy was glad she'd shared it with her chauffeur.

Cassie seemed relaxed as they drove down the country lane. If only she knew what awaited her tomorrow. "We actually have twins in my family. My mother has twin brothers, and two first cousins have had twin babies."

"Have you mentioned this to Greg at any point?" Bella asked with humor in her voice.

Cassie chuckled. "I thought it best not to say a word. Maybe when having a family gets closer to reality." She sighed. "I really want to marry Greg. I keep hoping that one day I'll be ready to plan the wedding."

They drove the back roads, with Bella pointing out the turns to take. Even GPS would have no idea where they were. Amy wasn't sure she could recreate this if she needed to. They pulled onto the highway and, after a short time, passed the seedy-looking motel on the right.

"Bella asked not too long ago if I'd like to have the wedding planned and just show up."

Amy held her breath, waiting for whatever else Cassie might add. She just hoped it wasn't, *I've been thinking about that, and I hate the idea.*

"Every time I think about that, I fall more in love with the idea. I'm just letting you guys know that if you want to take the reins on this, I would be thrilled. I just want a pretty wedding. I want to be beautiful for Greg. And I'd like to give my guests good food to eat. Other than that, I'm not caught up in all the *hows* and *whys.* I've planned so many weddings and attended so many others that I've seen it all. Simple would be great for my own."

Amy looked at Bella in the rearview mirror. Had they done a simple wedding? Maybe. Cupcakes instead of a big cake felt a little simpler. Henri had come through and knew Cassie wanted something like wildflowers.

"Everything you asked me the other day for the article, Amy, made me think more about my own wedding."

Amy wasn't sure what to say, but she felt she needed to say something.

Fortunately, Paige stepped in. "I haven't seen everyone's selections from the article, but I heard that Simone made cupcakes Amy and Cassie got to try. What flavor?"

Cassie licked her lips. "They were so good. Raspberry, lemon, and chocolate."

Paige grimaced. "Together?"

Cassie laughed. "No. Four different flavor combinations. And they were all good."

Bella nodded. "I agree. I stopped by Cassie's house for tea and got to try them. Delicious."

They finished the drive into the city talking about baked goods. By the time they arrived, Amy wanted to stop at the nearest bakery. Fortunately for her waistline, they had massages scheduled. They were brought right into rooms, and the relaxation began.

Bella had thought of this as a way to get Cassie out of town, and it was pure genius. Right now, for the first time in weeks, Amy let go of all her troubles and confusion. Thoughts about this wedding, Scott, the house with the rabbit, and business faded away. By the end of the hour, she felt calm. They went from the massage to a sauna and then a facial.

Just as she wondered how everybody was doing, she was back in a waiting area, and her friends were there.

Bella said, "This was fabulous. I need to have another day like this before the baby comes."

Cassie stared at her. "You said this was the last time you could get in before the baby was born. That's why we all made room in our schedules. Not that I'm complaining because it was fabulous."

Bella's eyes widened as she realized she'd said the wrong thing. "My schedule is pretty tight for the next month or so. I thought this was my last chance. But I feel so relaxed that I may be able to sleep. For that, I could squeeze in another massage."

Paige grinned. "I'd love a return visit. I'll drive."

After getting back into their street clothes, they headed for Amy's car. Then a discussion about where to eat their late lunch ensued. Amy suggested the Indian restaurant owned by a renowned Indian chef who was often on TV. Nashville had become a foodie center in the last few years, which gave them many options, some quite surprising like this one. After a wonderful lunch there, they went back to Two Hearts. Amy's tension increased with every mile. Had they succeeded in keeping Cassie away from wedding guests?

Greg would have pizza for Cassie at his apartment, one of the few places they knew she wouldn't see wedding guests. They were doing all they could to keep her from mingling with the people in town tonight. She may have said she wanted a surprise wedding, but that didn't mean they should tell her now. They'd leave the surprise for tomorrow when she couldn't as easily get cold feet.

CHAPTER TWENTY-NINE

Once again, Amy had trouble sleeping. In a few hours, the wedding would be over. Thank goodness! Scott would leave so she could have closure. Even so, she felt her heart start to shatter whenever she thought about him.

But she had a lot to look forward to today. Any thoughts of the bookstore were pushed to the side because a human being can only endure so much change at one moment. She had maxed out on hers.

Amy crawled out of bed when the sun blasted through her window. Since she hadn't gotten any late-night emergency texts, it seemed they had kept Cassie in the dark.

If she'd planned the wedding or found out earlier, Cassie would have been on a roller coaster of emotions. Had it been stressful for everyone else? Yes. But Amy would happily do it again. A hot shower revived her enough to make her way to the kitchen, where she poured a mug of coffee down her throat and reached for another one.

Her brother came into the kitchen. "What's got you up so early that *you're* making the coffee?"

Now that the day was here, she could tell Dexter about it. "We planned a secret wedding for Cassie and Greg."

"Whoa! Are they going to be happy about that?"

Amy chuckled. "Greg is thrilled. Cassie has told us she would love to get married as long as she doesn't have to plan it. My guess—my fervent hope—is they will both be thrilled."

Dexter pulled a mug off the rack and reached for the coffee carafe. "I know I wouldn't be happy if you planned a wedding for me."

Amy took a few more sips of the coffee, caffeine-fueled energy seeping into her body. "Unless I've missed something, you aren't dating anyone."

He grinned. "That much is true. I guess that's why I wouldn't be thrilled about a wedding, huh?"

Amy nudged him with her arm. "That would do it."

"Would you have wanted someone to secretly plan a wedding for you and Logan?"

She froze with her mug an inch from her mouth. Then relief surged through her that she hadn't married him. She'd thought he was a good guy, but in the end, she'd probably been more in love with love than with him.

"I'm relieved no one did." She felt completely different about Scott. Not that she wanted to get married to him today. But he felt honest and open. Logan never had. She'd just taken it as part of his personality—something else to love. In the end, it wasn't what anybody should have in a relationship.

Amy put on the aqua dress she'd bought on her last newspaper run to Nashville. She knew the color brought out the blue in her eyes and hoped Scott appreciated it. Then she slipped on navy blue shoes, which had enough of a heel to be pretty with the dress but not to cause her pain in what would probably be a long day wearing them. She was ready to go after a sweep of mascara and some blush.

Her first stop today would be a big one.

She pulled into Cassie's driveway with trepidation. The group had decided to have her pick up Cassie this morning on the pretense of taking photos for the article. She'd actually be taking Cassie to get the license.

Amy steeled herself for the job ahead. Cassie was waiting in her kitchen, wearing a pretty floral dress. Paige would be at city hall ready to snap photos for what Cassie believed was the newspaper article. Amy would use one of the photos in the paper, but the rest would be a keepsake for the happy couple.

"Ready to go? Paige is waiting for us."

Cassie closed the door, saying, "Romeo, you've already had breakfast." He meowed, so she added, "I'll be back. Don't worry."

In the car, Cassie said, "I could have driven myself. I'm not sure why Paige insisted on you driving me there."

Amy sought the right answer. "It seemed easier since I was going to be there, anyway."

When they drove by Paige's business, Cassie turned to her. "Aren't we going to her studio?"

"She set up a different location. We're almost there. And don't worry. I'm not an ax murderer driving you to an unknown location to commit a crime."

Cassie burst out with laughter. "That never crossed my mind." When they pulled up and parked on the street by the city hall office, Cassie said, "This is a weird place for photos."

When Paige came out the front door, camera in hand, Amy's nervousness ramped up. Showtime!

"I'm not sure what you have planned, but Paige is the photography expert, so I'll go with it." Cassie climbed out.

When Amy said, "Up the steps," Cassie gave her a questioning glance, but she dutifully went up them with Paige snapping photos. When she reached the top, Greg opened the door.

Cassie stopped in her tracks and stared at him. Amy had to admit the man looked good. His dove gray suit fit him like a glove, and the white shirt with a tie in coordinating wedding colors looked great on him.

His bride-to-be asked, "What's going on, Greg? That's a fancy suit you're wearing for conducting city business."

Greg held out his elbow for her to put her arm around. "Today, it's all about us."

Cassie slipped her arm around Greg's but quietly studied him for a moment. "What are you up to?"

"Only good things."

Amy and Paige followed the couple through the door and down the hallway, their footsteps on the old linoleum the only sounds. When they arrived at the clerk's office, Greg stared at Cassie, fear on his face, his confidence gone. He turned to the clerk and cleared his throat. "We'd like a marriage license."

Cassie gasped. "Am I getting married soon?"

The clerk, whom Cassie knew, said, "Honey, if you don't know, there's a problem here. Do you want this here license?"

Cassie turned to the three of them. "Do I?"

Amy took a step toward Cassie. "It will make the day we have planned go much smoother if you say yes."

Cassie grinned as widely as Amy had ever seen. Her eyes sparkling, she gave Greg a quick kiss before turning to the clerk and saying, "Yes, ma'am. I'm getting married. Today?" She looked up at Greg.

"I'd like that very much."

She leaned into his side. "Today," Cassie said with conviction. Once they had filled out the paperwork and had the license in hand, Amy expected a barrage of questions from Cassie, but she only asked, "What's my next stop?" as they went down the hall.

"Bella's place."

"That makes sense. She has the dress and accessories?"

"She does."

Cassie practically skipped down the steps.

As Amy drove Cassie to Bella's, she said, "I hope you don't mind that Greg saw you on your wedding day."

Cassie made a scoffing sound. "I definitely don't hold to those rules. Besides, I agree with you. Telling me in advance would've been a bad idea."

Amy's gaze jerked over to Cassie and then back at the road. "Would you have wanted us to cancel it?"

"I don't think so. But I definitely would have tried to take over. It's what I do. I wouldn't have thought you guys did a bad job, but your version of the wedding wouldn't have been exactly how I wanted it." She raised her hands in the air and smiled. "This way, I didn't have a chance to meddle, and I love that. Who was in on this?"

"Your future mother-in-law, Bella, Paige, Simone, Michelle, and their men. Scott. And Dinah. I also heard that Sam from the hardware store was helping out with some setup."

Cassie shook her head slowly. "I'm amazed I didn't catch a whiff of it. How did you do that?"

Amy grinned. "Let's just say it was worthy of a spy thriller novel. Lots of secrets and clandestine meetings. You didn't know it at the time, but you helped choose almost everything."

"You're good. Thank you."

Amy pulled in front of Bella's Brides. "Now for the pretty part of the day."

Cassie rubbed her hands together with glee. "I can't wait to see what Bella made for me."

The fit and flare dress Cassie had chosen from the sketch was even more beautiful in person. The narrow straps and fitted bodice with the flare to a fuller skirt suited Cassie and would be easy to wear for hours. The creamy color would be perfect with her dark red hair.

When Cassie saw her wedding dress on the hanger, she gasped. "It's the one from the sketch and with the changes I suggested." Hands on hips, she turned to Amy. "What you meant earlier about my choosing everything was that everything you'd said would be in an article was actually for my wedding, right?"

"Sort of. But not really. I am going to publish that article." Amy made an X over her heart. "The idea started as a way to learn what you liked but turned into a great article."

A beautiful, soft-pink knee-length dress hung beside the wedding dress. With a ribbon around the empire waist, it flowed loosely and would feel right next to the wedding dress.

Bella moved next to the pink dress. "I hope you don't mind. This is your matron of honor dress. And it's mine."

"Mind? I would have chosen you, of course. Other than the people I grew up with and, in general, haven't kept in touch with, you're my oldest friend. Not that you're getting old."

Bella chuckled. "Let's get this show on the road. You have two more hours of being single. Then there will be an unforgettable afternoon wedding."

"Afternoon. I like that. It's a little bit different. And on a weekday too."

Amy said, "There's a reason for that. If we'd chosen a Saturday or Sunday, you may have unknowingly booked a weekend wedding on your scheduled wedding day, but we thought it was unlikely you'd book a Thursday."

"Oh my goodness! There is a Saturday wedding." Her face fell. "I'd always pictured getting married and going on a week's honeymoon. It doesn't look as if that's going to happen."

Bella said, "You're leaving Saturday evening. It was the best poor Greg could do. He wouldn't tell any of us where he's taking you."

"And he's been in on this since the beginning?"

"Almost. We'd figured out some of the details before we invited him in. Greg has been happy to be on the sidelines." Amy knew that had made their jobs easier. "He hasn't needed to do much beyond buying a new suit and tasting cupcakes."

"My cake. Is it one of the flavors of cupcakes I tasted?"

Bella and Amy stared at Cassie. Amy knew Bella was thinking the same thing. *What if she doesn't want cupcakes and wants a cake instead?*

"We're doing cupcakes. I hope you don't mind?"

Cassie's expression turned gleeful. "I'm so happy. Everything is unconventional. Will we have music?"

"Yes. You'll enjoy the performer we chose."

"This is perfect." Cassie sat while a woman styled her hair into a beautiful knot with strands around her face. Makeup highlighted her eyes and coloring. Amy noticed Bella holding her breath as Cassie put on her dress.

When the zipper moved smoothly up the back, and the dress fit perfectly, Bella let out a big breath. "Phew! I'm glad you haven't gained or lost weight since I last measured you."

Cassie slipped on the creamy white shoes covered in beads. "I know how you got the dress size because you had that from wedding number one, right?"

"Yes. And you're wondering about the shoes. Do you remember a day about two weeks ago when I had been at your house and said I'd forgotten my purse? You were on your way somewhere, so you gave me your key. I went back to get my intentionally forgotten purse. I know I committed a horrible invasion of privacy when I scrounged around in your closet to check your shoe size."

"This *was* worthy of a spy novel. And since you've borrowed more than one piece of clothing from my closet, I don't consider it an invasion of privacy." Cassie grinned. She fastened a pearl necklace her mother had provided around her throat and put on matching earrings. "My mother kept this a secret?"

"She knew about it for less than a week."

"I'm sure she commented on the lack of tradition."

Amy laughed. "She did."

Cassie stood in front of the mirror. She made a stunning

bride. Out of the corner of her eye, Amy noticed a limousine pulling in front of the building. Bella gestured toward it.

"We were going simple, but Henri, your favorite florist, wanted to treat you. He said no beautiful bride should ride in the back seat of a five-year-old sedan. Apparently, he's been looking at my car," Bella said with a smile.

Cassie headed toward the door. "Where am I getting married?"

Bella answered. "The church."

"And the reception?"

Cassie had been so gleeful about everything so far. "Do you really want to know? You seem to be enjoying the surprises."

Cassie didn't speak for a moment. Then she smiled and said, "You're right. Yes, I do want to know, but then I'll start thinking about what it looks like and all the things. Surprise me. It's a beautiful day, one that reminds me of the day I rode in here, so I'm happy to just go along for the ride." She went out the door humming the wedding march.

CHAPTER THIRTY

When she pulled up to the church in a limo, Amy felt as if history was repeating itself. This time, though, the bride definitely wanted to be here.

Paige waited for the wedding couple, camera ready, and began snapping photos as they arrived.

Amy should have assisted the bride from the limo, but Cassie didn't wait for help. Wearing a wide smile, Cassie hurried up the church steps where Bella, looking beautiful in the dress she'd designed, waited to straighten the bride's gown before she entered the church. Once that was done to Bella's satisfaction, she shook her finger at Cassie. "Remember: you aren't in charge today."

"Got it. Not in charge." She went inside and toward what she knew was the bride's room.

Bella glanced at Amy with a frustrated expression. "It will be a miracle if she doesn't start making changes. We need to hold her to what we've done unless her change is simple."

Paige followed the bride into the church, staying off to the side and out of the way. Amy knew James would be waiting inside for additional help with the photography.

A woman about her mother's age waited by the bride's room. Elegantly dressed in a tailored lavender silk suit with a matching hat on her head and shoes on her feet in a slightly deeper shade of purple, she exuded money and an upper social class.

"Mother," Cassie said with a flat voice.

So this was the Mrs. Van Bibber she had heard about so many times.

"I'm glad to see you, my dear. It's been a while."

Amy knew Cassie avoided contact with her mother. It was one of those odd situations where she loved her, but being around her was almost always stressful.

They moved closer. Amy knew Cassie should be put in the bride's room, but her mother was between them and it.

"Mother, it's good to see you. Would you like to come into the room with me?" When Cassie's mother started to close the door behind herself, Bella gasped.

Amy heard Mrs. Van Bibber say, "I've grown to understand what you see in your small-town man, but I will never understand why you moved to this middle-of-nowhere place." Then the door closed before anyone else could enter.

Amy looked over at Bella. "Should we go in there to help her or leave her alone?"

Bella stared at the door. "It's a tough call. As maid of honor, I should be helping the bride. But I don't know how we would get her mother away from her. It's rarely a joyful moment when she's nearby."

Paige stepped beside them. "They're in there alone. This isn't good, is it?"

Bella shook her head.

"Can she be given some sort of task?"

"That's a great idea." Amy would like to find a way to help the situation. "As I go through the list of everything that needs to be done, nothing seems to be right for her."

Mrs. Brantley appeared. "Is there a problem?"

Bella explained in a hushed voice.

Mrs. Brantley turned to the door, rapped on it twice, then went inside without waiting for a reply. She heard Mrs. Brantley greeting Cassie's mother warmly. Then she said, "We suddenly realized we've neglected a certain task. It needs somebody in the wedding party with stature. Would you be willing to help?"

Amy could see Cassie's mother fidgeting in her chair, probably trying to find a graceful way to get out of it.

"Cassie normally has her team here, but we couldn't leak word of the wedding enough to bring them in. Someone needs to stand just outside the entrance to the sanctuary to make sure each person in the wedding enters in the proper order. Dresses need to be hanging correctly, and ties must be straight. I know this is a letdown because you're the mother of the bride, and you should be seated up front before the music begins. Do you think you'll be able to help us?"

As Mrs. Brantley spoke, Cassie's mother sat up straighter. By the time she finished, her shoulders were back. "I do like it when things run properly. I can make my way around to the front after the wedding party has passed by. Do you think that will work?"

Amy saw Mrs. Brantley glance subtly at Cassie, who gave a small nod. Mrs. Brantley reached down and tugged slightly on Mrs. Van Bibber's arm. "Let's get you in place right now. It's a little while before the wedding, but the extra time will help you get the lay of the land."

"It's a good thing I'm here then, right?" Mrs. Van Bibber said as she exited the room and passed them.

Bella whispered, "Mrs. Brantley never ceases to amaze me. Can I be her when I grow up?"

"She certainly is something," Amy said.

With the change in place, Bella went inside with Cassie. Amy felt someone at her side and turned to find Scott. "I thought you were supposed to be at the farm."

He nodded. "I received notice of reassignment this morning. Mrs. Brantley said she needed help here. I'm wearing one of Greg's suits." He gestured toward his clothing.

She grinned. "You look good in it." And he definitely did look good in the navy jacket and pants.

"I'm to stay by your side so we can make sure everything goes well."

Amy stared up into his eyes. Being at Scott's side sounded just right, but she had a feeling Mrs. Brantley was playing matchmaker.

When Greg arrived, Scott went into motion, taking the groom to the room he and Micah, the best man, would use.

Amy tapped on the bride's door when something occurred to her, opening the door slightly. "Cassie, I just realized something. We didn't ask your father about giving you away. Do you want him to do that?"

Cassie smiled. "I'm certain my mother has already taken care of that."

Amy glanced over and saw Cassie's mother straightening her father's tie and gesturing down the aisle with what must have been directions for him.

Amy's own mother was fun and, in general, pretty laid back. She'd be great to have at a wedding.

Time passed quickly, and soon Scott came over to tell them Greg and Micah were at the front of the church. Cassie's father waited just outside the door for her.

The ceremony went off without a hitch. Cassie's mother made sure everyone entered correctly, and she actually performed a necessary service because the order and timing were flawless.

After that, she gracefully went around the outside edge of the pews to the front to sit beside her husband.

When it came time for the vows, Cassie and Greg used traditional vows instead of ones they had written. Greg had told Amy that since Cassie wouldn't have time to create hers in advance, they would use the well-known version but without the word *obey*. He wanted a life partner, not someone in a different role.

After a kiss that made Amy remember kissing Scott—and wish she could have another one or a thousand more kisses with him—Cassie and Greg were pronounced husband and wife and turned to walk down the aisle. Amy had thought Cassie was smiling before, but now she could light up a room.

When they reached the back, Cassie hugged her and Bella. "Thank you for all the work you and everyone else put into this. I am thrilled beyond words that I'm now Cassie Brantley."

Greg asked, "Should we tell her where the reception is?"

Amy looked over at Cassie and shrugged. "Your call."

"I'm overjoyed with everything that's happening. Please tell me where."

"The barn at Cherry and Levi's."

"Oh, good! That may be my favorite venue in the area. I know the cupcakes are the ones I tasted and approved. Does that mean the food will be the appetizers Nick made?"

Greg grinned. "You should have seen the spymasters at work."

"This is the best wedding I could ever imagine. I didn't have to do anything. I wasn't stressed out. And you made sure to have things Greg and I would love. You guys are the best. But where's Simone?"

"She raced out after the ceremony and said she was on her way to deliver cupcakes. She didn't want them to sit out too long. By the time you arrive at the farm, Simone—and your cupcakes—will be there."

The crowd jostled around them as people moved toward the exit and off to the reception. When Cassie turned to greet people, Mrs. Brantley took her arm.

"My dear, there will be plenty of time to speak to all the guests at the reception. We'd better get you going with your photos. I know Paige is waiting outside."

As the couple went outside, Scott stood beside Amy. "I went to two family weddings, one for my sister and one for a brother. They were easy compared to this because I just showed up. I had no idea what went on behind the scenes."

"I think I'd like something simple for my own wedding." Amy gasped. "Not that I'm planning on getting married anytime soon. It's just an observation after being part of this."

Scott nodded, but he looked at her in a way she couldn't quite place.

The bride and groom got in their limo and left as soon as James and Paige finished with the photos. Amy and Scott followed behind in his truck.

CHAPTER THIRTY-ONE

hen Cassie stepped inside the barn and saw her country music star friend Carly warming up to perform, she squealed with delight and ran over as fast as her sparkly heels would carry her to hug her. When they stepped apart, both women were in tears.

The evening went surprisingly well, considering they didn't have a professional planner. Trays with appetizers circulated through a crowd that included college friends of Cassie's, former clients, friends of the family, and relatives. Michelle and Simone took care of passing out hors d'oeuvres. Amy kept an eye on the cupcake area to make sure it stayed tidy-looking. People kept pulling a cupcake out of the middle and messing up the heart shape Simone had worked so hard on.

Instead of cutting a cake, Cassie and Greg sliced into a cupcake and fed each other a bite. Simone had made the requisite tiny cake they could freeze and eat a year from now. Amy found that icky because almost no baked goods could survive a year in the freezer and still be tasty. But who was she to argue with tradition?

Amy kept on the move through the venue, ensuring things

were orderly and going smoothly. Every once in a while, she'd search for Scott. He'd be working security in one part of the venue or another. When the event started to wind down, Amy stood off to the side for a moment and watched him again.

Simone stepped to her side. "He's easy on the eyes, isn't he?"

Amy could play dumb, but she decided not to bother. "He is."

"You make a great couple."

Amy sucked in air as she fought for a response.

"You'd have to be blind not to see what is happening between you and Scott. And yet you'd let him drive away tomorrow and go back to Chicago forever, wouldn't you?"

Amy nodded quickly, fighting the tears that threatened. "He has a life elsewhere."

"Who cares? People move all the time. Do you really think Scott would be upset about moving if he thought you cared about him?"

Scott smiled at her and gave a small wave.

Simone said, "I rest my case. I saw that little thing between the two of you there. Don't let him go." Simone punctuated every word by tapping on Amy's shoulder. "When you find a good one, and it all seems to click, don't let it go."

Amy felt her lip quiver as she thought about him leaving. She breathed in and out slowly a few times, focusing on the wedding around her. She'd get through this. The event officially ended when the bride and groom stood, ready to leave.

The couple passed by her on their way out. Cassie leaned close and whispered as she went by, "Don't let him get away."

Greg, apparently overhearing, said, "My thought exactly."

Two of her friends and one of his had weighed in with their opinions about her love life. Was anyone telling him things like this? She picked up a napkin and plate that had dropped to the ground and threw them away. Scott came over and lobbed a cup in the trash like a basketball.

Just having him beside her set off a chain of emotions. "I need a breath of fresh air." She hurried toward the exit.

He kept pace with her. "I could use a breather too."

Standing beside her and staring up at the stars, he said, "We were supposed to have one more proposal before I left."

Amy nodded. "Life became so busy that my push to grow the newspaper was set aside. I'll have to find another man to do the proposals with me."

"I'd rather you didn't. I'd like to be the only one who proposes to you."

She turned toward him, the moonlight overhead glazing the top of his head with a glow. When he didn't say more, she asked, "What do you mean? I'll have to be proposed to again to continue the articles." And she hoped to be proposed to— someday—by a man who loved her and wanted to marry her. She'd even eat year-old cake for their anniversary.

Scott leaned closer and tucked her hair behind her ear. "Amy, I mean it. I'd like to be the next person to propose to you. But not here, not now."

She realized he wasn't talking about the newspaper. "I want for you to be the only man who proposes to me," she said, laying her cards on the table.

Scott grinned and picked her up, spinning her around in a circle before he set her down and kissed her.

"Does that mean you'd like to have me stay here in Two Hearts?"

"What kind of question is that? Of course, I want you to stay in Two Hearts. But your life is in Chicago."

"You used the wrong tense. You need to say my life *was* in Chicago. My mother reminded me that Archer, a college buddy of mine, has wanted to start a computer coding business with me. I'd ignored his repeated offers and all but forgotten about them because I loved my job. There was no point in even considering what he'd suggested. When she mentioned it, my mind started to wonder if it was possible. I've spent hours on the phone with Archer in the last few days."

Amy started to feel a glow from the inside. "You decided to take him up on it?"

"I did. I have a lot to wrap up in Chicago. My family won't like it that I'm moving so far away, but they'll be happy I found you. I know they'll love you."

Amy met him halfway when he leaned down for a kiss.

When they broke apart, Amy couldn't fight the grin on her face. "I know you need to leave to wrap things up in Chicago. Take as long as you need but not a second more."

"I'll be back in a month."

"And this proposal, how long do you think I'll need to wait for it?"

He pulled her close and held her in his arms. "We'll have to figure that out. But I have a feeling you won't be waiting too long."

Neither did Amy.

EPILOGUE

*A*my added a collection of mysteries to the shelf in her bookstore. The tall wooden bookcases she and Scott had found online from an old bookstore in Missouri that had closed filled the space perfectly, giving two rows of shelving that ran nearly the length of the room. They'd had to rent a truck to bring them here, but they made the store exactly as she'd pictured. About seven feet high, these gave a cozy, intimate feeling to her store that she loved.

She straightened the row of books in the wedding section, and, instead of the tension she felt when Scott had first suggested the idea, a giggle bubbled up.

Soft footsteps came down the wooden floor toward her, footsteps she knew without turning had to be Scott's because they were alone in the store. He wrapped his arms around her. "What's so funny?"

She turned to face him. "I actually *like* the idea of weddings. This shelf makes me happy now."

He quirked an eyebrow. "Happy? The entire wedding section of your store still feels like foreign ground to me."

Her head dropped forward as disappointment surged through her. She had thought Scott had become more interested in weddings, at least when it came to the two of them.

"Hey." He tilted her head up. "Why so glum all of a sudden?"

Amy glanced around, hoping to find something to blame for her disappointment. The front door chimed as a customer entered, saving her from a reply. Before she took a step in that direction, a second chime sounded. Then a third and fourth.

"There seems to be a rush." She hurried down the row of bookcases but found the front of the store empty. A quick scan down the aisles of shelving turned up nothing.

Scott stood a few feet away, leaning against a bookcase. He rubbed his hands together in a way she'd describe as nervous. She wondered what on Earth had him fidgeting when he followed that by rubbing the back of his neck. Then he pointed to the front window and asked, "What's that?"

"What's . . ." Amy followed his guidance and found a two-tiered cake in her favorite colors of lilac and pink. Nosey sat perched on the green and gold patterned upholstered chair she'd placed near the window so the reader would have good light. "Scott, I don't understand. Why is there a cake, and what is Nosey doing here?"

"The cake is the chocolate cheesecake you love. Nosey is here because he's important to you, and this is a significant moment you'll always remember."

Her birthday wouldn't be for months. Maybe he'd done this to celebrate her store's first week of business. "This is all lovely." When Amy turned to thank Scott, she found him on one knee with an open ring box in his hand.

She put her hand to her heart and gasped.

"Amy Marchant, would you do me the honor of becoming my wife?"

She tried to speak but only a squeak came out. Amy cleared her throat as she tried again.

"I love you, but this floor is even harder than the ground at the farm."

That broke through her tension. Laughing, she ran over to Scott and gave him a quick kiss. "Of course, I'll marry you. Today, tomorrow, any day."

When he stood, he pulled her in and his lips again covered hers. "We should have a better kiss than that."

Amy agreed. When they broke apart the next time, Scott said, "I think we should give our families a few weeks to get ready."

"And Cassie. I know she'll do a great wedding for us." *Us.* She stared at the man she loved. "Moving to Two Hearts has been full of surprises. You're the best of them."

Nosey jumped to the floor, following that with a jump and spin she now knew was called a *binky*. "You too, Nosey."

Scott wrapped his hand around hers. "Ready for cake? Our friends are outside waiting. I knew you'd want to tell everyone right away. Paige wanted to take pictures, but I told her we were keeping this story to ourselves."

Warmth flooded through her. He'd chosen well. So much of her life had been put online to help the newspaper, which had thankfully worked and brought in subscribers. But this moment was only for the two of them. "Let's bring everyone inside." Not letting go of him, she pulled him over to the door, peered out, and found a group of friends waiting off to the side, including Bella with her new baby girl.

Amy held up her left hand. "I said yes!"

Join Cathryn's newsletter to learn about sales, giveaways, bonus short stories, and when the next book is coming out. And if you've missed it, HOW TO MARRY A COUNTRY MUSIC STAR is the prequel to the series. You just read about Carly,

Cassie's friend and the singer at her wedding. In HOW TO MARRY A COUNTRY MUSIC STAR, she's a down-on-her-luck country music star. Jake is the wealthy man who hires her to be his housekeeper. Get the ebook FREE today at cathrynbrown.com/marry

ABOUT CATHRYN

Writing books that are fun and touch your heart

Even though Cathryn Brown always loved to read, she didn't plan to be a writer. Cathryn felt pulled into a writing life, testing her wings with a novel and moving on to articles. She's now an award-winning journalist who has sold hundreds of articles to local, national, and regional publications.

The Feather Chase, written as Shannon L. Brown, was her first published book and begins the Crime-Solving Cousins Mystery series. The eight-to-twelve-year-olds in your life will enjoy this contemporary twist on a Nancy Drew–type mystery.

Cathryn's from Alaska and has two series of clean Alaska romances. You can start reading those books with *Falling for Alaska*, or with *Accidentally Matched* in the spin-off series which includes *Merrily Matched*.

Cathryn enjoys hiking, sometimes while dictating a book. She also unwinds by baking and reading. Cathryn lives in Tennessee with her professor husband and adorable cat.

For more books and updates, visit cathrynbrown.com

www.ingramcontent.com/pod-product-compliance
Lightning Source LLC
Chambersburg PA
CBHW060704190726
48289CB00002B/529